MAY   2014

ONCE
UPON A
LIE

Center Point
Large Print

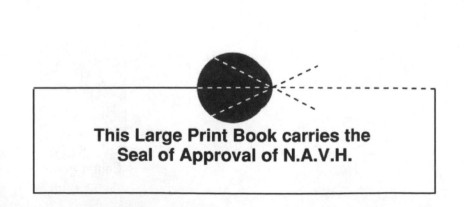

**This Large Print Book carries the
Seal of Approval of N.A.V.H.**

ONCE
UPON A
LIE

Maggie Barbieri

CENTER POINT LARGE PRINT
THORNDIKE, MAINE

This Center Point Large Print edition is published
in the year 2014 by arrangement with
St. Martin's Press.

This is a work of fiction. All of the characters,
organizations, and events portrayed in this novel
are either products of the author's imagination
or are used fictitiously.

The text of this Large Print edition is unabridged.
In other aspects, this book may vary
from the original edition.
Printed in the United States of America
on permanent paper.
Set in 16-point Times New Roman type.

ISBN: 978-1-62899-092-8

Library of Congress Cataloging-in-Publication Data

Barbieri, Maggie.
Once upon a lie / Maggie Barbieri. — Center Point Large Print edition.
pages ; cm
ISBN 978-1-62899-092-8 (library binding : alk. paper)
1. Bakers—Fiction. 2. Women—Fiction.
    3. Cousins—Crimes against—Fiction. 4. Family secrets.
    5. Large type books. I. Title.
PS3602.A767O53 2014
813′.6—dc23
                                                    2014001387

To Jim, Dea, and Patrick

Acknowledgments

Without the support and constant encouragement of Deborah Schneider, my wonderful agent, and Kelley Ragland, my incredible editor, I would never have written this book. They told me to go "big." (Fortunately, as the saying goes, they never told me to "go home.") This book is my attempt at going big. So, my heartfelt gratitude goes to two people with whom I have had the privilege of working for the past nine years and without whom I couldn't face the darker thoughts that lurk in the recesses of my imagination.

Thanks, too, to Cathy Gleason at Gelfman Schneider, a woman of grace and humor who makes everything seem easy.

To Andy Martin, Sarah Melnyk, Hector De Jean, and Elizabeth Lacks at St. Martin's/Minotaur Books, a hearty thank-you for everything you do to make sure that every book I publish is one of which I am proud.

And to my family, "thank you" doesn't seem like enough but it will have to do.

Chapter 1

The recipe was simple:

Take one old guy with budding Alzheimer's, a cast of characters who had never met a potato they didn't like, and a dead body in a closed casket. Add accusations and recriminations to taste. Mix well and bake for two hours from either three to five or seven to nine.

Voilà. Once everything cools to a simmering rage, you have an Irish wake.

Maeve had set aside exactly seventeen minutes for paying her respects to her cousin Sean. Any longer than that and she'd be late for Rebecca's soccer game, something she had promised her oldest would never happen again after last week's embarrassment. Being late to the game was bad enough, but forgetting the cut-up oranges? Apparently, that was an offense punishable by death. Or at least the collective stink eye from a bunch of mothers whose greatest daily decision was *grande* or *venti*.

Traveling with an octogenarian with a faulty short-term memory was slowing her down; she was now down to thirteen minutes. Add to that the uncomfortable creeping of a pair of unruly Spanx and Maeve could feel her composure begin to crack. "Come on, Dad. Let's get in line," she said after signing the guest book. She looked at the names of the other mourners who had signed in before she did and noted all of the usual suspects: the McDonoughs, the Dorseys, the Trainors. All were people from her past, and all were people who, if asked, would say that they had helped raise poor, motherless Maeve. All were people who probably felt at least partially responsible for the meager success she had achieved in life. All were people who had turned a blind eye to her situation and who were therefore partially responsible for what had happened to her.

She spied her father heading toward the Giordano wake across the hall; she grabbed his arm and pulled him back. It seemed definitely more appealing as wakes went, what with the tiny yet vociferous mourners and the misplaced scent of salami wafting out, but it was not Maeve and her father's ultimate destination. Now down to just ten minutes of meaningful visitation, she hustled him into the black-clad queue of visitors that had formed in the short time it had taken her to write her name and address in the guest book. In her head, she was listing all of the items she'd need to pick up from the store after this jaunt, spectating at a soccer game, and shuttling her dad back to the assisted-living facility. Sean Donovan's death, and the scheduling of his wake, had proven to be incredibly ill timed.

As they approached the casket, which was

closed—much to the disappointment of the gaggle of Irishwomen from the neighborhood who had turned out—Maeve surveyed the room, her eyes settling on two guys who could have been family members, their ruddy complexions and ill-fitting suits two defining features of the Conlon men. It dawned on her quickly: cops. She had been raised by one and had spent enough time around his friends that she could spot one a mile away. Two? That was easy. When they traveled in pairs, they really stood out in a crowd. The rumpled blue suits and worn cordovan loafers were a dead giveaway, no pun intended. She didn't have to wonder what they were doing there; Sean had been found in his car in a deserted section of Van Cortlandt Park, a hole in his head that he really didn't need, as he was prone to saying while he was alive. That his pants were around his knees and he had a glove box full of unopened condoms didn't lend credence to his wife's story that he had gone out for a gallon of milk, but it did lend a layer of sordidness to the story that Maeve found more than a little amusing.

"What're the po-po doing here?" Jack asked, nodding in the direction of the cops. Over at the inappropriately named Buena del Sol, a land-locked facility for people like Jack, they watched MTV a little more than Maeve would have cared for.

She shushed him and pulled him closer. His

were failing faculties, but he was in good physical shape; even still, his strength, as he tried to pull away from her, was surprising.

"Why are we here?" he asked for not the first time that day.

"Sean, Dad. He died."

He gasped, as he did every time she reminded him of the fact. "From what?"

In the past six days, she'd made up a different cause of death every time he asked, and she was running out of reasons her healthy, a little-over-half-century cousin had passed on. "Chronic diarrhea."

"I hear that's a terrible way to go," Jack said, shaking his head sadly. He seemed genuinely chagrined despite the fact that Jack's nickname for Sean while growing up was "shit for brains."

Funny. She'd always thought that Jack would kill him.

The widow Donovan, Dolores, rooted in her rightful place in front of the casket, beckoned Maeve forward; Maeve felt that she had to oblige. She pulled Jack along with her, his focus on Sean's toothsome eldest daughter, a girl who apparently thought that wearing a low-cut cocktail dress was the way to go at her father's wake. When they finally arrived to pay their condolences, Dolores threw herself into Jack's arms, the old man not entirely sure what he was to do with a hundred and eighty pounds of soft, quivering, taffeta-encased flesh. Maeve interceded and wedged herself between the woman and her father, whispering her condolences while wondering how she could extricate herself and Jack and get the hell out of Dodge without attracting anyone's notice.

Two minutes to go. She raced over to the casket and knelt beside her father, his eyes closed in prayer. He may not have known who was in the casket, but he certainly remembered how to say a prayer for whoever it was. Jack was a daily communicant at the assisted-living facility, not remembering that in his old life—pre-Buena del Sol—he was a shitty Catholic who hadn't been to church since his beloved wife's funeral almost four decades earlier.

Maeve took in the flower arrangements piled high around the gleaming mahogany coffin; Dolores had spared no expense. She looked at the photo collage that Dolores had undoubtedly implored her daughters to create on behalf of their beloved father. Sean at the beach; Sean at the Yankee game. Sean with his hand on the shoulder of his nephew Brian as Brian was confirmed. Dolores and Sean's wedding day. Maeve eyed the rosary beads draped over the top of the casket, wondering if Sean had even known how to say a decade of the rosary while he had walked the earth. To anyone watching, Maeve must have looked like a grief-stricken family member whispering her last good-byes to a beloved relative. She was certain she heard the sympathetic clucking of the old women who sat in the row of chairs directly behind her, touched by her studied composure in the face of an unspeak-able tragedy.

Truth be told, she had more feelings for old man Giordano, laid out in the room across the hall, going to his eternal rest amid the cries of more emotional mourners, than she did for the man who lay beneath the wood on which her fingers were splayed.

"Bye, Sean," she whispered. "See you in hell."

Chapter 2

The Spanx notwithstanding, Maeve was in a black mood by the time she got to the soccer game. Someone else had brought the oranges today; apparently, if the girls didn't have them on the sidelines, one of them might die. But as with many things in her life, Maeve didn't have the energy or the intensity to bring to the task and was glad that in addition to attending a wake in the Bronx, she hadn't been given the role of "refreshment mom" today. She was already teetering on an emotional precipice and needed only one small push to send her careening over the side.

It was October, and with the dawning of the

month came soccer and an inordinate amount of talking about citrus fruit and electrolytes. Maeve had been through it before and knew the script by heart.

Her car sat perpendicular to the field, offering her a splendid view of the game. Her cell phone rang as she was making the decision between removing the offending undergarment in her car or in the Porta-Potty adjacent to the field, both options presenting unique challenges. Charlene Harrison, the director of Buena del Sol, was in her usual high dudgeon. This time, she didn't even offer a greeting when she heard Maeve's voice.

"If he gets out again, he's out of here."

"He didn't get out, Charlene," Maeve said, hiking her skirt up. She did a quick check around the parking lot to make sure everyone was fixated on the game and not on her striptease. "I took him to a wake." Jack was a wanderer, and the staff at Buena del Sol had strict orders—the guy got signed out by a responsible adult or stayed put. No ifs, ands, or buts. Jack, however, had other ideas, ideas that took him to the far reaches of Farringville and anywhere else he saw fit to go. As he reminded her almost daily, he was a grown man and grown men could do what they wanted, a statement that was only partially true. Grown men who had all of their faculties could do what they wanted; the others had to stay in the care of the staff of their assisted-living facility.

"Well, you didn't sign him out."

"I'm sorry?" Her dress now pulled up around her waist, she hooked a thumb into the waistband of her girdle. Charlene Harrison apparently had no idea that Maeve had more pressing matters, namely a pair of recalcitrant underpants that might require the Jaws of Life to free her from its binds.

"You should be. Do you know we almost called the police?"

"But you didn't, right?" The last thing Maeve needed was to see her name, or that of her father, in the local paper's police blotter. That would have tongues wagging for weeks, and she was already suspect, having gotten divorced several years earlier from a man who apparently preferred his spouses younger, fitter, and formerly the trophy wives of fellow parishioners at Blessed Sacrament Roman Catholic Church. She rolled down one side of the spandex underwear. "So we're good?"

Charlene was letting out exasperated sighs on the other end of the phone. "We're not good. We're less than not good. The other night? That was inexcusable."

"What happened the other night?"

"He was gone five hours as far as we can figure out," Charlene said. "Could have been longer."

That was news to Maeve. "Where was he?"

"We don't know. All we know is that he came

back on his own. So God knows, Ms. Conlon." She paused. "God knows."

"What night was this?" Maeve asked.

"Saturday. The twenty-ninth."

Saturday, the twenty-ninth was the day Sean was murdered. Maeve would ask him about it, but it wouldn't do any good. He wouldn't have any recollection of where he had been. He told her once that he liked to walk to the park down by the river, but that was a good three-mile walk from Buena del Sol. At eighty, was he really capable of making a six-mile round-trip journey? If so, Maeve gave him credit. He couldn't remember where his shoes were, but he could find his way to and from the park. The mind— his mind—was an incredible thing.

Charlene was still talking. "Just remember to sign him out next time."

"Will do," Maeve said, and snapped her phone shut. Both hands free, she pulled off the Spanx, one leg getting tangled in her stiletto heel before she threw both of them on the passenger seat, taking in deep breaths. Never again would she take for granted the ability to breathe deeply from her diaphragm. She leaned her head back and closed her eyes, wondering how long it would be before she had to tackle the onerous task of finding another home for Jack. This was his second, and the last one in the immediate vicinity. He had a bit of a wandering jones, and that made him wholly unsuited to life in an assisted-living facility, where people like Jack needed to be present and accounted for at all times.

She wondered how to get him placed under house arrest. An ankle monitor on her elderly father would be just the ticket to take one stress off her plate, but she was sure they were practically impossible to come by on the open market.

Now that she could breathe, she watched the game, noticing Rebecca on the sidelines scanning the crowd for her mother. Maeve knew she couldn't spend the entire game in the car, even though that was her inclination and something she did on a fairly regular basis. It didn't endear her to the other moms, and it incensed Rebecca, who felt that her mother needed to be front and center, cheering for the daughter who was playing for a college scholarship and a way out of this "sucky town," as she liked to refer to it. Maeve had the good sense not to tell her it was actually a sucky "village," Rebecca not really caring what Farringville was, technically.

She put her shoes back on and made her way down to the bleachers, her high heels unsuited to picking over gravel and grass, her dress feeling tighter now that she didn't have anything pushing her belly back toward her spine. She passed a group of mothers, some of them her friends, most with an unnatural devotion to soccer, and took her place on the lowest bleacher in the stands, closest to the field but with the best view of the chain-link fence. She didn't have the energy to climb any farther, so it would have to do. During the next time-out, she waved to Rebecca, making sure her daughter saw that she was there, in the stands, and cheering as though her life depended on it.

Sitting on the top row was her fifteen-year-old, Heather, and with her was a boy that Maeve recognized from Rebecca's grade who was grade-A trouble. Maeve filed that away for later, thinking that she would have to tread lightly to find out about this new boy and what he had to do with her youngest. Heather avoided her mother's gaze and was probably trying her best to squelch the embarrassment she felt at having a mother who thought nothing of showing up at a soccer game in a black dress and heels. Heather wasn't much different from Jack when it came to memory; although Maeve had reminded her that she would be attending Sean's wake, by the time the sentence was out of her mouth, Heather was on to something else, something in which she was the star and the only person who mattered.

If hell had a sound track, it was the sound of a bunch of overeager suburban mothers screaming the names of their daughters over and over and over again. If Maeve never heard Marcy Gerson scream the name "MEER-ANNN-DAAHHH" again, it would be too soon. That high-pitched wail haunted her dreams, even though otherwise she found Marcy pleasant to be around. Maeve plastered a smile on her face and clapped enthusiastically as the girls ran back onto the field, their time-out over.

She looked up to see her ex, Cal, slide in next to her, his infant son strapped to his chest, facing forward, his little arms flailing as Cal rearranged himself so that he could sit comfortably on the bleacher. Devon was Charles "Cal" Callahan's latest accessory, the baby's mother, Gabriela, being the second. He turned and waved at Heather, who gifted him with a big smile and a wave that looked sincere.

When it came to her daughters, Maeve accepted her role as creator and nurturer of all things bad and inconvenient, but she didn't relish it.

"Glad you could come. What's Gabriela up to? Writing a column telling us all why we should be wearing cerulean this season?" she asked, not proud. Sarcasm in this instance was beneath her, and she bit back more biting words that would just illustrate how bitter she was that her one-time friend was now her former husband's wife.

"What's the score?" he asked, ignoring her. He was good at that.

Maeve pointed at the scoreboard. "Three–two. We're losing."

Cal gave her a once-over. "I didn't realize this game called for formal attire," he said, pulling a cloth diaper from his back pocket and wiping the baby's mouth.

"Sean's wake."

"Oh, right." Cal focused on the game while continuing the conversation. "How was that?"

Maeve pulled a pair of sunglasses out of her purse and put them on. "The usual. A bunch of old biddies from the neighborhood, Father Madden . . ."

"He's still around?"

Father Madden had married them a long, long time ago and had been very disappointed to learn that the vows hadn't "taken." "He is. He's doing the funeral in the morning."

"You going?"

Maeve jumped to her feet as Rebecca launched one toward the goal, hitting the goalpost. A collective groan spread through the crowd. "To the funeral?"

"Yeah."

"Probably not."

The baby started fussing and Cal pulled a bottle out of his cargo shorts. He handed it to Maeve. "Hold this?" He unstrapped the baby and took him out of the contraption on his chest, sitting him upright in his lap, still facing forward. The baby was obviously a soccer fan; he was more animated than Maeve had ever seen him. Cal put the bottle in the baby's mouth and he sucked greedily. "There was never any love lost between the two of you."

"Me and Sean?" she asked. "You think?"

Cal watched the game until the ref blew the whistle, signaling the end of the first quarter. "I could never figure it out. He seemed like an amiable sort."

They always do, Maeve thought. Instead, she shrugged in response.

"Jack doesn't want to go? Granted, he was your mother's nephew, but still . . ."

"Jack isn't entirely sure who died or why. I think he'll be fine with not attending."

The baby finished the bottle in record time, and Maeve braced herself for the inevitable projection of undigested formula that was bound to come her way. Cal threw the baby over his shoulder to burp him. "How's business?"

"Great," Maeve lied.

Cal gave her a sideways glance. "Still making your fortune one cupcake at a time?"

"Something like that."

"You'll let me know if you need help? Especially with the wholesale thing? That's where the money is." The baby let out a burp that sounded as if it had started at his toes; Maeve put a little distance between herself and the baby, but the burp was unproductive. "Let me know," he repeated.

Never. "Of course. We're doing great, Cal. No worries." It was typical of most of her conversations with Cal: he knew just enough and not really enough. As a result, he was low on the list of people from whom she sought advice. She went to him only if she had to and could count on one hand how many times that had been.

He finally got caught up enough in the game to leave her alone. Although he was now a stay-at-home father, the attorney in him had never completely disappeared. Once, she was used to his interrogations, but now she was out of practice and had to stay on her toes so that she didn't let on the things she didn't want him to know. The wholesale deal was done, gone the way of a larger manufacturer in Brooklyn who could produce cookies at an alarming speed and for far less money than Maeve's two-person operation.

She was able to cheer when Rebecca scored a goal early in the third quarter, and feel dismay when the game became a runaway for the other team in the final minutes of the fourth. Her mind was still in the Bronx, though, and back at the funeral home. She wondered just how much damage the bullet had done to Sean's brain. Was death instant or had he lingered even a few seconds before dying? Did he know what was coming—not him, obviously—when the passenger-side door of the car had opened and someone had slid into the seat? Did he know it was the end or did he think he deserved one more chance? Did he have any regrets at all?

She wondered about all of this, not noticing that Cal was talking to her. "Huh?"

"A hobby," he said, taking the baby off his shoulder.

"For me?"

"Yeah. You work twelve hours a day and when you're not working, you're taking care of the girls. Or your dad. You need a break." He shoved the baby's chubby legs into the carrier. "You need to do something for you."

"Like tennis?" It was the only thing she could think of that women her age did when they were at a loss for other things to do.

"Sure. Like tennis."

Maeve mulled that over. A hobby.

"Find something meaningful. Something that would help you relax." He stood, pulling the baby's feet through the holes in the carrier. "Or if it makes more sense, something that would help other people. Because if I know you, that drives you more than anything." He was smiling, but she could sense the dig inherent in that. Doing for others and not for him. For him, that had been the downfall of her marriage.

Maeve's mind was racing. "Or a combination of all three of those things." You know what would help me relax? she thought. You shutting up. The smile never left her face.

Cal looked as though he had hit on something. "Right! Meaningful, relaxing, and helpful to others. That sounds like the perfect combination for you." He leaned over and kissed the top of her head. "Now you just have to figure out what that might be."

Maeve looked up, her ex-husband's handsome face backlit by the late afternoon sun. She smiled. "I'll give it some thought, Cal." She was glad she had left the Spanx in the car. If they'd been in her bag, handy, she might have been inclined to strangle him with them, right in front of every mother in the stands. No jury in the land would convict her, she always thought, particularly if it were truly a jury of her peers: overworked, under-appreciated wives and mothers who just wanted someone to clean the toilet when it was dirty and pick up a gallon of milk when there was none. Instead, she continued smiling, thinking of how she used to ignore the way he patronized her, sometimes even finding it just short of charming, chalking it up to his concern for her. Now, though, it got under her skin the way a lot of things did, things that never used to bother her but now made her blood boil, like rude customers at the store or people who let their officiousness and position hold sway over her, making her fear the worst. People like Charlene Harrison, who couldn't contain one old man in an assisted-living facility that was a good three miles from the river the man loved so much.

"Hey, what are you thinking about?" Cal asked.

Nothing. Everything. "Just all the things on my to-do list."

"I've got the girls this weekend," he said.

She knew. Unlike him, she never forgot where the girls needed to be or what they required to live happy lives in this little village. Her brain was full, way fuller than his, with details about everyone else's lives. How she managed to keep everything straight, while he could barely account for himself most days, was a mystery she had yet to solve. Maybe it was like the late George Carlin used to say: Women are crazy and men are stupid. And the reason that women are crazy is because men are stupid. Maeve ran through the list of activities scheduled for the girls while in Cal's care. "And don't forget that Heather is grounded."

"She's here now," he said, pointing to his middle child, high up in the bleachers.

"This doesn't count. She's supporting her sister," Maeve said, although she didn't entirely believe it. "She wants to go to a party this weekend, but she's grounded from going."

Cal raised an eyebrow. "For?"

"Unauthorized Facebook use."

"I don't even know what that is."

"And you don't want to know," she said, adjusting herself on the bleachers. It entailed putting something on Rebecca's wall that detailed her older sister's extensive morning toilette, inviting derision from many of Rebecca's own classmates, not to mention Heather's. "She doesn't go to the party. Under any circumstances."

He gave her a salute. "Got it, chief."

She let that go, as it wouldn't be the last time she would tell him about the grounding, nor would it be the last time he gave her a contemptuous salute. Pick your battles, she said to herself, breathing deeply. Even those that she chose to fight she might not win, so choosing carefully would be her goal. She looked up at him again.

Why did I ever love you? she thought. She probably knew the answer to that question, but sifting through the various emotions would take time she did not have.

Chapter 3

Rebecca was still in uniform when Maeve got home, working on math at the kitchen table. Her dark head, her hair the same color as her father's, was bent over a textbook filled with symbols that Maeve didn't recognize from any math course she had ever taken. Fortunately for her, Rebecca had inherited her father's good looks—his deep brown eyes, his full lips—and his aptitude for anything that required logic. Maeve could create anything from scratch but failed when it came to writing anything down that would approach a recipe, one with fractions and precise measurements.

"What are we having for dinner?" she asked by way of greeting.

Maeve hadn't thought that far ahead, but one thing the Culinary Institute had taught her, besides great pastry skills, was how to turn whatever was in the refrigerator into a meal. That is, if the refrigerator held any food whatsoever, which hers didn't.

"Order a pizza?" Maeve asked.

The look of joy on Rebecca's face at this news was out of proportion to the simple idea of a pizza for dinner. The girls had made it known that they hated most everything Maeve cooked, mostly because every meal was accompanied by two vegetables. She had learned to turn a deaf ear to their protestations, but after putting in a full day at the shop, sometimes it was hard.

"You played great today," Maeve said.

"Thanks."

"Homework?"

Rebecca looked at her. "What do you think?"

Rebecca was in the homestretch, giving it all she had in order to get her GPA to where she wanted it to be, and where she wanted it to be was Vassar-ready. Maeve tried not to think about the tuition that went along with a Vassar education, hoping that Cal had been as good with his money as he claimed he had been, socking it away and making dividends that would get their oldest—the more ambitious of the two—to where she wanted to go.

He told her not to worry, but worrying was second nature to her. Her daughters knew that better than anyone.

Maeve kicked off her shoes and went to the sink, dealing with a pile of dishes left over from breakfast. She was surprised when Rebecca asked her how the wake was, queries into Maeve's well-being or activities never really being part of any conversation with her teens. Was it true what people told her about a college-bound kid? Would Rebecca really start to come around and maybe like Maeve just in time to leave? Maeve found the whole concept depressing, as if her entire life revolved around hoping for the day when her daughters would see her as a comrade and not as an adversary. She hoped she was around when the day finally came. "It was a wake. With a bunch of Irish people. You know the drill," she said. She thought back to her mother's wake, the one that she really didn't understand or want to be at, the old Irish ladies clucking over her, promising to take care of her, some of them—the widows—eyeing Jack as if he were a rib roast on sale at the local butcher. He had never remarried, and none of them came through on their promises.

Maeve had been seven, the memories of her beautiful mother laid out in a stylish off-price suit that she remembered her buying in Brooklyn one fall Saturday, the casket open only from the waist up. Maeve remembered telling her father that the shoes her mother wore matched her suit perfectly and should be displayed, but his only response had been to smile sadly before breaking out into heart-wrenching sobs that no one should have had to hear, let alone a little girl who pleaded with the body in the casket to wake up.

"But I'm sure Grandpa had a great time," Rebecca said, showing a flash of the sense of humor she had inherited from her grandfather. "He loves wakes. Especially the ones with the open caskets."

"He loves any time he can get out of Buena del Sol," Maeve said, a little tingle, fear, traveling up her spine. How far did he actually get the last time he left the facility? And where had he gone?

"Sean seemed nice," Rebecca said.

Maeve focused her attention on a wineglass with a smudge of lipstick on the rim. "Yeah," she said, as noncommittal as she could sound. Water sloshed over the edge of the glass and onto her dress. The last time they had all been together had been for the Donovans' annual Fourth of July party a few months earlier, held under a huge white tent in the backyard of their Fieldston manse, the girls unwilling participants in the extended Conlon-Donovan reindeer games. Maeve had managed to beg off on this invitation year after year, but this year, Dolores Donovan had gotten crafty and sent an invitation directly to Jack, who had informed Maeve that they all were going because he would need a ride.

She thought back to the day they went.

"Why do you want to go, Dad?" Maeve had asked, not relishing the thought of seeing her cousin—really, her childhood tormentor—host a grand party for two hundred.

Jack had listed the reasons. "Free lobster. Good whiskey." He had hesitated before offering the last reason, the only one that made Maeve acquiesce, even though she wasn't sure it was the best one. "And apparently, there's a rumor going around that I've lost my marbles, and I can't have that. I've got to show everyone that I'm still the same Jack Conlon, witty raconteur and all-around smart guy."

So they went, Maeve second-guessing her decision the minute they walked through the door. Heather had been particularly miserable, as the keg was closely guarded by a waiter in a crisp white shirt and black pants, while Rebecca, good-natured firstborn that she was, made the best of it, bringing a summer AP assignment and availing herself of the quiet of Sean's wood-paneled library. Jack had been in rare form, hitting the bar hard and regaling the kids of Maeve's cousins with stories of his derring-do on the police department, stories that were only half-true, most of which had been perpetrated by someone else. Maeve had kept her distance from both Dolores and Sean, spending time with Dolores's sister, Margie, someone Maeve remembered from the neighborhood as being one of the nicer Haggertys and the one least likely to throw an unnecessary barb her way, the Haggerty sharp tongues being their stock-in-trade.

Margie was the one Fidelma Haggerty had pinned her hopes on, the one she hoped would go into the convent and forever be the link between the Haggerty family and the kingdom of God. Margie, an avowed atheist and, as it turned out, lesbian, had other ideas, joining the Peace Corps instead and setting out for remote parts of Africa that Maeve hadn't even heard of. Maeve, a few years older, was long gone when she left and hadn't seen her since they were kids, each trying to avoid her own kind of trouble. For Maeve, it was Sean. For Margie, it was her own father, a drunk and a malcontent. It wasn't until Margie sat down next to her under the grand white tent at a table sparkling with little votives that Maeve realized how little she knew of Margie but how much she remembered liking her.

Margie was well into her second or third glass of beer by the time Maeve sat down, her eyes shining. "I thought I could avoid this by planning a side trip to Egypt, but the revolutions put an end to that."

Maeve did a visual around the room and located Jack talking to some of his old cronies from the neighborhood, people that the Donovans probably invited to parties so that they could show just how far they had come from the old neighborhood to the south. "Not having fun?" she asked.

Margie ran a hand through spiky black hair. "Remember *Sesame Street*? 'One of these things is not like the others'? I think that may apply," she said, clinking her glass against Maeve's. "And to think that my wife actually wanted to come to this." Maeve wasn't sure which of them she was referring to; neither of them belonged. She had never felt comfortable among the Donovans, neither the blue-collar ones they'd been nor the upper-middle-class ones they had become. "To say that I have been a disappointment to my family would be an understatement."

And apparently, there was no love lost between Dolores and Margie. "I always tell my sister that she can have all this money, send her kids to the best schools, but she'll never have class," Margie said, draining her beer. "Marrying a nitwit didn't help." She let out a soft belch. "Sorry. I know he's your cousin."

Maeve waved it off. "Not a problem. 'Nitwit' is being kind." She kept her eyes trained on her youngest and the keg. Her peripheral vision held Sean, who was glad-handing the men in the room, being the big *macher*, as her one employee, Jo, liked to say, his Rolex dangling from his wrist and catching sunlight. He caught her looking and gave her a sly wink followed by a thumbs-up in Heather's direction. The gesture made her freeze.

Margie was talking, but Maeve caught only part of what she was saying. "I always felt like the guy had a cruel streak. I guess that makes him well suited to Wall Street," she said.

"That's what my father always says." Maeve turned, spotting Sean making his way toward Heather.

"My sister will overlook a lot for money. My parents, too." She waved around the tent. "This would have sent my dad over the edge. To be the big guy in the neighborhood, even if the money wasn't really his? That would have made him so proud," she said, her voice tinged with disgust. "Too bad he died right after they got engaged. He didn't get to see all of this."

Maeve remained silent.

Margie's diction was getting a little fuzzy. She smiled at Maeve. "We were a couple of terrors, huh?"

"You and me?" Maeve asked.

"Yeah," she said. Maeve wondered just how much Margie had had to drink, because she had been anything but a terror. Maeve had been good and obedient and hadn't said a word unless spoken to. "I can't count how many times you ended up in the emergency room. You were kinda clumsy, right?"

"I guess you could say that," Maeve said, for

lack of a better response. "Clumsy" was an adjective that Maeve wore with considerable unease.

"My mother never thought your dad was doing a good enough job of looking after you."

Maeve bristled at that. "Oh, really?" she said, fixing Margie with a withering look. "And just what did your mother think that my father should have been doing better?" Maeve remembered the Haggertys—Fidelma and Marty—and didn't think either of them would have won a Parent of the Year award.

Margie drew back, just sober enough to realize that she had really touched a nerve. "I'm sorry," she said. "You just always seemed kind of sad."

"I lost my mother when I was seven. You would have been sad, too," Maeve said, and then flashed on the hard, cold face of Fidelma Haggerty and thought Or maybe not.

She left out the part where Sean Donovan, Margie's brother-in-law and Maeve's sometime childhood babysitter, had pummeled her to the ground one day, "wrestling" being his favorite form of entertainment, dislocating her shoulder. He'd popped it back into place before Jack had come home from doing a day tour at the precinct nearby, the memory of the pain making the adult Maeve wince. Or the part where he'd pushed her down a slide at the playground with such force that she had tumbled head over feet, getting a huge bump on her forehead that had turned the colors of the rainbow before finally fading.

Clumsy? Hardly. *Sad?* Very much so.

Margie pointed at Maeve's glass before heading back to the bar. "Want another one?"

Maeve looked down at her half a glass of Chardonnay and decided it would be best if she didn't push it. One unhappy drunk at a Fourth of July party was enough. Two? That was trouble. She stood, ready to gather her daughters, her father, her wits. They were leaving.

Before Margie walked away, Maeve asked her the question she should have been asking herself. "If you hate being here, why did you come?"

Margie took a look around the room, her eyes settling on her mother seated a few tables away, on her face the unhappy, pinched look that Maeve remembered her having thirty years before. "Oh, you know. Family loyalty and all that." She looked at Maeve over the top of her cup, held aloft. "And you?"

Maeve's eyes settled on Jack. "I guess it's the same. My dad really wanted to come," she said, unable to keep the disbelief out of her voice.

Margie laughed, a tinkling, mirthful sound that brought Maeve back to their childhood. "You're a good daughter, Maeve. So we've got that in common." She hoisted her glass high, as if to toast. "Maybe more, but we'll never know," she said, "because something tells me I'll never see you again."

Maeve started to speak, but before she could follow up with Margie, she was gone, the keg her destination, lost in the throngs assembled around it.

She grabbed her purse from the back of the chair and gave a wave to Heather. "Find your sister," she mouthed.

"Divorce suits you, Mavy," came the voice from behind her, making the hair on her neck stand at attention. The arm around her waist, the finger pinching too hard through her linen top, it was textbook Sean and his maneuvers, every attempted show of "affection" tinged with cruelty and just a touch of pain.

"Only my father is allowed to call me 'Mavy,' " she reminded him, pushing her chair under the table.

He leaned over and whispered in her ear. "And me, of course," he said.

He was a bully and always had been, and she hated herself for seizing up when he was around. Let it go, she told herself. Move on. But she couldn't. Not when there were family gatherings to attend and no excuse in the world that she could give Jack as to why they couldn't go and eat lobster and shrimp under the stars of an exclusive Bronx enclave, watching fireworks as they exploded overhead. She saw later on, much later, that she was in control. They didn't have to go. But Jack wanted to be here, and she was

35

always the good daughter, the one who couldn't not let him have those short-lived memories of being among his family in his eightieth year. So she came, letting him experience the love of the extended family, giving him the chance to show them that he hadn't "lost his marbles," carefully nursing her Chardonnay, giving a wide berth to her hosts.

"The girls are beautiful," he said, his face close to hers.

"I know," she said. "And if you touch one hair on either of their heads, I will—"

He cut her off, laughing. "Don't push it, Maeve. Just have a good time." He ran a hand down her back. "You never did know how to have fun."

I'm an adult now, she reminded herself. There's no reason to fear him, she intoned mentally. But she felt the way she had all those years ago and more than that, angry at herself for letting herself be manipulated into doing things she didn't want to do. Back then, it was one thing, but now, she had control. She stood silently and waited for him to lose interest in her, something he eventually did, seeing Dolores trying to get his attention. He slithered off, but not before giving her a chaste peck on the cheek in a way that almost made her imagine that she had dreamed everything. A kiss between cousins. Family affection.

She watched him slide past Heather, a hand lingering on her back just long enough to make his point, but not long enough to arouse suspicion in anyone else. If it rested much longer, she might have snapped, but as always with Sean, she was never entirely sure of what she had seen or what had just happened. The end result of being in Sean's sights? An inability to discern truth from fiction.

She texted Rebecca in the library and Heather, still lingering by the bar, to meet her at the car. She found Jack and dragged him away from the clutch of men who were enthralled by his semi-true stories. She had been sleepwalking, she decided, and now, for some reason that she couldn't figure out, she was wide awake. They had left the party earlier than Jack wanted—just an hour after they had arrived—long after the girls wanted, and right when Maeve wanted.

Jack had always said what a good girl she was; Margie had told her she was a good daughter. Stupid and manipulated was more like it. As she drove down the highway, away from the party and her cousins, all she could think was that good, stupid, or manipulated, all of that ends today.

She was still at the sink, lost in thought when she heard Rebecca speak.

"Kind of cute, too."

Maeve looked up, not realizing that her daughter had been talking the whole time. Her hands were still in the water, red and waterlogged after her extended mental trip down memory lane. "Cute?"

"Yeah. Sean."

Maeve didn't see it.

"Like an older Ryan Gosling."

"Really?" In her mind's eye, Sean looked like pure evil. To this day, she couldn't describe one characteristic of his face beyond his eyes, which were blue, mean, and devoid of any emotion beyond hostility and menace.

"Do the police know who did it?" Rebecca asked.

Maeve flashed on Jack and his disappearing act. "No. I don't think so."

"Probably a robbery, right?" Rebecca said, probing more, suspecting that she had hit on a topic her mother didn't want to discuss. Usually, Maeve was chatty, bringing up things that she liked to talk about but that made her daughters sick to their stomachs. Topics like safe sex, responsible drinking, and a host of other things that she probably read were good topics to have conversations with her teens about but in which they were loath to participate. If she really wanted to get them talking, she made vague references to getting an eyebrow ring or a tattoo with their names on her forearm, anything to start a conversation. "Or something else?"

The glass slid out of Maeve's hand and clattered to the floor, breaking into more pieces than she would have imagined. Months later, she'd still find a shard, like a memory long forgotten, sticking up from the floor, waiting to pierce a bare foot or slice a toe. No, they'd reappear when she least expected them to, hopefully not doing any damage. She gripped the edge of the sink. "Probably a robbery. Right." She bent down and picked up the largest piece of glass, the stem, and held it in her hands. "If I asked you to stay with me and never leave, what would you say?" she asked, intending for it to sound like one of her regular pleading jokes about missing Rebecca when she left for school. But this time even her daughter picked up on the hint of desperation in her voice. When Maeve took in Rebecca's worried expression, she quickly added, "You can't leave me here alone with Heather. You know that, right?"

Bonded in their mutual fear and trepidation for the younger Callahan, a girl who could push her mother's buttons with the greatest of ease, they managed to get back on track. "You are so screwed," Rebecca said, laughing.

Maeve hated that she couldn't leave well enough alone, but that was an ingrained part of her nature. That and a feeling that if she failed to protect her girls, as she herself had been left unprotected, she would never forgive herself. "You never have to do anything you don't want to do."

Rebecca responded with a groan.

"I know I'm a broken record, but it's just—"

Rebecca threw her mother's words back at her: "You'd never forgive yourself if something happened to me."

Maeve bent down and saw she was surrounded by broken glass, each shard a threat. Rebecca, finally realizing that her mother was stuck, got up. "Careful," Maeve said.

"That'll leave a mark, right?" Rebecca said, echoing one of her grandfather's favorite sayings.

"Right," Maeve said, her mind on other things. "That'll definitely leave a mark."

Chapter 4

On Monday, after the bakery closed at four, Maeve made an unscheduled visit to the assisted-living facility. When she got to Buena del Sol, she found out that Jack was in the weight room, an idea that frightened Maeve more than the fact that he had snuck out several nights earlier.

The "concierge," a young woman who sat at the front desk, a stuffed monkey attached to her shoulder, gave her a warm smile. When Maeve asked her what kinds of weights one found in the weight room of an assisted-living facility, the monkey did the talking. "Nothing too heavy, Miss Conlon," the monkey said by way of the woman's hand. Maeve stared at the woman's mouth, noting that she was a pretty good ventriloquist while also being completely insane. "And our residents are completely supervised while in there. Isn't that right, Doreen?" the monkey asked the woman around whose waist its long legs were attached.

The woman nodded vigorously.

"Doreen?" she asked. "Could you ask my father if he could meet me in the community room?"

Doreen affected the husky voice of her stuffed simian counterpart, her lips not moving. "Doreen can't, but Caesar can," she said.

Maeve was used to seeing the staff talk to the residents like children, but this was the first time she had ever been treated that way herself. Rather than dwell on the fact that Doreen really took her job seriously—or rather, Caesar did—Maeve went with her fallback position: Doreen was crazy. She waited patiently while Doreen, using her *Planet of the Apes* voice, paged Jack in the weight room. When she gave Maeve the high sign, in this case a regular old thumbs-up with one of her own opposable digits, Maeve started down the hall, taking one deep breath before she hit the community room, a place that invariably smelled like a combination of oatmeal, disinfectant, and something else that she would never attempt to discern, no matter how curious she was.

She took a seat by the window, looking out over the back lawn and the various residents who were taking advantage of an unseasonably warm October day. Some were in wheelchairs, while

41

others wandered freely. Two, to Maeve's surprise, were engaged in a rather passionate kiss, confirming her suspicion that life at Buena del Sol was a hell of a lot more interesting than Maeve realized. To the best of her knowledge, Jack wasn't involved in a romance, but nothing would surprise her. While he talked a good game about breaking hearts left and right during the five o'clock supper hour, his own heart was still devoted to his lovely Claire, long gone but still a presence in his fragile mind and memory.

He arrived a few minutes after she sat down, by now fully engrossed in a home improvement show that boasted that she, too, would be able to make her own valances by the show's end just like the show's trained designer. Now that Jack had arrived, she'd never know. Jack was wearing a tank top that showed off his ropy yet still muscled arms and the slight paunch that had developed only since he had discovered the joys of assisted-living dining hall chocolate pudding. His smile widened as he got closer, the look on his face one that greeted her every time they came together and one that she would treasure, even when it eventually would hold no recognition of who she was or what they once meant to each other. "Mavy!" he exclaimed, leaning over and giving her a big kiss. He pulled out the chair across from her.

His pants were on backward, the drawstring for his sweats trailing down over his backside.

"The concierge is interesting," Maeve said.

"Doreen?" Jack said. "She's two sandwiches short of a picnic." He leaned in and smiled conspiratorially. "If I do say so myself."

Maeve smiled.

"To what do I owe this enormous pleasure?" he asked.

"You lift weights?" she asked.

"Amazing, right?" he said, flexing a bicep in her direction. "Give me one other guy at seventy who can lift as much as I can."

"I can't think of anyone, Dad," she said, but then again, she didn't know too many seventy-year-old men, and even if she did, he wasn't one of them. But she didn't share that with him.

"I can bench-press more than Lefkowitz," he said. "And he was Golden Gloves back in the day."

"Impressive, Dad," she said, sneaking a look at her watch. "Listen, I have to talk to you about something."

"What did I do?" he asked, his brow furrowed. Anytime Maeve had to talk to Jack, it usually meant trouble of some sort, and he was smart enough to know that.

"You didn't do anything, Dad," she said. She didn't think he had, but she couldn't be sure. She looked out the window, the lovebirds drifting by, their arms entwined.

"Get a room," Jack mumbled.

She knew it was useless to ask, but she had to.

"Dad, where were you a week ago Saturday?"

Jack screwed up his face, deep in thought. As if that would help. He searched his brain for the answer and came up empty, using what he always did when he was at a loss: a big smile. "Not a clue." He took a gander at his left bicep. "Do you know where you were?"

"At the shop," she said. He looked at her quizzically. "The Comfort Zone?"

"Ah, yes," he said, but she wasn't sure he knew what that was.

"I'm easy to keep track of." She tried again. "Think, Dad. A week or so ago?"

He gave it another shot. "Church?" He wiped a bead of sweat that had appeared on his forehead, the fruits of his exertion still exhibiting themselves in little ways. "Why?"

"Were you really at a church?" she asked.

He knew the jig was up. "What did that old battle-ax Harrison tell you? She's framing me, I tell you. It's a frame-up!" he said, cracking himself up with his own joke.

Maeve knew better than to get frustrated with him and offered a little laugh in return for his overacting. "She's not framing you, Dad. She just let me know that you weren't here and nobody signed you out. She was wondering—I was wondering—where you might have gone."

"What difference does it make?" he asked, his own frustration at his lack of memory showing its face. He turned around and glared at the man sitting by the television and in an uncharacteristic display of ill temper yelled at him to turn the volume down. "I hate when you do this, Maeve. I'm a grown—"

"Man," she finished. "I know. You're a grown man. But I need you to stay put, Dad. I really, really want to keep you here."

As quickly as the anger came, it was gone, replaced by the Jack she knew and loved. "And what would be the big deal about a week ago Saturday?" he asked.

"Nothing," she said. "No big deal. You were probably at the river, right?"

"Probably," he said. "That's my favorite spot, you know."

It wasn't the first time he had told her, nor would it be the last.

"A week ago Saturday, you say?" he asked. The set of his mouth told her that he was absolutely sure about what he was going to say. "It was book club. We read *Water for Elephants*. Brand-new book. Had the library in the village hold it for me. Hated it. Don't like elephants. Never did."

The book wasn't brand-new, nor did Jack have borrowing privileges at the village library; the fines for his overdue books had become too steep for Maeve in spite of her friendship with the head librarian. As Jack waxed poetic on the finer plot points of the book, all of which were correct and astute, Maeve's mind wandered back. A week ago Saturday. Jack wanted to know what would be the big deal about that day, but she would never tell him, even though he would forget anyway.

She wondered how long it would be before he asked again, because it was the night that Sean Donovan had gone out for a gallon of milk supposedly and ended up with a hole in his head he didn't need. Some things the old guy just didn't need to know.

Chapter 5

Maeve started her day earlier than anyone she knew: her alarm went off a little past four thirty, and she left the house at five thirty that next morning, just like always. Although she planned her days and her baking with precision, there were always things that needed to be done, coffee to start, and papers to arrange so that she could open at six on the dot. Her one employee, Jo, was not the most punctual, but Maeve cut her some slack. They had been friends for years and had been through a lot together: Jo's cancer treatment, her divorce, and a host of other life experiences that neither had foreseen but both had weathered together.

The Comfort Zone was walking distance from

Maeve's house, but she always drove. The people in the village of Farringville—a forty-minute train ride to Grand Central Station in New York City—took their morning commute seriously, and many cut it close when driving to the local train station. The last thing she needed was to be walking along a dark street in the wee hours of the morning, a speeding commuter mowing her down as she traversed the one stretch that had no sidewalk.

The shop was dark when she entered, the only light coming from the alarm system by the back door. She thought it sounded clichéd—and it was—but this was her favorite time of the day. Once Jo arrived, her chatter filled the silence in between customer visits, and the big mixer on the table provided background music to her latest musings on the women in town and her general take on everything from the best Chinese food to be found locally to the state of Maeve's blond hair, usually not to Jo's liking. The empty store, the scent of fresh-baked scones part of the permanent smell that greeted her every day, was the place she most identified with the word *home*.

She had set up the front of the store to resemble a café she remembered from her honeymoon in Paris, procuring spindly iron chairs and tables for customers who ate in and hanging cheap prints of scenes from the City of Lights. It was bright and sunny when the sun reflected off the nearby Hudson and displayed none of the blood, sweat, and sometimes tears that she put in every day to fill the glass-front cases with a mix of sweet and savory items: cupcakes for those who wanted a sugar rush, quiche for the harried commuter on the go who was out of ideas for dinner. Bread and rolls on the shorter side of the L-shaped counter, cookies on the long part. It was all there and it was all done by her, and when people asked how she did it all, even she couldn't figure it out.

As the coffee dripped into the pot, she picked up the papers that were delivered every morning and that sat on the small patio in front of the store. Various headlines bemoaned the loss of titan of industry Sean Donovan, his death still a mystery, a cause for concern among the people who lived in the neighborhood where he had been killed. One of the headlines was tawdry and unnecessary, putting a voice to the fact that he was not where he should have been, another focusing only on the devastated family, the sordid nature of the story buried in the last paragraph. She closed the papers and folded them flat, then stuck them beneath a large stack so that no one would know they had been read.

The morning rush went smoothly, Maeve having prepared just enough scones and muffins so that only a few were left by the time midmorning rolled around. Jo had handled the front of the store with an ease and flexibility Maeve hadn't really seen to date, and she wondered if this was a

Jo she could rely on completely if she wanted to take a vacation day in the near future. By lunchtime, though, Jo's energy was flagging and they fell into their usual roles of stressed-out baker and hapless assistant.

Instead of working, Jo was reading aloud from the village's local rag, the *Day Timer*, and her favorite feature, the police blotter, which was particularly entertaining that day.

She was draped over the counter, her long legs stretched out behind her, her short hair sticking up in a number of different directions. Her overalls were covered with flour, making it appear that she had worked far harder at baking and with more efficiency that morning than she actually had. "Get this one," she said. " 'A woman called the Farringville Police to report that she didn't like the e-mail alert on her new cell phone. An officer responded and changed the ringtone to one the woman found more pleasing to the ear.' "

Maeve was restocking the front glass case with cupcakes, red velvet this time, her biggest seller. "You're making that up."

"Hand to God," Jo said, putting a hand over her heart. "Our tax dollars at work. Listen to the next one. 'Picnickers at Farringville Park called to report an auspicious diver in the Hudson River.' " She waited a beat. "You heard me right. Auspicious. As in 'providential' or 'fortunate.' "

"Must have been a good day for diving." Maeve

49

pulled the empty platter out of the case. "What did the police do with this charming fellow?"

"Nothing. Blotter says he was just looking for fish."

"As only an auspicious diver can," Maeve said. She pulled off her apron. "Sorry I have to leave you to close," she said. "I would say that I'd be back by four, but I know how long these Conlon-Donovan things take."

"I still think my people have the right idea," Jo said, folding the paper into perfect rectangles. "Die one day, bury the next."

"Yeah, but then you have that whole sitting-on-a-box thing for seven days, right?" Maeve grabbed her peacoat from the back of the kitchen door and put it on.

"With the best bagels and lox known to mankind on the buffet," Jo said. "The Jews can take any event and make it a deli day." She grabbed a bottle of glass cleaner and a roll of paper towels from under the counter. "Go," she said, shooing Maeve out the door. "Who wouldn't want to go to an ash scattering in the middle of a gorgeous October day?"

Maeve hesitated. When she put it like that? Not her.

"You bringing Jack?" Jo asked.

"He wouldn't miss it," Maeve said, offering a little laugh. For the comic relief alone, she had to bring Jack. His asides would be the only thing keeping her sane during Sean's dispersal from the banks of the Hudson River, a journey south that would take her to her old Bronx neighborhood.

So why was she going? Maybe to make sure he really was dead.

Jo bowed at the waist and offered a benediction in Hebrew.

Maeve asked for a translation. She had gotten used to most of Jo's Yiddish and Hebrew expressions, but this was a new one.

"Stay strong," Jo said, focusing her attention on the glass case and the myriad fingerprints that had appeared there.

Maeve went out to the parking lot and noticed the stiff breeze that had kicked up between the time she'd left the house and arrived at the store. Not really the perfect weather for scattering ashes. She drove the short distance to the assisted-living facility, fetched Jack, and headed south on the parkway.

"Hated the snot," Jack said. "Hate that Dolores even more. She's a wailer."

That was putting it kindly. Maeve would remind him of this the next time they were invited to a Donovan family party, even if they had lobster and Johnnie Walker Blue. Jack often talked about how much he hated Sean but seemed to have forgotten when he got that invitation to the Fourth of July party in the mail. Turned out Jack Conlon's love could be bought for a two-pound lobster and a shot of good whiskey, not to mention an opportunity to prove to everyone that he was still the same old Jack.

Maeve had heard through the family grapevine —namely an e-mail from Margie, who seemed to want to reconnect with Maeve suddenly —that the widow Donovan had tried to follow her deceased husband's casket into the back of the hearse that would take him to the crematorium before one of the stronger relatives stopped her. All for show or truly an exhibition of a lost love? It was hard to tell, hard to know. Although Maeve had done her fair share of family parties, and with the exception of the July Fourth extravaganza, she hadn't spent a whole lot of time around Sean and his family after she had left for college, and that was the way she liked it. Sean made her skin crawl, while Dolores had been a neighborhood girl and a not very nice one at that, so Maeve had no interest in keeping that relationship going. Familial loyalty and devotion went only so far, and Sean didn't deserve any of hers. Margie seemed nice enough, but Maeve wasn't all that keen at rekindling what had been a casual friendship at best.

Jack blathered the whole way down, and although he protested vehemently about being "ripped from the warm confines of the community room" to attend the ash scattering of the "little puke," he was more than delighted to be traveling alongside his daughter on a jaunt that was sure to be interesting, given the players. Maeve had also promised him a late lunch at his favorite clam joint on City Island, and the prospect of that had him on his best behavior. He was dressed today in a natty tweed blazer, pressed khaki trousers, a bow tie, and loafers. The only sign that he had maybe lost the mental thread while he was dressing were the two different socks—one black, one green—that Maeve could see peeking out from beneath his cuffed pants.

"You look handsome, Dad," Maeve said.

"Mimi Delaveaux helped me pick out this outfit," he said, pulling at his collar. "I think she wants to get in my pants."

Maeve cringed.

"You think the bow tie is a bit much, don't you?"

"I didn't even know you had a bow tie," Maeve said.

"There's a lot you don't know about me, daughter of mine," he said, but there was no humor in his voice, and that worried her.

They were silent for most of the ride, Jack coming to life a little bit when they passed their old street. He craned his neck toward the window. "I can see it," he said. "The old house."

"Do you want to drive by?" she asked, praying that the answer would be no.

Her prayers were answered. "No," he said. "Too hard." He turned back around. "I loved it here, though. Didn't you?"

The number of lies she told herself, as well as her father, grew with each passing day. "Loved it," she said flatly.

They came to a stoplight on the avenue. Jack whispered as if they weren't alone in the car, "I know why you asked, you know."

She wasn't sure if this was one of his tangents or if he had something on his mind. She waited.

"About that Saturday?" he said. "That's when Sean died." His voice got a little louder. "And I know that he didn't die of those things you told me. I have eyes. I read the paper."

She made a left turn onto the avenue, keeping quiet. It was better that way.

"You think I forget everything, but I don't. I remember stuff."

"So where were you, Dad?" she asked quietly, not wanting to arouse the ire that he displayed infrequently but enough to keep her on her toes. From what she had read, the anger was part of the dementia that was slowly stealing his mind and his essence, the thing that made him Jack.

He turned into a petulant child, his arms folded across his chest. "I don't have to tell you every-thing, you know."

"No, you don't." She wasn't sure she wanted to know everything anyway. She waited. "So where were you?"

His voice was as tangled as if a clump of cotton were stuck in his throat, and when he spoke it came out thick and hoarse. "That I can't remember. That's one of the things."

She knew he was upset. It was these times, when he had the realization that his grasp on what was now and what was then was tenuous, that made him scared. It scared her, too. She changed the subject. "Tell me about *Water for Elephants*."

"Now why would you want to know about that?"

She pulled up at another light. She leaned over and gave him a quick peck on the cheek. "Because unlike you, I happen to love elephants."

Maeve had printed out directions, but she didn't need them. She drove the narrow, windy streets of her old neighborhood and wended her way down to the river, just past the train tracks and into the parking lot of the Metro-North station, where she parked the car illegally. She figured she could keep a watch from where they stood so that if the police came, MTA or city, she would be able to move quickly.

Twenty or so people had gathered riverside, the blowsy Dolores clad in an expensive black pantsuit, the jacket of which was stretched across her broad back. She was wailing openly, just as Jack had predicted. He got out of the car and surveyed the scene. "Why are we doing this again?" he asked.

That was a very good question. She didn't tell him that Dolores had specifically requested his attendance, saying that Sean had loved Jack like a dad—Maeve was pretty sure that that was an out-and-out lie—nor did she mention the fact that their nonattendance at the funeral had been duly noted by the entire family. She guessed that their attendance at the wake didn't count. Apparently, it was the funeral that mattered. Maeve wasn't sure why she cared, but she did, more for Jack than for herself. She counted the number of people whose wakes or funerals she would be required to attend and came up with exactly four. Once those people were gone, she could quietly fade into the sunset, never to be seen again by any members of this wholly dysfunctional family.

She and Jack found themselves in the large throng. Dolores made a show of giving Jack a big hug and an even bigger kiss, one that he wiped away when she wasn't looking. She proclaimed loudly that now that the "latecomers had arrived," they could commence with the service.

No Irish family is complete without one priest to call their own, be it a relative with a vocation or a parish priest who had seen his fair share of goings-on and had heard the confession of every member of the extended family. Today, the go-to guy was the ubiquitous Father Madden, the same guy who had married Maeve to Cal all those years ago and who now looked at her with a mixture of sadness and disappointment because he knew she was divorced. Despite preaching to the crowd about the resurrection, he seemed to seek her out specifically, making eye contact with her the whole time, maybe trying to make her understand that the rising of the Lord on the third day applied to dead marriages as well. On that account, she was a nonbeliever. She held his gaze, having found over the years that the person first commit-ting to the stare was usually the first one out when it became a two-person contest. She listened with faux rapt attention to his droning about Jesus and how He died for our sins.

If that were truly the case, He would have died a second time knowing that He had created the ultimate sinner, Sean Donovan. Or at least turned over in His tomb.

A priest was supposed to preside over the burial of ashes, not the scattering of them, but Maeve knew from the e-mail that had circulated that Dolores had every intention of throwing Sean into the Hudson. She didn't know if Father Madden knew this or was turning a blind eye, the Donovans being solely responsible for the new gym floor at St. Augustine's. That Madden had sold his soul for a stretch of hardwood didn't surprise Maeve.

Margie stood on the outskirts of the family, a tall, attractive woman by her side. The wife, Maeve presumed. Margie eyed Maeve warily, either embarrassed by how much she had drunk at the barbecue a few months earlier, the last time she had seen her, or regretting their conversation, the one that had left Maeve a little upset and feeling less than warm toward the long-lost Margie, e-mails replete with family gossip notwithstanding. Clumsy, she had called her. Maeve thought the word sounded sinister in her brain, given how inaccurate it was. I guess that's one word for it, she thought. She did the right thing and shot Margie a warm smile, one that hopefully evoked the sadness that she was supposed to feel at the situation and the forgiveness she felt was necessary for biting the woman's head off at the family party.

The grand finale—the sprinkling of the ashes—came a lot sooner than Maeve could have hoped for. Next to her, Jack had begun to shiver in his tweed blazer, his hands jammed down deep in the pockets of his khakis. Dolores held the urn aloft and turned toward the river, her wailing becoming one long, steady sob that transcended even the noise of the commuter train rumbling behind them. She beckoned the group closer so that everyone could see the remains of her beloved husband scattered into the river he loved so well, if his fifty-foot sailboat was any indication.

Dolores pulled the top off the urn and turned dramatically, flinging ashes into what turned into a very stiff north wind. Jack had the good sense to zig as the ashes zagged, leaving Maeve open to the vagaries of the windswept remains of a cousin she had been glad to see go. A few flecks of Sean Donovan landed on her shoulders and on her sleeves. Her stomach did a flip as she took in the amount of ash in which she was now covered, noticing that everyone else seemed to have been downwind of the ashes' trajectory and clean of any soot.

Jack looked at her mournfully. "I guess this means we can't go for clams."

Maeve managed to hold down the muffin she had eaten right before she had left the store, but yes, it still meant that they weren't going for clams.

It was as if Sean were laughing at her from his grave. See? he taunted. You'll never be rid of me.

Chapter 6

"Speed dating."

Maeve looked up from the mixing bowl. "That's funny. I thought you said 'speed dating.' "

"You know you want to." Jo hoisted herself over the counter and into Maeve's work space, something that Maeve had asked her several times not to do, but that she persisted in doing. Jo was a former gymnast, and she still carried herself like one all these years later. She had competed until she had gotten too tall—topping out at a hair below five feet nine—and left her little spandex-suited teammates behind to throw themselves up and over and around the mats at the gymnastics academy where she still held a couple of scoring titles. Reed thin, long-legged, and graceful, she hid her lithe body behind baggy overalls and Doc Marten boots. She never did a backhand spring or anything else to give away her background, but the ease with which she could bend from the waist to pick up a dropped knife or stand on her toes to get something on a tall shelf was a dead giveaway that she was a former athlete and made Maeve, a hair over five feet, envious.

"You know?" Maeve said, watching Jo's eyebrows go up in anticipation of her acceptance of the plan. "I really don't." She held up her spatula, letting the ganache she was making trail back into the bowl. "Does the consistency of this look right to you?"

Jo shrugged. "Looks okay. Put a dollop on top of the cake and see if it holds." It was the first reasonable thing she had said about baking the entire day.

The store was quiet that morning, despite it being a typical workday. Maeve handed Jo a muffin tin, the idea being that she would actually bake.

"It will be fun," Jo protested.

"The last time someone said that to me, I ended up throwing up, upside down, on a roller coaster in Seaside Park." Maeve licked the knife that held a dollop of cream cheese frosting. "It won't be fun. It will be a disaster. Thanks, but no thanks."

Jo looked at her forlornly, reminding Maeve that she was much newer to the realm of divorce than Maeve was, although Maeve had never had a longing to pair up with anyone after her marriage had ended. In the space of eighteen months, Jo had lost her breasts and her husband to cancer, the former to the actual disease, the latter to the fallout from more than a year of treatment and all its attendant horrors: chemotherapy, hair loss, and, ultimately, a body that didn't resemble the one that he thought he had taken possession of ten years earlier at their wedding.

To say that Maeve didn't like Jo's ex was a massive understatement.

Jo was still talking, but Maeve realized she wasn't listening. She was fantasizing about killing him. And not in that abstract way in which you thought about making someone—a nuisance, really—disappear. It was all very clear to her, and she figured it would take about fifteen minutes; if she budgeted her time correctly, she could fit it in between Heather's tutoring session and Rebecca's haircut.

"Maeve?"

"What?" she asked, noting the empty muffin tin in Jo's hands.

"It's one night. And there's free booze," Jo said.

"You really want to do this?" Maeve asked.

Jo looked at her beseechingly. "It's that or I put an ad on Craigslist. You don't want that, do you?"

Maeve reached into the huge stainless steel refrigerator in the kitchen and handed Jo a tub of muffin mix. "And what would that say?"

Jo thought for a moment, putting down the muffin tin. "Breastless woman with boundless sexual energy seeks to make the carnal acquaintance of man with penis. No experience necessary. On-the-job training available." Jo had had a reconstruction after her surgery, but it hadn't gone well, her body too battered, her skin too thin, another nail in the coffin of her marriage.

Maeve took off her apron, still clean, and hung it on the back of the door. "Very enticing. Alluring, even." She pulled open the kitchen door, staring out into the empty space in the front of the store. "Okay, I'll think about it."

Jo clapped her hands together excitedly, a gesture that belied her almost forty years on the earth. "I'll drive. I know how you get around free Chardonnay."

Maeve was halfway out the door, another soccer game on her schedule, when she reminded Jo that she hadn't actually said yes.

Cal and Gabriela were already at the game when she got there, and she did her best to hide the hitch in her step as she approached the bleachers, the one that indicated that, yes, she was surprised to see them, and no, she wasn't happy to see Gabriela. Her flat-ironed hair was motionless on this breezy day, held in place by countless applications of some kind of product Maeve would never buy or use on her own curly blond tresses, preferring a stretched-out elastic band or a headband to deal with the strays that inevitably made their way onto her face. Next to Gabriela was a purse big enough to hold a case of wine, its soft, buttery leather containing the contents of one very glamorous woman's life. Maeve knew for a fact that Gabriela had gotten the bag at a photo shoot a few years earlier because she had offered it to Maeve, her unkempt and not-stylish friend married to the man she had set her sights on, a gesture that Maeve now knew was a guilt offering. At the time, Gabriela had been sleeping with Cal on a regular basis, and it seemed that Maeve was the only person who hadn't known.

Maeve wished she had taken the bag. It was worth twenty grand on eBay, its salmon color making it a rare and exotic breed of designer handbag. She had looked it up.

The baby was strapped to Cal, as usual, Gabriela's crisp white dress shirt not the place to put a baby whose reason for being was to dribble and drool as much as possible. Cal's second wife looked up as Maeve climbed into the bleachers, taking a seat behind them. She was happy to notice, looking down at Gabriela's head, that a thin spot had begun to appear right at the crown of her former friend's head, pink scalp starting to peek through black tresses. Karma really was a bitch. That, or Gabriela's aggressive straightening treatments were wreaking havoc on her scalp.

Gabriela's modus operandi was to behave as if nothing had changed between them. She looked behind her and gave Maeve a big smile. "I left work early so I could see the game," she said, her Portuguese accent covering every word like a cashmere blanket, soothing and comforting. Maeve knew better, though; beneath the earth mother persona lay a spoiled, rotten witch who got what she wanted, when she wanted it, regardless of the cost. Like the bag. And Cal.

The baby was the icing on the cake. Sure, he was adorable and completely innocent in this whole situation, but watching Cal parade around like Father of the Year when he had been completely absent for the better part of his first two daughters' fleeting childhoods, was hard to take. Cal decided right around the time that Gabriela announced her pregnancy, with some creative math that made Maeve realize in hindsight that perhaps Gabriela had been pregnant before Cal had really bolted the family nest for good, that he was burned out on corporate law. That plus the fact that he now had a wife, two children, and a pregnant mistress was enough to burn anyone out. It was depressing him, making him question if he really was living his best life, sentiments that were the hallmarks of a traditional midlife crisis. Maeve watched from the sidelines as he struck a deal with his new wife to stay home and take care of little Devon while she continued her career at a second-tier women's magazine—*Frou Frou* was no *Vogue* and never would be—dispensing advice as to how to wear the newest nail polish colors and when to wear fishnets. Her magazine was for women with a lot of time on their hands and even more disposable income; it didn't interest Maeve in the slightest.

So why had they been friends? Maeve asked herself that every day. They had met at church, when Maeve was still going, and served on the hospitality committee together. From what Maeve knew, Gabriela still went to church every Sunday and, like some of her Donovan cousins, was quite the donor. The church benefited from a beautiful statue of Our Lady of Fatima, which Maeve knew that Gabriela's ex-husband had paid for but for which she took complete credit.

Maybe Maeve, like her former husband, had been a little bit in Gabriela's thrall, her beauty making her overlook what turned out to be an indefatigable shallowness hidden beneath a thick layer of gloss and shine, two things that Maeve had lost so many years before. Maybe she hoped that Gabriela was only kidding when she called her first husband's children the "little rotten bastards," or that she really didn't mean it when she'd called her former husband—while they were still married—"the troll." When the dust had settled and Gabriela had ridden off into the sunset with Cal, Maeve came to the conclusion that what she had once written off as witty insouciance turned out to be a deep-seated maliciousness that Cal seemed to take to like a bee to honey. While Maeve had tried so hard to be the good girl, it seemed that her former husband was drawn to the bad girl.

To this day, she had never seen Gabriela hold the baby.

Maeve reiterated her request that Heather not be let out of the house the Saturday upcoming. Gabriela gave her a sly smile. "Getting a little too hot to handle?" she asked.

"I guess you could say that," Maeve said.

"That will be up to this guy here," Gabriela said, patting Cal on the shoulder. "I've got my hands full with the little one," she said, pinching the baby's cheek in a way that suggested she had just met the boy and found babies, in general, a level just above detestable.

Rebecca finished her workout with the team and scanned the crowd as she always did for her mother, who returned her daughter's wave with an enthusiastic one of her own. When the game started and everyone became involved in the heated rivalry that was Farringville versus Lake

Monroe, it was as if Maeve had become invisible to the couple in front of her.

As she washed the dishes in her kitchen sink that night, she realized that Gabriela hadn't expressed sympathy at her family's loss of Maeve's cousin. She wondered if Cal had even told her, the subject of Maeve and her family something he probably didn't bother himself with beyond his concern for Jack.

She hoped they were happy—really, she did—but then wondered if that was even possible, given the players.

Chapter 7

Maeve never said she would actually speed date, a fact that she reminded Jo of when they arrived at the hotel conference room the following evening. She pointed at the lobby bar as they strode past, telling Jo that she would wait for her until she was done.

Jo was not happy. "I thought we could do this together."

"Aren't we? I'm here, aren't I?" Maeve might have given Jo the impression that she would actually participate in ten dates in fifty minutes, but when it became clear what speed dating actually entailed, Maeve said that she had never gotten on board to talk to strange men, in person, in a hotel ballroom. "And why did we have to come to the Bronx again?"

"Looking for tribe members," Jo said. "I figured it would be easier to meet a single Jewish man in this part of the city than where we live."

"There are Jews in Westchester," Maeve reminded her. "And Eric was Catholic. Since when did you get so religious?"

"Since I married a cheating goy who never once told me I was beautiful," she said, attempting a joke that fell flat because it was true and not remotely funny. "I'm off Catholics for the time being. No offense," she said to Maeve.

"None taken."

"So let's try a Jew!" Jo said. "Now get your head in the game."

"It is," Maeve said.

"Not really."

She was right. Maeve wasn't into doing this with Jo, and she wasn't really there mentally. She thought of one more potential "out" and raised it to Jo. "I didn't sign up!" she said, trying to sound apologetic and failing miserably. "I think you need to register for these events. I didn't register."

Jo was one step ahead of her. "I signed you up yesterday," she said. "Problem solved." She pushed Maeve gently toward the door to the ballroom, where a group of singles, men and women, had gathered in anticipation of a night of possibly meeting their soul mate. Before they entered, she said, "You owe me thirty bucks."

Speed dating didn't come cheap, another reason Maeve stood fast; clearly, speed dating was not for her. "You do it," she said. "I'll wait at the bar." Jo pouted while she waited for Maeve to change her mind. Maeve could see she wouldn't win this one and threw up her hands. "Fine."

Jo smoothed down the front of her dress. "How do I look?"

"You look great," Maeve said. In a tight black dress that showed off her slim build and sky-high stilettos, Jo did look great. Maeve hadn't put as much thought into what she would wear and ended up in her best pair of jeans and an untucked oxford shirt, sensible flats on her feet. Next to Jo, she looked like someone's maiden aunt. Someone's tiny maiden aunt.

"I'm wearing a Wonderbra," Jo said. "Do you think that's false advertising?"

"No." She thought for a moment of what other advice she could give Jo, who was more invested in this process than Maeve would have thought or even liked. "I wouldn't mention how much you hate cheating Catholics, though."

"What about how Eric never satisfied me sexually?" she asked, only half-joking.

Maeve pretended to think it over. "Uh, no on that one as well."

"I bet you're going to have a good time." She smiled hopefully, and it was that smile that came close to breaking Maeve's heart. It was also what made her enter the ballroom with Jo, against her better judgment.

The minute she entered, she was sorry she had, but she put her feelings aside, paying attention to the rules, planning on breaking several if the spirit moved her. She took her place at a small table and waited until bachelor number one, a tall drink of water named Doug, took his place across from her. She wished she were thirstier, but Doug wasn't the kind of guy who was going to slake her thirst. He was thirty-nine, Jewish, never married, and a C.P.A. Maeve listened to his litany of academic and athletic accomplishments and then beckoned him closer.

"Turn around slowly," she said, watching his eyes as he did as he was told. That was a plus in his favor: he could follow directions. "Do you see the fantastic-looking brunette over there? The one who looks like a taller Natalie Portman?"

He turned back around, keeping one eye on Jo. "Uh-huh."

"She's thirty-eight, Jewish, a former gymnast, divorced, no kids."

"Keep going."

"She likes the Knicks. And she makes the best pot roast you'll ever have. Bar none."

"My mother makes good pot roast," he said.

Great. A mama's boy. "Play along, Doug," Maeve said.

"Okay," he said. "What else?"

"What else is there?" she asked.

"Does she want to get married again?" he asked.

Maeve considered this, not sure what the right answer was. But Doug made it easy for her. "Because I'm looking to settle down," he added.

"Definitely," she said, as if that had been her answer all along. She wanted to advise Doug not to show his hand so easily; that always led to trouble. "She's dying to get married again." Of that she was fairly certain.

His eyes narrowed. "What's in it for you? How do I know that you're not just trying to get rid of me? What if I wanted to date you?"

"You're a Jew. I'm a Muslim. It would never work," she said just as the air horn sounded. Doug looked at her quizzically, then jotted something down quickly on his date sheet before sauntering off. Maeve watched Doug's Dockers-clad backside sidle away, his attention still on Jo. Mission accomplished.

Maeve leaned back in her chair, her work for the evening complete. Another candidate slid into the chair across from her, talking while she continued to focus on Doug, wondering if he was good enough for her friend or if her usually correct instincts had let her down.

The new bachelor rapped his knuckles on the table. "Hello?"

Maeve dragged her eyes away from Doug,

calculating that the air horn needed to sound three more times before the round robin brought him to Jo's table. "Um, hi?" she said, focusing on the man in front of her. The face that stared back at her was mid-forties, black, brown-eyed, and handsome in a way that suggested this wasn't his first rodeo. But he looked tired. Really tired. As tired as she felt.

"Your name?" he asked, looking down at his date sheet. "Or are we just going to use numbers?"

"What are we supposed to do?" she asked.

"Not sure. I wasn't really paying attention during the instruction portion of the evening," he admitted, but he held out his hand anyway. "I'm Rodney."

"Maeve," she said, taking his hand.

"What kind of name is Maeve?" he asked.

"Gaelic."

"What does it mean?"

She had been hoping he wouldn't ask, but now that he had, she had to tell him. " 'Intoxicating,' " she said, blushing. "The original Maeve was a warrior queen in first-century Ireland. She wielded a pretty hefty sword, according to Irish lore."

"And you?"

"Just a spatula," she said.

"So what brings you here, Maeve?" he asked, folding his arms on the table.

"Speed dating," she said as convincingly as she

could muster. Something about him made her want to tell him the true story, but she held back. The people here were taking this whole exercise much more seriously than she was, and she couldn't recommend that every man she met date Jo.

"You don't sound very convincing," he said.

She shrugged. "Giving it my best shot."

"Me too," he said. "What do you do?"

"I own a gourmet shop in Farringville. The Comfort Zone?" she asked, but she could tell by his face that he either had never been to Farringville, despite its relative proximity to the speed-dating location, or he didn't eat gourmet or comfort food. "What do you do?" she asked.

"This and that. Import/export."

She didn't know why, but she liked his deliberate vagueness. Maybe it allowed her to create an identity for him that suited what she wanted to think. "Well, if your 'this and that' takes you to Farringville, make sure you come in and visit," she said, sounding far more confident than she felt. "It's only about a half hour from here in Westchester."

He studied her for a minute. "I just might do that," he said. "So what are you doing here?" he asked in a rephrase of his earlier question.

"Speed dating," she repeated.

He continued to look at her. "I don't think you are."

"Well, you'd be wrong." She decided that turning the tables was the only way to go. "What are you doing here?"

"Looking to find a good woman to date."

"I don't think you are." She paused a minute, the truth hitting her so hard that she was surprised she hadn't figured it out earlier. "You're a cop."

His calm façade cracked slightly, but not enough so that Maeve could tell if she was right. A slight shrug was all she got in return. He tried to tell her she was wrong, but he couldn't; the word *no* stuck in his throat.

"You've got cop written all over you."

"Really?"

"My father was a cop. I can spot you guys a mile away."

He regarded her coolly.

She sensed she wasn't going to get the truth, so she tried another tack. "Okay, Officer. We've got work to do here. What would a date entail?" she asked after a few seconds of silence.

A smile played on his lips as he looked off into the expanse of the ballroom. Finally, he brought his attention back on her. "A bottle of Côtes du Rhône. A meal we cooked together. Dessert? Definitely." He leaned in and whispered conspiratorially. "And I ain't talking chocolate mousse here."

She wondered why the hair at the nape of her

neck was damp, but she didn't have time to really process it; the air horn sounded and Rodney moved on to the next table, his seat being taken by a bald guy wearing a loud paisley shirt more colorful than should have been legally allowed. She followed Rodney with her eyes, wondering what a cop would be doing at a speed-dating event and why, in spite of knowing that, she was intrigued. Maeve had tamped down any thoughts related to love and lust long ago and was surprised, sitting there, to find out that they still held a little place in her brain.

The guy at the table wanted to know her "sign." She made up a story about being on the cusp with Aries rising, which got him talking about her tendencies and why they were a perfect match.

Sometimes, she was her own worst enemy.

Her attention previously trained on Doug, Maeve now watched Rodney move fluidly through the room, wondering what he was really doing there. Because that was a man who, in a five-minute interlude, had managed to pique her curiosity, something no one had been able to do in a very long time.

Maybe ever.

Chapter 8

Kids' birthday parties were the worst.

Maeve had to remind herself several times during a party why she had started this part of the business. Oh, that's right—seventy-five dollars a head with a minimum of ten kids. Throwing just two parties a month paid her rent and kept her going. Otherwise, it was muffin by muffin, scone by scone, as Cal so wisely pointed out, and even with the free help her two teenage daughters occasionally provided, it was tough going. She had her one paid employee, but Jo preferred to work the "front of the house," as she liked to call it, passing up the opportunity to spend an afternoon with icing-covered kids.

After she'd hosted just a few, word had gotten out that a birthday party at The Comfort Zone was worth every penny, and soon Maeve was booking back-to-back parties every weekend.

Too bad she hated kids, her own notwithstanding, although even they made her question her devotion to them from time to time.

Before the party, she had visited her father again at Buena del Sol. She reminded him that he couldn't leave the premises without her, even if it was just to go across the street to the deli to get a six-pack.

He responded by reminding her that he was sixty-eight years of age and that he didn't have to listen to anyone. He was a grown man.

Once again, she didn't have the heart to tell him that he was really eighty and that he did have to listen to her. And while he was a grown man, he was one whose brain didn't fire on all cylinders. That conversation was like a broken record, and it didn't matter how many times she told him; it only made her feel better for a short time and made him more determined to grab hold of his freedom. She had enough on her plate without tracking down another facility that wouldn't just sedate him, strap him in a wheelchair, and wait for him to die. She kept all that to herself, though, extracting a promise from him—probably already forgotten—that he would stay put.

Once, he had been a detective from whom other detectives sought advice; he had spent thirty years on the police force, working far longer than he had to to collect a significant pension. It was the work that he loved and that kept him at it. Some days, he would regale her with stories that she had never heard, and she was still surprised to find that she was fascinated; she thought she had heard them all. His gift had been his gab, as he liked to say, Jack Conlon being the guy who was called when all else failed, when even the right series of questions in an interrogation didn't elicit the right answer in a given situation. He could find common ground with anyone, and that made him trustworthy to even the crustiest of criminals.

He wasn't a shadow of his former self; there were still flashes of that great sense of humor, and physically the old guy could probably take out men half his age. She wondered, though, how long it would be until he forgot her completely, looking at her as if she were the greatest mystery he had yet to solve.

Going from her visit with Jack straight to the party had been a bad idea. It was hard to be festive for a bunch of little kids when all she could think of was the next time he was found on the side of the road by a passerby or a cop, a newspaper tucked under his arm, a six-pack swinging back and forth as he made his way to a destination he wasn't entirely sure of. Home? If asked, he would have no idea where that was.

She had a hard time getting her daughters to work the parties anymore, so today she was on her own; the girls had their limits, apparently. There were only nine girls for this party and they were fairly well behaved, the birthday girl's parents' bickering not an indication of the kids' demeanors. One of the invited children hadn't shown up, and it was clear that the father of the birthday girl—one Michael Lorenzo—was angling for a discount, one that Maeve was not prepared to give. The final count had come in the day before, as she requested, her policy set forth in the original contract that Cal had drawn up and that the parents had signed. Any no-shows on the day of the party were to be paid for in full, no exceptions. At the time, she'd wondered why Cal had worded the contract to make it sound as though any deviation from the final number would land the signer in the guillotine, but now she was glad for his legalese. It was right there in black and white, but that didn't mean the fat guy in the Ed Hardy T-shirt wasn't going to give her a hard time.

Mrs. Lorenzo had seemed like an agreeable woman when she had come in to book the party and then again to sign the ironclad contract. Maeve hadn't been able to put her finger on it, but she found the right word when she compared the wet dish towel in her hand to the woman sitting on a chair by the kitchen door. "Sodden." That's all that Maeve could come up with. Today Tina Lorenzo wore a tight-fitting top that despite its fit seemed to be trying to pull away from the woman's skin. Although she was fairly fit, Maeve wanted to tell Tina Lorenzo that a shirt that tight was off limits after your thirty-fifth birthday. Maeve didn't need to see her eyes, always hidden behind dark sunglasses, to know that they spoke of pain and of sadness. Her body told a tale that no one but Maeve—or someone like her—would be able to guess. Whatever "it" was, it was there and on this woman; there was no hiding it. The woman pushed a lank lock of hair behind her ear, taking in the party from her perch on a stool that Maeve used when icing her cupcakes. She didn't seem overjoyed at what seemed like her little girl's dream party. She didn't seem happy with the half-eaten cupcake in her lap on a crumpled paper plate.

As a matter of fact, to Maeve she didn't even seem alive.

Maeve poured another round of juice into the girls' cups, brushing past the birthday girl's mother and feeling an electric jolt of depression as her back touched the woman's knees. That was every-one's mistake: they thought depression meant that you were dead inside, that there was no spark. There was a spark all right, Maeve thought; it was just a spark that deadened you from within with each passing day, taking energy from its source.

The father was yammering into his cell phone, presumably talking to one of the parents of the missing child, threatening them with an invoice if they didn't show up at the shop within the next thirty minutes to pay for the party their kid was missing. By the way he was talking, though, Maeve determined that there was no one on the other end of the conversation and that what he was doing was just for show.

She shot him a look, thinking, So that's how you want to play it?

"The Comfort Zone?" he asked the imaginary person on the other end of the conversation. "More like the Suck-Ass Zone."

Classy.

One spilled juice and nine overly decorated cupcakes later, it was time for the cake. As Maeve passed by the mother again, her arms laden with a heavy three-layered cake just as Tiffany, the birthday girl, wanted, she noticed a bruise peeking out from the side of the sunglasses, a mark that the woman had taken great pains to hide behind a thick layer of gloppy makeup. Inexpertly applied, it only brought more attention to what Maeve could see was a fresh injury and one that would take a few days to show its true colors.

She put the cake on the stainless-steel table, around which sat the perfectly behaved children, and picked up her cake knife, the one with the serrated edge that made the cleanest cut. She smiled at the group. "Girls? I just need to run outside for one quick minute to get some candles I left in my car," she said, fingering the box of candles that sat in the front pocket of her apron. "I'll be right back."

Lorenzo looked at his watch and tapped the face, letting her know who was in charge.

You think so, huh? she thought as she exited through the screen door. Let's see.

Outside, it was easy to pick out the minivan that had transported the dysfunctional family to the party, the family with the child who was afraid to get icing on her hands, the mother who either endured abuse or had had a run-in with the old standby—the doorknob—and the father whose silly fashion sense betrayed a sinister side that Maeve could almost smell on him. The minivan—with a Mad River Glen bumper sticker on the back—was the only other car in the back parking lot, parked beside and almost on top of her sensible but aging Prius in which she found the candles. She wedged herself between the two cars, and she indulged in a fantasy in which she ran the knife down the side of the van until she got to the end; it was far enough down on the body of the car that it wouldn't be noticed immediately. In her mind, the final flourish came when she carved "F U" right above the fender.

But she didn't do any of that. She'd had every intention of doing it when she had left the store but knew what would happen if the car was found with a scratch on it. First, Mr. Lorenzo would take her to task for allowing people to drive erratically in the lot, as if she had any control over that. With her luck, he'd blame it on Jo and then Maeve would really have to kill him. Then, he'd take out whatever pent-up rage was left on his wife and possibly his kids. He had no self-control, while she had it in spades, and that's what separated her from him. With a satisfied smile on her face, she walked back into the store, the candles held tightly in her hand.

"Now who wants a piece of chocolate cake?"

Chapter 9

Maeve wanted to remind Julie Morelli that when they were in yoga class, and corpse pose in particular, there was no talking.

She would have liked to put Julie in corpse pose for good, but that wasn't polite. Even Jack, who had met her in the store once, couldn't stand her, and he didn't remember anyone long enough to form an opinion. Julie was different, though. "Could talk a dog off a meat wagon," he liked to remark in her presence, but she was too stupid to realize he wasn't talking about canines and hamburgers in general. Maeve always thought that no jury in the land would convict Julie's husband—also known as "the Mute" to Maeve and her friends—if he smothered her while she slept, the only time her mouth wouldn't be working overtime. Maeve turned her head to the right and smiled at Julie, when in her heart she wanted to tell her to shut the hell up.

Julie took Maeve's smile to mean that talking was now appropriate. "So sorry about your cousin," she said. News traveled fast. Maeve had told only one person besides Cal—Jo—that Sean Donovan, the guy whose murder had been all over the papers, was her first cousin. Maeve had been counting on the fact that there would be nothing to connect her to him and on the fact that over two weeks later, the media attention would start to wane. Apparently, she had been wrong. "Were you close?"

Maeve looked back up at the ceiling, her legs stretched out, her arms held tightly at her sides. That was the funny thing about yoga: although Maeve had taken it up for the relaxation it supposedly provided—and to replace the meditation on Sunday that going to church used to provide—she was more tense than ever when she left, and Julie Morelli had nothing to do with that. Maeve wondered if she was just wired to be continually wound-up. While everyone else in the room was close to a comatose state, she and the woman on the next mat with the mouth that wouldn't quit were wide-awake and not focused on their deep breathing.

Julie was still talking. "Kids? Wife? Did you see him on holidays? Did you grow up together? How was the wake? The funeral?" The questions kept flying, so fast that Maeve had a hard time keeping up.

Maeve could dig a hole.

"Is his wife set financially?"

And push Julie in.

"And the kids? Will they be able to go to college?"

And then shoot her in the head.

"Did anyone see who did it?"

Nobody would be the wiser.

She was enjoying the fantasy so much that she didn't hear the soft voice of Tamara, the yoga instructor, bid everyone "namaste." Namaste, my ass, Maeve thought. Get me the hell out of here. How did you translate that into Hindi?

Maeve rolled up her mat and stood. Julie grabbed her in an embrace and pulled her close.

"I don't think there is anything worse than losing someone you love so violently," she whispered into Maeve's ear, Maeve's diminutive frame looking as if it were being swallowed whole by the almost six-footer.

Yes, there is, Maeve thought, but she remained silent. And she had never said she loved him.

"Such a violent, violent death," Julie cooed. If Maeve didn't know better, she would think that Julie was actually getting turned on.

As she got into her car, the unseasonable October heat enveloping her like a wet blanket, she thought about the new one she was going to rip Jo. It's not that her relationship to Sean Donovan was a secret, but Julie Morelli? Not telling her was a given. She thought Jo understood that the fastest way to keep the gossip moving in town was to tell Julie. Maeve had certainly kept her mouth shut during Jo's very public, and very painful, divorce from Eric, but everyone had found out the gory details regardless. How? Maeve had given Jo one guess when her friend had come to her in tears. Julie Morelli knew it all and had told everyone.

Cal knew. So did Gabriela. Maeve was sure, though, that neither would say a word. Cal was discreet and Gabriela couldn't give a damn about anybody but herself. She had probably already forgotten that Sean had been Maeve's cousin; she was like that.

She pulled in behind the store. Once inside, she peeked through the porthole in the kitchen door, seeing that Jo was perched on a stool, reading the local paper. Maeve knocked on the glass and beckoned Jo back into the kitchen area.

The paper tucked under her arm, Jo greeted her warmly. "How was yoga?"

"How was yoga?" Maeve asked, pulling a knife from the magnetic strip above the sink. "Julie Morelli couldn't wait to ask me everything there was to know about Sean's death."

Jo tried to hide the fact that she knew where Maeve was going with the conversation. "Really?" she asked, playing it cool.

"Really," she said, opening the refrigerator, taking out a carton of eggs, and slamming them down on the counter. When she opened the container, three were broken.

Jo flinched. "I'm sorry."

"It may be hard for you to understand this, but I really don't want to be associated with the man who was murdered, with his pants down, in Van

Cortlandt Park. What don't you understand about that?" she asked, feeling a momentary flicker of remorse when she saw tears well up in Jo's eyes. If she had learned anything about herself over the years, it was that it took a while for her anger to dissipate, and until it did, she had to let it out, one way or another.

"His pants were down?" Jo asked, her eyes wide.

Maeve shot her a look that let her know they weren't going down that path.

"I made a mistake," Jo said. "That's all I can say."

Maeve put down the knife and gripped the sides of the counter. She breathed in the scent of the cupcakes that Jo had baking in the oven, a scent that brought her back to the first kitchen she had ever baked in in the semidetached house on Independence Avenue, right off the main drag and around the corner from the park. She thought about Jack tasting her first homemade cupcake and bragging about it and her to his brother in the living room. She remembered being in the kitchen and Sean taking one, pretending he was going to eat it, but pressing it into her mouth instead, acting as though it were all great fun until she started crying, loud, gasping sobs, her bottom tooth, the first adult tooth that she had, chipping in half. He told her father she had fallen. She had been eight years old. After a few seconds, in which she erased the memory of her cruel cousin and replaced it with those of her father, she raised her head. "It's okay," she said. Jo was crying openly now. "It's okay," she repeated.

"I would never do anything to hurt you," Jo said, making her way around the counter.

Maeve held up a hand to stop her. If Jo hugged her now, she would crack into a million pieces. "I'm sorry. I just want to distance myself as far as I can from this. It would be bad for business . . . ," she started, looking at Jo. "It will be bad for business," she amended. Because the cat was already out of the bag, and in due time, everyone would know.

Chapter 10

Maeve was wrong: it was great for business.

She never could have anticipated what the murder of her cousin would bring her in terms of profits, but it seemed as though everyone wanted to pay their condolences to her and, while doing so, place an order.

"I'll have two dozen of the mini chocolate cupcakes," Sarah Teitelbaum said.

"Four dozen of the large gingersnaps, please," Carolyn Bain said when she called.

"Can you make one of your chocolate cream cakes? Enough to serve thirty people?" Barbara Worthen asked.

Sure. I can do all of that and then some, she thought. Even the distributor had contacted her again, out of the blue, and asked if her operation had grown at all since the last time they spoke. She didn't honestly believe that he had called because of the murder, but maybe her luck was changing. That first day after it seemed like everyone knew, she posted record sales and was able to put half of the next month's rent in an envelope under the register drawer. Might as well pretend it wasn't there; if she kept it in her possession, it would be gone before the month was over.

She had smoothed things over with Jo, too. Nothing like making change for a fifty-dollar bill, or even a hundred, to make her forget that one slip of the tongue had revealed something she had wanted to keep to herself forever. She even gave her friend and only employee that afternoon off to study for the upcoming test she would be taking; a master's in social work was something Jo had always wanted but never had time for when she was married. Now on her own, she had decided to pursue her dream. The Comfort Zone was Maeve's dream come true, but not Jo's. Hers was to help the less fortunate, those in need of assistance. Maeve's was to keep everyone well fed; she guessed that she could also make the world safer, just in a different way.

Maeve had underestimated just how nosy

people were and how they loved a good tragedy. A sordid one? Even better.

Two nights before, Cal had asked her if she had found a hobby yet.

"Still working on it," she had said, turning away from her computer to stare at the stack of bills she needed to pay and, for once, would be able to.

"Well, keep thinking about it," he had said. "I'm sure you'll find something." And then he had kissed the top of her head in that annoying way he had and taken the girls out to dinner at a new pasta place they were dying to try. She wondered how he would fork pasta into his mouth with young Devon strapped to his chest, but if she knew Cal, he would find a way.

That kid was never going to learn to crawl if Cal didn't unstrap him soon.

"Try the red velvet. You won't be disappointed."

Maeve's head snapped up from behind the glass case. She'd been so engrossed in rearranging the refrigerated display that she hadn't realized she wasn't alone. Marcy Gerson was doing what she always did when she came to Maeve's store: hard selling other customers who couldn't make up their own minds because of her incessant chatter.

"And have you ever had her brownies? Scrumptious!" she said, her face taking on the look of someone in the rapture.

Maeve pulled a box of cupcakes out of the case and pushed them across the counter to Marcy;

the order she had called in was ready and waiting for her. "Fourteen fifty, Marcy."

Marcy was still doing her best to convince the handsome African American man that the red velvet cupcakes were the way to go. Don't bother, Maeve thought. He's not here for the cupcakes.

Marcy turned back to the counter. "How much do I owe you?"

"Fourteen fifty," Maeve repeated.

Marcy pressed fifteen dollars into Maeve's outstretched hand. "Keep the change," she said, winking. She left the store, giving the man a last glance as she sashayed past, leaving a cloud of musky perfume in her wake.

The man looked at her. "A whole fifty cents. Whatever will you do with such largesse?"

"I could buy you a half a cup of coffee, Detective," Maeve said, putting the money in the register and dropping fifty cents into the tip jar that she left out for Jo.

The man did his best to look impassive, but Maeve could tell that he wasn't used to being "made" so quickly even this second time.

"Daughter of a cop, Detective. You guys don't exactly blend. Know what I mean?"

"Is there somewhere we could talk?" he asked, gesturing toward the kitchen. There was the cop thing, but he also had a college professor thing going on, what with the tweedy sport coat, pressed slacks, and loafers. The thinking man's

91

detective. She should have been wary, but his posture—a little slumped, slightly morose—didn't engender that feeling in her.

Maeve didn't think that it would do any good to protest, so she put a sign in the door that indicated she would be back in fifteen minutes, locked it, and led the detective around the counter and into the kitchen. Once behind the swinging doors, he pulled his badge out of his pocket.

"Detective Poole. NYPD Homicide." He smiled slightly. "But you already knew that."

Maeve's face gave nothing away; it was as if a visit from a detective were an everyday occurrence in the bakery. She'd known he was a cop almost as soon as she had seen him at the speed-dating event. She saw him studying her expression before deciding to reveal the reason he was there. "Why were you speed dating?" she asked, cutting to the chase.

"Believe it or not, it's germane to the case," he said.

She appreciated his honesty, even though there wasn't a lot of detail there. "How so?"

He smiled in a way that told her she wasn't going to get an answer.

Out of the corner of her eye, she spied her purse and resisted the inclination to reach across and shove it down toward the end of the counter. The better course of action, she decided, was to pretend it wasn't there. In it was Jack's service revolver, the one that she had taken possession of years ago when it was obvious that no good could have come from him having it. She had planned on putting it in a safe-deposit box at the bank, its age now rendering it a law enforcement relic, but that meant she had to go to the bank and rent one. She didn't have that kind of time. As sympathetically as Rodney Poole looked at her, Maeve didn't think that he'd take kindly to her having a weapon in her bag.

"Sean Donovan was your first cousin?" he asked, pulling a small notebook out of his pocket. He dug deeper into the inside pocket of his jacket, rooting around for something clearly not there before going to his pants pockets and then the pockets on the outside of his sport coat.

Maeve let him go through the entire search. "Pen?" she asked, taking one out of the pocket of her apron. She motioned to a wooden stool on his side of the gleaming stainless-steel countertop. "Have a seat."

He perched on the edge of the stool and opened his notebook. "Sean Donovan was your first cousin?"

"My mother and his father were siblings."

"Were you close?"

At one time, yes, she thought. "No." She leaned on the countertop. "Is it customary to question family members in a murder investigation?"

"Depends on the murder investigation," he said.

They stared at each other for a few seconds before Maeve reached onto the rack behind her and selected a red velvet cupcake for him. He looked more tired, more spent, than anyone she had ever seen. Behind his brown eyes was something that she could almost put her finger on, almost place, but it eluded her. It wasn't exactly sadness, but it was close. "Here. You look like you could use a sugar injection. And I'd be happy to pour you fifty cents' worth of coffee, if you're interested."

"If you pour me a whole cup, I'll give you the other fifty cents."

She pretended to consider that for a moment. "You know what? You seem nice. I think I'll stake you to a whole cup. It's on me." She paused at the door. "Milk? No sugar?"

"That's it," he said, seemingly surprised that she had guessed correctly.

She left the kitchen and went into the store, gathering her thoughts as she pulled the lever on the coffeepot. Granted, she didn't know how most murder investigations went, but she had watched enough detective shows on television to know that they didn't question people without cause. She also knew, and was always surprised, that the people they questioned seemed put out by the intrusion of one or two detectives. She decided that she would play against type and make him comfortable. Unless he was there to find out exactly what went into her oatmeal cookies, there had to be a reason he had driven all the way to Farringville, a good half hour to forty-five minutes from the city, no traffic.

She snapped a lid onto the coffee cup and took a deep breath before returning to the kitchen. She handed the cup to the detective. "I'm not sure, but I think this may be a dollar twenty-five's worth."

"You're very generous," he said, taking the lid off before taking a small sip. Maeve noted that the cupcake was gone, a crumb-filled wrapper all that was left. "Your father and his brother-in-law. Any bad blood?" he asked.

"We're Irish, Detective. Define 'bad blood.'" She crumpled up the wrapper and tossed it into the can behind her; she pushed another cupcake in his direction. "If you mean garden-variety grudge holding, then yes. If you mean something more serious, then, no."

She wasn't sure what he was writing in his notebook, but she didn't think it was her definition of "bad blood."

"And your cousin? Your relationship with him? Your father's?"

That was trickier, and she gave herself a few seconds to think. Any longer than that and it would appear that she was trying too hard to put her feelings into words that wouldn't incriminate her. "Pleasant."

He flipped back through his notes. "He was"

—flip, flip, flip—"six years older than you?"

She felt that a studied nonchalance was her best posture in this situation. "I guess that's right. It's hard to remember. I have a lot of cousins." She traced a pattern on the countertop. "Boom, boom, boom. One right after another. I think there are twenty-six of us altogether."

"Twenty-seven," he said, looking down at his notebook. He realized why she had come up with the count. "Right. Twenty-six with the passing of Sean." He went back to the notebook, not looking at her. "And you?"

"Only child."

He let that go. "Your father. He lives in an assisted-living facility close by?"

She nodded.

"Still drives?"

She laughed. The thought of Jack behind the wheel, not sure of where he was going or how he would get there, would be almost comical to think about if it weren't so sad. The most tragic day of Jack's life—a close second to the day his beloved Claire was buried—was the day that Maeve had sold his 1964 Mustang three years earlier when it finally became clear that his mental slide was due not to dehydration, but to dementia. The look on his face when she told him it was gone, having brought him the check from the new owner to endorse, was etched in her brain. It had taken him only a day to forget that he had ever had a Mustang, let alone that it had been a classic in mint condition, but she remembered. She would never forget. It was the day she had broken his heart.

Poole was sipping his coffee and looking at her. "So the answer is no?"

She realized that she had never answered him. "The answer is no."

"You're sure?"

"I'm sure," she said. "Why?"

He didn't respond. "Does your father still know how to take public transportation? Have friends who drive?"

"No and maybe. I don't really keep track of who has a license at Buena del Sol." As she watched him write in his book, she felt the knot in her stomach, the one that had started when she had laid eyes on his badge, begin to grow. Was this actually going where she thought it was going? If so, her worst fear had been revealed, taking shape right in front of her eyes. She looked at Poole, now finished writing, staring back at her, watching her face for any betrayal of the truth. She shook her head slowly. "Not him, Detective. Not my dad."

"We have to cover all bases, Ms. Conlon."

"He's an old man with a brain that doesn't let him remember what he had for breakfast by the time he gets to lunch."

"You said it yourself: you're the daughter of a

cop. And only a cop could know some of the things that this perp knew."

"Please. You have to believe me. It's not him."

He looked at her sadly. "Then who?"

She realized that she had slumped a little bit over the counter, her hands reaching out to him, pleading with him to believe her. She sat up straighter. "I don't know."

Poole snapped his notebook shut and put it into his pocket. He handed her the pen that she had lent him. "We'll need to talk to him."

She nodded, her head feeling wobbly on her neck. She thought back to the night that Sean had died and how Charlene Harrison had later reported that Jack had gone wandering that night. Great. Now he was a senile octogenarian with no alibi.

"If you think it would be better to have a lawyer present, you can arrange that." He held her gaze. "It's just a formality," he said. "Covering all of the bases."

"That won't be necessary," she said quickly, thinking that by doing so, she'd be helping to implicate Jack. When she thought about it, though, she knew her first call was going to be to Cal. She was sure he would have a different take. She'd have to remind him that having the baby strapped to his suit jacket wouldn't be appropriate or appreciated.

They moved back into the store and she unlocked

the front door. Poole turned, his hand on the doorknob. "Really, why were you speed dating, Detective Poole?"

He was considering whether or not to answer. He kept it simple and vague, just as he had the night they had first met. "Part of the case."

A little sliver of fear pierced her brain. Was she part of the case because of her relationship to Jack? Or was there someone involved who was at the event? Was it the guy who wanted to know her sign? The tawdry-looking blonde with the big boobs who had gotten the attention of every man there?

He continued to linger by the door, studying her as she puzzled through the different scenarios in her mind. "I know this is more than a little strange, under the circumstances, but can I buy something before I leave? My littlest one would love some cupcakes, I imagine."

If this was his way of leaving on good terms after practically accusing her father of murder, he was almost successful. Maeve went back around the counter on shaky legs and took out a box. "How old?" she asked, grateful to be asking questions and not answering them, even if moving on to something as benign as a discussion of his children was completely out of left field.

"Nine. I've got a couple of others, but they're in college."

It was out of her mouth before she could even

process that it was a highly inappropriate question. "Change-of-life baby?"

He smiled. "More like save-your-marriage baby." He shared her chagrined look, seeming to wonder why he had let that slip. "Anyway. I'd like four of those red velvet cupcakes. And if you have another four chocolate, that would be great." He reached into his back pocket for his wallet. "Wife will never forgive me if I don't get her favorite."

Maeve handed him the box, her signature raffia bow on top, a sticker with her lopsided cupcake logo holding it down. "It's on me, Detective." She pushed the twenty-dollar bill that he had laid on the counter back toward him.

He pushed it back toward her. "I can't. For real," he said.

Bribery, even in the form of cupcakes, was frowned upon by the NYPD. She took the twenty. "It wasn't a bribe, if that's what you were thinking," she said.

"If it was, it would have been the best one ever," he said, giving her that sad smile.

"I'd usually say, 'Come again,' but in this case, I don't think I will. I hope that's okay." She handed him his change.

He nodded slowly. "I think that's just fine."

If it meant getting him to stop looking at her father, she would give him a daily supply of cupcakes.

After he left, and she watched his police-issue sedan roll out through the parking lot, past the stop sign, and onto the main road in town, she perched carefully on the edge of the stool behind the counter, her hands beneath her to steady them.

She thought about Poole's theory that a cop had been involved.

Jack had been a cop once and a good one at that, but she felt sure that even after all this time, he would say that he was in the business of saving lives, not taking them.

Chapter 11

Jack was sitting on her back porch, a healthy pour of whiskey in a heavy tumbler in front of him. Although Maeve talked a good game, when he came to their house for dinner, she always allowed him a drink or two. She was less inclined to let him have his favorite cheddar cheese and buttery crackers, but tonight she had bent the rules to accommodate him. She wanted him to have the things he loved.

Maeve raised an eyebrow when she took in the thick slices of cheddar sitting atop crackers lined up in front of him. "Go easy, Dad. Pace yourself."

He dismissed her with a flick of his hand. "When you get to be almost seventy like I am, you can eat all of the cheese and crackers you want. Look it up. It's a law."

As always, she didn't correct him and tell him his real age. She found it amusing that his age always varied; some days he was in his fifties, on others he was closing in on seventy. Whatever it was, he always skewed younger. She was pretty sure he knew that eating cheese and crackers wasn't on the books either, but she wasn't sure. "Just this once," she said, knowing that she couldn't deny him even if it wasn't just once.

He picked up another cracker, put a thick slice of cheddar on top of it, and popped it in his mouth, washing it all down with the last of his whiskey. He gave her a devilish smile. "If I'm going to the chair, I'm going with half a bag on," he said.

Maeve and Jack were all that was left of their family, Maeve's mother's death denying Jack more children, Maeve more siblings. Jack's stock answer, whenever she asked him why she'd been an only child, was, "Why have more when the one we have is perfect?" She had craved the companionship of a sister, even a brother, but what she lacked in siblings, she was lucky enough to have in a cadre of cousins: all of Jack's siblings had at least five in their individual broods, ten at the most. She was never alone.

Except for when she was. And that's when the trouble came.

Maeve knew, because Jack told her, that the

"sun rose and set on her." She always sensed that he felt if he loved her enough, it would be all she needed. He didn't know she needed to be protected, too.

"I had something to tell you, but I forgot what it was," Jack said, his reading glasses, the only other sign that he was advancing in age, slipping down his nose.

Maeve took a seat across from him at the wrought-iron table. "Did it have to do with book club? Weight lifting with Lefkowitz?"

He shook his head. "That's not the name of the book."

"I know, Dad," Maeve said, resisting the urge to laugh. It wasn't the name of the book, but it was a good title if she ever decided to try her hand at writing. She served him another cheese-and-cracker sandwich, which he gratefully accepted.

"Oh, and did you hear what happened?" he asked, already forgetting about what he wanted to tell her and on to the next thing.

"No, Dad. What happened?" she asked, preparing herself for a long story about trouble at Buena del Sol. He might not remember where he was and what he was doing most of the time, but he was very attuned to the social machinations of the seniors at the home.

"Sean died," he said, obviously shocked by his nephew's untimely passing. "Do you remember him?" He was always forgetting, so he assumed everyone else was, too. "Or was it Declan?" He scratched his head, leaving a speck of cheddar in his thick mop of white hair.

Maeve reached over and flicked the cheese away. "It was Sean, Dad. Remember? We went to the wake?"

Jack looked up into the cloudless sky and pondered that. "Yes!" he said as the light bulb in his brain went off. "That's right. That miserable wench Dolores had me in a headlock for most of the time we were there, right?"

"That's right."

"And Margie's now a gay."

"That's one way of putting it."

"She told me she got married to another woman. Have you ever heard of such a thing?" he asked.

"Yes, Dad. Civil unions are legal in New York now."

"What did he die of?" he asked.

"Who?"

"Sean," he said, exasperated, as if she were the one having a hard time keeping up.

"Dutch elm disease," she said. He looked confused, so she prodded him gently. "Do you remember what happened to Sean?"

He thought for a moment. "Don't care. Hated the kid."

That wasn't exactly news, but the way he said it was more direct than Maeve had ever heard him verbalize.

"I seem to remember a cruel streak. Am I wrong there?"

Her silence served as tacit agreement.

"No wonder he worked down on Wall Street. Probably among his kind there." He shook his head. "Pass that cheese."

Maeve pulled her chair closer to his, thinking that the proximity would allow him to understand what she was going to say. She had five minutes or so before the girls came home, and she needed both to tell him about the circumstances of Sean's death and his possible questioning by the police and leave herself enough time to deal with his reaction. "Dad, listen. A policeman was by the bakery. He said they are questioning family members."

He looked puzzled. "That's strange. Now why would they be doing that?"

She looked at him, raising her shoulders slightly in question. "Sean didn't really die of Dutch elm disease," she said.

"You don't say," Jack said, revealing that he was in on the joke.

"He was murdered."

"I know. Buena gets the papers delivered daily."

"Does anyone know he was your nephew?" she asked.

"Just Moriarty," he said, referencing his best friend, another retired cop, though his problems were different from Jack's. Although he had bounced back nicely from his last stroke, he still bore the evidence of what it had done to him, mainly slurred speech that made him sound as if he'd had a few belts with his turkey chili and rice pudding. Otherwise, he was totally fine. Hale, even. Maeve made a mental note to find out if he still drove.

"They can't think that one of us did it, can they?" Jack repeated. Maeve hadn't heard him the first time, deep in thought about Jimmy Moriarty and his ability to drive. She didn't want to tell him that the "us" he was referring to—her and him—was really only "him." They thought he did it.

"They might, Dad."

She continued to look at him, watching the synapses firing for the first time in a long time.

"Fools."

Not really. Both Jack and Maeve had plenty of motive—and a little opportunity—to kill Sean. "Where were you on the night Sean died, Dad?" she asked.

He didn't hesitate. "I went to a Knights of Columbus meeting at the church. That idiot Maloney wants to make the communion breakfast a monthly event. Moron. We can't even get people to come once a year."

Jack hadn't been a member of the K of C since 2002.

"Then, I went to the Steak House for a pint."

The Steak House was around the corner from

106

their old house. Maeve felt an electric charge of anxiety run through her veins. This wasn't going to be easy. She knew it was useless to ask him these questions, but she'd figured she would give it a try.

"Oh, well," he said. "Poor bastards are just doing their jobs." He tinkled the ice in his empty glass. "Just let me know when I have to talk to them. I have a pretty busy schedule," he said. "Book club this month is going to be a humdinger and I don't want to miss it."

"Why's that, Dad?"

"We're reading *Fear of Flying*. I thought it was about nervous airline passengers." He gazed off into the distance. "I'm so happy I was wrong."

Chapter 12

"God, what do you have in here? Your bag weighs a ton," Jo said, moving Maeve's purse from the counter to the table next to the back door.

Maeve grabbed her bag and stowed it on the top shelf of the standing metal rack next to the five-pound bag of sugar and the ten-pound bag of flour that she kept in the event of an emergency. Jo was responsible for placing the dry goods order, but her lack of punctuality was matched only by her incredible forgetfulness when it came to ordering. Maeve had thought that giving

Jo more responsibility was a good thing because it took things off her own plate, but it was still an evolving process.

To wit: They were out of butter.

She was headed to the grocery store, leaving Jo in charge of making another batch of cupcakes. The two dozen that they had made that morning were already gone. She grabbed her bag from its place next to the sugar and the flour and hefted it over her shoulder. It was heavy. Too heavy. She had to do something about that. She added that task to the list she was keeping in her head, the one that was blank every morning when she got up because she'd forgotten everything while sleeping.

"I'll be right back," she said to Jo.

"And I'll be right here," Jo said, pulling a chair up to the stainless-steel counter, positioned so she could see customers coming into the shop, and opened the textbook she was now bringing to work so she could keep up with her schoolwork. Baking, apparently, was going to take a backseat to social work.

At the store, Maeve resisted the urge to do her regular grocery shopping, knowing that she would spend way too much and not have enough time to unload before going back to the shop. A few things caught her eye that she couldn't resist, though—the cheap shampoo her kids hated but that was half price, another box of Band-Aids for the shop, discounted pasta—and she filled up her cart more than she had originally intended.

In the checkout line, Maeve felt a tap on her shoulder.

"Excuse me?"

This was her second pass through the checkout. Butter was on sale and wouldn't be this cheap again for a long time, so she bought as much as the store would allow at one time and made multiple trips through the checkout line to pay. She hoped the bags that she garnered in her first go-round didn't mark her as a scofflaw. She turned around.

A young mother, a baby in the front part of the cart, a toddler in the cart itself, was pointing at the floor. "Your purse. I think you have a hole in your bag."

Maeve looked down, spying money on the ground along with a tampon whose wrapper had secn better days, along with the pen she had lent Rodney Poole. And trying to make its way through the ever-widening hole in the fake leather was the barrel of the gun that she had kept close to her ever since she had removed it from her father's house. She had deemed her original hiding place, a shoebox on the shelf in her closet, unsafe, and she still hadn't gotten to the bank to rent a safe-deposit box. So she was left to carry it around, its heft reminding her that she needed to find a good way to dispose of it and fast. She quickly pulled the purse to her chest, pushing things back through the hole in the bottom and throwing the butter onto the counter as the person in front of her finally figured out how to use the keypad on the credit machine.

"Bonus card?" the checkout guy asked her. "You know it's only eight to a customer, right?" he asked, pointing to the butter.

She dug through her bag and pulled out her card, which he swiped and handed back. She positioned herself so that the bags already in her cart wouldn't be so obvious. "I know," she said. She didn't tell him about the other pounds of butter that she had already put in her trunk, probably melting into the environmentally conscious bags that she had remembered to bring into the store. "How long is the sale on?" she said, her hands shaking at the thought of how close she had come to exposing the gun in her bag.

"Over at the end of the week. Eight to a customer."

"Got it," she said, throwing butter into another bag as quickly as she could. She'd be back the next day and purchase another gross. Seriously. What were they going to do? Throw her in coupon jail?

In the parking lot, she took deep breaths, trying to calm down. As she passed the two handi-capped spots nearest the store, she spotted Tina Lorenzo struggling to disengage a jammed cart from a long line of other carts sitting under a canopy. In her arms was a toddler who was squirming to get away and holding her free hand was Tiffany, the little girl from the birthday party, who still wore the same placid look that she had that day in the store, her blond curls billowing around her head like bleached cotton candy. Like that day in the store, she was singing a song to herself when she thought no one was watching.

Maeve put the thoughts of the gun out of her head and rushed over to help the woman free a cart from the massive chain of immovable metal. After Maeve stowed her cart, she put her purse into the bag with the butter, figuring the gun had less of a chance of falling out if it was secured in yet another bag. "Here. Let me help you," she said as she wrestled with the last cart in the line.

It was the little girl who recognized her first. "You're the cupcake lady."

She guessed that was one way to identify her. "Yes. I'm the cupcake lady."

Tina Lorenzo wasn't wearing her sunglasses today, and Maeve could see that the troubled look she suspected lived behind them was in full evidence in the harsh sunlight of the fall day. "Thank you. Tiffany had a great time at the party."

"I'm so glad."

Tina put the baby in the cart and hoisted Tiffany up and over the side and into the back. She turned so that her back was to her children. "I'm sorry about my husband."

Maeve waved a hand dismissively. "Don't worry."

Tina reached into her own bag and pulled out her wallet; she took four twenties and pressed them into Maeve's hand. "Here. I haven't been able to get to the store to pay you directly, but I hope this makes us even." She zipped her bag shut. "Keep the change."

Maeve clutched the money in her hand and looked at Tina Lorenzo. Something hung in the air between them. Maeve wanted to tell her that there was a way out of her situation, but she didn't know this woman from a hole in the wall. And when she thought about it, was she the right person to be doling out advice? A woman who had an unflattering running commentary in her head every time her ex-husband was around? A woman who wanted to kill Jo's husband and had even crafted a plan for doing so and getting away with it? A woman who wasn't a wee bit sad that her cousin had been found with a bullet in his head in the middle of a dark and deserted park? All Tina had to do was ask Cal, and she'd know that Maeve didn't handle conflict with anything approaching reason. With nothing left to say on the subject of leaving, she thanked Tina and walked away.

"It's complicated," Tina called to her back.

Maeve paused. She supposed it was.

Chapter 13

Jo had no idea that when Doug from speed dating had called her, he already knew that she was Jewish and single and made a mean pot roast. She was so excited to share the news of their first date that she was actually blushing. And Jo did not blush. She was way too jaded for that.

"Do you remember him from speed dating?" she asked Maeve. "You must have met him."

"Tall, light hair, nice eyes?" Maeve asked, doing her best to look as if she were searching her overcrowded memory.

"Dockers, though? With pleats?" Jo said. "If we're going to get serious, the first thing we're going to do is go clothes shopping."

"Remember, Jo," Maeve said, pulling a loaf of bread out of the oven, careful to keep her hands away from the heat, "you can change a man's wardrobe, but you can't change his taste."

Jo found a broken cookie amid a pile of perfectly round ones and shoved it in her mouth. "Yeah, but the Dockers will have to go."

"Give the guy a chance," Maeve said. "If he's the guy I remember, he seemed nice."

"Yeah, but he was speed dating," she said derisively.

"And so were you."

"I know, but that's different."

Maeve didn't have time to get into why that might be; the corkboard over the sink held orders that had piled up and needed to be filled if she was going to stay in business. "Before you go, can you give me a hand?" she asked. "Like do your job?"

Jo's mind was still on the date and stayed that way while she attempted to start a batch of brownies. "Will you drive me to the train station later? We're meeting at Grand Central."

They closed at four, and Maeve spent the next hour mopping the front of the store while Jo transformed herself from shopgirl into femme fatale. As Maeve was putting the mop away, a little song played on her cell phone, letting her know that she had a text. It was from Cal. He had let her know that morning that he was taking Jack to the Bronx to be questioned. As a result, she had been a nervous wreck the entire day, waiting to hear from him.

His text was short: "Met with Detective Poole. Talk soon."

She wrote Cal back to thank him for letting her know. An image popped into her head: her father wearing a sport jacket and two different shoes, being coached by Cal, wearing the baby like the plastique worn by a suicide bomber, arriving at the precinct.

Jo emerged from the bathroom and Maeve was astounded at the transformation. Her friend now wore a pair of tight black jeans, a white shirt, and high-heeled black boots.

"Yowza," Maeve said. "Who needs speed dating when you look like that?"

"I did," Jo said. "In the worst way. It was either that or move out of this town. There's not a decent man who's not already married, divorced with issues, or not aware that he's really gay."

Girl had a point. Maeve put on the alarm and locked the back door.

"Doug does seem nice," Jo said, hope creeping into her voice. "You know what he said?"

"What?"

"That pot roast is his favorite meal," she said. "My signature dish. If that's not serendipity, I don't know what is."

It was rush hour, commuters fleeing the parking lot of the train station as if they were being chased by zombies. People were running to their cars, hurling themselves into the rides waiting for them, or hustling toward bus stops that would take them to various points in town and beyond. Maeve steered the Prius toward the drop-off point at the bottom of the stairs to the ticket office, giving Jo a quick peck before sending her on her way. In front of her was a minivan with a Mad River Glen bumper sticker on it, and descending the stairs, walking right past Jo, was Michael Lorenzo, the last of the commuters exiting the most recent train to arrive in the station.

Maeve put the car in drive but noticed something on the seat next to her: Jo's wallet. She put the car back in park and jumped out, calling Jo's name, even though she knew Jo couldn't hear her. As she passed the Lorenzos' car, she could hear Michael screaming at Tina for being late, for not being where she said she was going to be, for not doing exactly what he wanted at exactly the time he needed it. As Maeve stood beside the car, staring in through the passenger side window, Tina stared straight ahead, not making a sound, doing nothing to defend herself from the verbal attack. Maeve clutched the wallet in her hands, the zipper pressing into the soft flesh of her palm, the pain of it not registering in her overcrowded brain.

The abuse continued while both children in the backseat began to cry. Michael was screaming, "Drive!" while his wife sat behind the wheel, seemingly frozen, incapable of moving forward, getting out of the car, or even reacting. He responded by reaching across the backseat and slapping Tiffany, the girl to whom Maeve was the "cupcake lady," across the face, silencing her. Her stunned, tearstained face was the last thing that Maeve saw before the car drove away.

She was still standing there when Jo came back down the stairs, muttering about forgetting her wallet.

"Hey!" she said, not getting Maeve's attention

on the first try. "Can I have my wallet, please?"

Maeve turned slowly and looked at her, not really seeing anything but the face of the little girl. She handed Jo the wallet, her head still somewhere else. "Do you need a ride home or will you get a cab?" she asked.

Jo regarded her with her own strange expression written on her face. "Cab. Are you okay? You look like you've seen a ghost."

"I'm fine," Maeve said. The van was reaching the crest of the hill that led out of the train station.

Jo looked at her watch. "I've gotta go or I'll miss my train. See you tomorrow?"

Maeve waved but didn't answer. She was walking around to the driver's side of the car, her destination clear.

Chapter 14

Maeve waited until she was sure that they would be back and she called Cal. Gabriela answered. "Hi, sweetie!" her ex's new wife cooed into the phone, as if they were best friends and she wasn't the woman who had created an irrevocable division between Maeve and the only man, besides Jack, that she had ever been able to trust.

"Is Cal there?" she asked, skipping the niceties. She was civil to Gabriela, but that was it.

"Oh, sweetie, he's with the baby."

"I really need to speak to him."

Everyone wore two faces; Maeve had heard that somewhere. But Gabriela wore only one, and it was as dumb as a sack of hammers. "With the baby," she repeated in that annoying chirp, the one heavily inflected with Portuguese, that she had.

"Put Cal on the phone, Gabriela!" Maeve yelled into the phone. If she wanted to play games with Maeve, that was fine. But this had to do with Jack, and Maeve wasn't in the mood for the runaround.

Cal was on the phone in seconds, out of breath and clearly having gotten a little tongue-lashing from his wife. "Did you have to yell at her?"

"Yeah, I did." She looked at the clock. "I only have a minute. How did things go with my dad and the detective?"

"Fine. I think they just wanted to see firsthand how out of it he really is," Cal said. "When he went into his whole theory on the Marilyn Monroe suicide, I think that sealed the deal. Once they realized that he thought it had just happened, they were content to let him go. They may want to talk to him again, but I didn't get the person-of-interest vibe from them."

Maeve hadn't realized that she had been holding her breath. She exhaled loudly.

Cal mistook her relief for embarrassment over her father's dissertation. "It wasn't a big deal. He always blames the Mob. Never the Kennedys. The Irish Mafia is still held in high regard."

"Not that," she said. "I couldn't care less if he gave them every theory he has. As long as they think he's as confused as he really is, I'm happy."

"They definitely got that impression," Cal said. "But one question."

"Shoot."

"Where was he on the night Sean was killed?"

"What did he tell you?"

"Stations of the cross at St. Margaret's."

"He told me he was at the K of C meeting. He apparently got into a fight with old Mr. Maloney. Guy's been dead since 1982."

Cal laughed. "But he seems happy, Maeve. He's actually happier than when he had all of his faculties."

She knew that, and as a result, she prayed for early-onset Alzheimer's for herself.

She told Cal to give the girls a good-night hug from her before she hung up. She put her coat on and grabbed her purse. She was going out.

The thing about hobbies is that you never know if you're going to be good at them until you jump in and try.

That's how Maeve had learned that she could bake.

It was also how she learned that she was a good shot.

Nothing had scared Jack more than letting Maeve go off to Hyde Park, a land that seemed so far away to him; but let her go he had, and she got her degree at the prestigious Culinary Institute of America, with pastry her specialty. Not too many fathers would require that their daughters get not only a gun, but a gun license, and learn how to shoot, but Jack Conlon wasn't most fathers. He was a father who saw danger around every corner, one of the perils of his job. He was also a father who had one daughter, and he was going to do everything in his power to keep her safe.

He had tried. But he had failed. How much he knew of his failure Maeve had never figured out.

People hurt other people every day, but people hurting children? That was just something by which Maeve could not abide. And if you were so quick to hurt your own child's mother, you were hurting your child by extension. That was a fact. Hurting the mother was a gateway; abusing that little girl, if the slap to Tiffany Lorenzo she had witnessed was any indication, was rapidly on its way.

Maeve wished someone had been looking out for her, but that was a long time ago and people— her family—didn't know as much about the topic. It was years before anyone wrote about spanking as an ineffective and abusive disciplinary method, never mind child abuse. Kids played outside in those days and they got hurt. They played in the street, and slid off slides, and jumped off swings, all activities that could lead, reasonably, to an injury. Maeve showed no signs because Sean knew how to do it, how not to get caught. And the people in her life didn't see the signs because they didn't know what the signs were. So she had suffered in silence, just as she had been taught to do by the other women in the family, the ones who occasionally got a rough slap to the face or a push to keep moving, and no one was the wiser. That way, no one else got hurt and she was never to blame.

She pondered this as she sat in front of the Lorenzos' house, a brick monstrosity that spoke of a large mortgage and high taxes but which had no pleasing aesthetic qualities whatsoever. If she were to guess, she would have surmised that they lived in this part of town, the one where new money moved in and looked down on the longtime villagers and even those with old money. Old money, to them, spoke of the past, and they were only about the future, if you asked them. New money sat on the zoning board and allowed these "homes" to be built. Build the tax base. Keep the local Hummer dealer in business. That's how it went these days.

Maeve looked at the house; it seemed as if every light were on, even though the family couldn't have been in every room of the house. It was just that big. She wondered if Mr. Lorenzo turned the lights on when he beat his wife and slapped his kids or if he preferred to do that in the dark. Maybe she'd ask him the next time she saw him. This wasn't the direction she had planned on going, but in her mind, it was a good way to start.

She wouldn't have to wait long. The garage door began its slow ascent as taillights winked beyond it in the garage. She sat up in the front seat of the Prius, just enough to see over the bottom of the window, and watched as Michael Lorenzo took the minivan out for a spin. She'd had no idea that he would be going out; this was just a bonus.

She was going, too. She made her mind up in an instant and pulled the Prius away from the curb, keeping a safe distance between it and the van.

It didn't take her long to figure out where he was going. The man-made dam in town afforded the perfect cover for anyone meeting up with someone. At this time of night, it was empty, all of the people out for a hike or taking their dog for one last stroll already safely behind the locked doors of their homes. It had started raining lightly, too, keeping away even a stray nighttime jogger. She waited on the main road above the dam until she was sure he was in the parking lot and then started her silent descent, her Prius making not a sound as she rolled down the hill, her lights off, and into the far end of the lot.

Even in the dark, the mist turning to a steady drizzle, she could make out the structure below. It defied her own limited comprehension of physics and construction in general, but she knew a little about the dam's history, mainly that it had taken fourteen years and countless men to construct and what was left, after all that time, was something majestic and awe-inspiring to behold. While most women took their kids to the local parks with their rubberized turf floors and safe gym equipment, Maeve had always preferred a picnic beside the churning waters of the dam, a Wiffle ball and bat to keep the girls occupied when the sandwiches and chips were gone.

Circling the dam were hiking paths that led nowhere and stone edifices that spoke to structures long gone and never to be rebuilt. Hiking along those paths, Maeve had always joked that they should never stray from the path lest they get lost in the thick copse of trees that flanked either side of where they walked. The girls were as taken with the mystery and aura of the dense woods, the water bellowing in the background, and the feeling of relief and awe when they finally emerged on the footpath over the crescent-shaped pool at the bottom, where water collected, still on calm days, roiling and angry on stormy ones. Their faces pressed between the secure bars, they stood there for longer than two little girls should have been able, impressed with something that their mother found endlessly fascinating.

She could make out one other car in the lot, a sleek-looking sports car, the furthest thing from a sensible hybrid that she could imagine. She wondered to whom it belonged and, more important, who would think that an evening tryst with Michael Lorenzo was a desirable way to spend time. She waited, in the dark, watching the car rock slightly, resisting the urge to gag. The guy was fouler than she had imagined.

Twenty minutes later, a woman emerged, adjusting her yoga pants and walking, a little shakily, toward her car. Six feet if she was an inch, she wasn't moving her mouth for once, but Maeve could still tell who she was.

Maeve had a newfound respect for Michael Lorenzo. Finally, someone had found a productive use for Julie Morelli's constantly moving—and open—mouth.

Maeve waited until Julie drove by, the woman yakking on her cell phone as if her life depended on it, and then emerged from her car, a baseball cap pulled down over her eyes, the collar on her denim jacket pulled up to her ears. Maeve knew that it would be only a few seconds before he started the van and pulled out of his spot at the opposite end of the lot, so she jogged, her sneakers slipping on the wet macadam. She circled around the back of the car, surprising him when she appeared in the driver's side window. She tapped lightly on the glass.

He rolled down the window. "What are you doing here?" he asked, the zipper on his pants still down. Perfect. The irony wasn't lost on her. It was almost identical to the way her cousin had been found. "Is this about the party? The money?"

She fingered the gun in her jacket pocket. "Sort of. That and other things."

He looked around, the realization dawning on him that seeing her at the dam, at night, was not the most normal thing in the world.

"How much will it take to make all of this go away?" he said, suddenly willing to negotiate. He must have realized that she had seen Julie.

"Nothing."

He looked back at her, blank faced. "Nothing? Come on. We're talking seventy-five bucks."

"Your wife already paid me," Maeve said. She had changed her mind, the reason she was here not clear to her anymore. "You need to stop hitting her. And your daughter." She was sure about Tina, but not about how much it affected Tiffany. Though if he wasn't hitting her on a regular basis yet, it was only a matter of time.

He zipped up his pants. "And you need to mind your own business." He put his seat belt on, the conversation over as far as he was concerned. "It's none of your business."

He was right, but that didn't mean she wasn't going to make it her business.

"Leave her alone. Leave me alone. Go back to your little bakery." He smiled smugly. "Everyone will be much happier that way." He started the car. "I'll send you a check. Just forget what you saw."

The butt of the gun was smooth against her

fingers. It wouldn't take much, just a quick draw and a simple shot and he would be taken care of forever. He'd never know what had hit him.

That's not who I am, she reminded herself. I'm better than that.

Then he laughed, and in her head all she could hear was Sean Donovan's high-pitched bray as he pushed her—not long after her mother's death—in the swing set in the backyard of his parents' house. So high, in fact, and with such force, that the chain link, rusted and weak from years in the scrubby backyard, broke free, sending her hurtling toward the metal garbage cans at the side of the house, her arm snapping on impact. She touched the gun in her pocket, but the car was gone and all that was left was a puff of dust where it had been.

That's not who I am, she thought as she imagined the next time they would meet.

Or maybe it was.

Chapter 15

The woman kept looking from Maeve to the cake on the counter and back at Maeve.

"This is a Batman cake," the woman said, pointing at the giant cake, enough to feed a hundred people, a perfect replica of the Caped Crusader down to the fondant codpiece.

Maeve nodded. "Right. A Batman cake."

The woman inhaled, exhaled, and then let it fly. "I ordered a fucking baptism cake."

Behind Maeve, Jo let out a little snort and then, under her breath, a contrite "Sorry."

Maeve looked down at the Batman cake, the one that she had spent two laborious days creating from a photograph. She herself had taken the order, and when she looked at her handwriting, the description so clear, she almost started to cry. She looked back at the woman, who looked on the verge of tears herself. "When is your event?"

"In two hours."

Maeve grabbed an order pad and a pen. "Give me your address. I'll have a cake to you in two hours that will serve a hundred people. It will be a rectangular, standard sheet. Are you okay with that?"

The stress of the party for a hundred, coupled with her child's christening, pushed the woman over the edge and she started to bawl. "I wanted a cake in the shape of a goddamned cross!"

"I'll never be able to make that in two hours," Maeve admitted, feeling sick. "But I'll create a cross to put on top."

The woman looked at Maeve and then at Jo, who was nodding vigorously as if letting the woman know what she should do. Finally, the woman let out a long breath and looked up at the ceiling. "Fine."

Maeve grabbed a few napkins from the holder

on the counter and pushed them into the woman's hands. "It's on me. And I'm terribly sorry." She turned to Jo, standing silently next to the coffee-maker. "Jo, get all of the necessary information while I start baking."

Maeve was halfway through mixing the batter for a full sheet when Jo walked into the kitchen. " 'A fucking baptism cake'?" she asked, bursting into hysterical laughter. "Isn't it kind of not really Christian to curse the sacrament your kid is about to receive?" She was doubled over, laughing now that the woman had left the store and a new cake was taking shape. "I know I'm a Jew, but seriously?" She adopted a Yiddish accent. "Hello, Moishe, Sadie. We're so happy you could come to little Chaim's fucking bris. Now pass the goddamned gefilte fish."

"Could you hand me that sugar?" Maeve asked, pointing to the metal shelf by the door. "You're delivering the new cake, so pull yourself together."

Jo was still laughing as she approached the shelves. "Batman?" she wheezed.

Maeve took her attention from the mixer. "I've been a little preoccupied." And exhausted. And burning the candle at both ends. And constantly monitoring the movements of a very angry, very violent man. It had been three days since she had seen him at the dam, and between working and taking care of the girls, she had done a few nocturnal reconnaissance missions, not sure why, but feeling as if it were her calling, her hobby. Mainly, she just drove past his house, something, when she thought about it during daylight hours, that seemed like something a crazy person would do.

Oh, and let's not forget trying to keep track of an aging, senile lothario who thought he was the resident Rock Hudson of Buena del Sol. In Jack's mind, Rock was still alive, straight, and quite the ladies' man.

Jo stood on her tiptoes and reached for the sugar, on the top shelf next to Maeve's purse, the one that Jo said looked as if it had previously belonged to a tranny hooker working Twelfth Avenue. That's a pretty specific insult, Maeve recalled telling her, but Jo did have a point in addition to pretty accurate fashion sense. Maeve had remembered to staple the bottom of the bag shut, and it was holding for now. What she hadn't been able to do was take the gun that was inside and find a new hiding place for it. There really was no good place to put it. She had had it at home but was terrified that one of the girls would find it, despite the fact that they didn't know how to find the vacuum or clean towels when they needed them. She couldn't keep it at the store. Chances were Jo would unearth it and raise all kinds of alarms regarding a firearm in their midst. And giving it back to Jack? Well, that was out of the question, for obvious reasons.

So, it stayed where it had been for close to six

months already, poking a hole through the cheap lining of her tranny hooker purse. The only comfort she got was that if someone wanted to hold her up, there was a possibility the bag would be close enough for her to get the gun and she could shoot him.

Who was she kidding? That sort of serendipity never existed in real life.

She was moving fast, scraping the sides of the bowl to get all of the batter into the pan while figuring out if she had enough icing to cover a double sheet. While she was muttering to herself, she heard a little sound escape from Jo's lips, a small protest. It was as if she knew what was coming and was helpless to stop it. It all happened in slow motion: Jo reaching high for the sugar, Jo moving the purse, the purse crashing down on Jo's head and opening a cut so quickly and so deeply that they both fell silent after the initial shock of the injury. Jo looked at Maeve, her eyes wide, the blood draining from her face as quickly as it was leaking from the top of her head. Maeve felt her own skin go clammy at the sight of thick, dark blood mingling with the waves of Jo's cropped black hair.

"I forgot," Jo said, just before passing out on the floor, "you're not a blood person."

She was right: Maeve wasn't a blood person, much preferring to deal with stomach issues with her kids than injuries. Maeve turned the mixer off and dialed 911. While waiting for the police and an ambulance to arrive, she knelt beside Jo, blood leaking from the horrible-looking wound on the top of her head, and pressed a clean towel to it. As the towel soaked up the blood, she grabbed the purse and threw it into a cabinet under the counter. She didn't know if Jo knew what happened to her or would even remember, but in Maeve's mind, she wasn't going to blame it on the weight of her purse. Rather, she thought as she pulled the metal shelf away from the wall, she was going to blame it on the imaginary contractor who hadn't secured the shelf to the wall. It came down with a crash, sugar, flour, and an assortment of other items that she couldn't afford to lose all scattering across the tile floor.

Jo was coming to, trying to sit up as the sounds of sirens filled the back parking lot. Maeve pushed her down gently. "Stay down, Jo. The ambulance is here."

"Ambulance?" she asked. She touched the top of her head, feeling the wet towel and her soggy hair. "Why do I need an ambulance? Is that blood?" she asked, waggling her fingers in Maeve's face.

Maeve pointed to the shelf. "The shelf came down and hit you in the head. You may need a couple of stitches." Or a couple of dozen, she thought.

Jo looked at Maeve, her eyes glassy and unfocused. "Stitches? Oh, I hate needles."

Two police officers came in through the back door, three local EMTs behind them. The officers hoisted the shelf up to make way for the stretcher, kicking the broken bags of sugar and flour to the side.

She moved to the side of the stretcher and touched Jo's arm. "I'll meet you at the emergency room," she said.

Jo pointed over her shoulder at the mixer, picking the perfect time to become cogent. "Keep baking. You'll never make the delivery if you don't get that cake made." She smiled at Maeve. "Remember: baptism. Not Batman."

Maeve recognized one of the cops; he did crowd control at the big soccer tournament every fall. "Can you wait for her and drive her home when she's done?"

His look said it all, but he added, "Do we look like a taxi service?"

"No," Maeve said, "but I have to get this cake done and delivered in the next two hours. How long do you think it will take for her to get stitched?"

"Lady," he started, "I don't know what you thought you were getting when you called 911, but in addition to not being a taxi service, we are also not prognosticators. I know you pay a lot of taxes to live in this town, but seriously?"

Someone's jockey shorts were too tight. "Fine," she said, turning back to Jo. "Listen, I'll get the cake done and head straight to the hospital. Wait for me, okay?"

Jo was resting on the stretcher, the blood seeping through the makeshift bandage that one of the EMTs had placed on top of it. "I'll call a cab."

Maeve grabbed her chin and pulled it gently so that Jo was looking at her. "No, you won't. I'll be there in a little over two hours. You may not even be done yet, but I'll wait for you in the waiting room." Maeve had been in that emergency room enough times to know exactly how it was laid out. She also had been there enough to know that the staff at the admitting desk wasn't the most agree-able, sort of like the cop who was using precious time to tell her what wasn't part of his job description.

Jo lifted her hand and put it on Maeve's shoulder. "Fine. I'll wait for you." One of the EMTs put the sides up on the stretcher and prepared to roll Jo out into the ambulance. "Hey," she said, grabbing Maeve's arm. "What do you have in your purse, anyway? That thing weighs a ton."

Chapter 16

The icing barely had time to set, the cake was still warm, but Maeve made it work and managed to get it into the car and over to the baptism lady's house in under two hours. The woman had softened a little bit, but not as much as Maeve would have hoped.

"On the house," Maeve reminded her, feeling as if she were glued to the front porch of the beautiful Colonial, not moving forward to hand it to the woman, unable to take a step back and get away from the woman's stink-eye glare. Cars lined the driveway, and out of the corner of her eye, she could see a tent in the side yard, the party well under way. When the woman made no move to take the cake from her hands, Maeve rested it on a wicker table next to the door and lifted the lid. "Take a look. I hope you like it."

In spite of the circumstances surrounding her creation of the cake, Maeve thought it had come out pretty well. And if the woman didn't think so, well, there were three dozen cupcakes to sweeten the deal; that box was already on the chair next to the table. The woman peered into the box, and even she had to admit that it was pretty damned good given the amount of time Maeve had had to make it happen.

"It's beautiful," the woman said. "Listen, I'm sorry . . ."

Maeve held up a hand to stop her. "No apologies necessary. My fault entirely. I hope you'll come back to The Comfort Zone soon so I can continue to make this up to you." She resisted an urge to look at her watch, her only thoughts with Jo, hopefully still at the hospital and not in a cab on her way back to Farringville. "Enjoy the rest of your party," she said to the woman, now smiling, before scurrying down the porch steps and walking to her car as fast as she could without breaking into an all-out sprint.

The hospital was twenty minutes away on a stretch of road with too many stoplights, all of which were red when Maeve hit them. She had texted Jo at one of them, taking care to make sure there weren't any pesky cops in the vicinity, and instructed her to "WAIT." She tapped the steering wheel impatiently at the third light, unable to think of anything but her friend, blood pouring out of her head, and the gun that was starting to cause too many problems despite its lack of use. Where to put it? That was something she was going to have to mull over when she had more time on her hands and fewer details in her head. When she thought about it that way, she had to laugh. The day she had more time on her hands and less to think about was a mythical day far in the future and probably would never come to pass.

Jo was still getting stitched up when Maeve arrived, lying on her side on a stretcher in one of the ER bays, her face as white as the sheet covering half her face and the right side of her body, doing her best to look brave. She wasn't successful. She looked terrified. Maeve knew that Jo hated being in the hospital; something like this brought out her darkest fears even though it had nothing to do with cancer. Jo had kept a gall-bladder filled with stones rather than go through elective laparoscopic surgery, so getting her head sewn up had to be unearthing some of the feelings that she tried to bury under a thick layer of sarcasm and black humor.

Maeve ignored the doctor sitting behind Jo, even though he was youngish, cute, and exactly Jo's type. She grabbed her friend's hand instead. "Hanging in there?"

Jo looked up at her miserably. "I think he's sewing my entire head back on."

The doctor pulled a long thread away from a bald patch on Jo's head. "Almost done," he said. Maeve didn't think it would be the appropriate time to ask Jo to tell the guy something about herself, something related to her gymnastics background or her amazing pot roast. Jo treated every situation as a potential for a hookup, but even this scenario had its limits in that regard.

"That's what you said fourteen stitches ago," Jo said. "Yes, I've been counting." Whatever pain-killer they may have given Jo had done nothing to quell her ire over being hit in the head with the world's ugliest purse. "And seriously? What the hell did you have in your bag?" she asked.

Maeve didn't answer, preferring instead to put a hand on Jo's sweaty brow. "Stay still and be quiet. You'll get out of here faster."

The doctor fiddled around at the back of Jo's head. When he was done, Jo looked like one of those Revolutionary War reenactors, the one who had to wear a bandage wrapped around his head while playing "Yankee Doodle" on a flute, marching with a pronounced limp. "And we're done!" the doctor said, helping Jo into a sitting position. "I'll go write you a prescription for Percocet so you can get through the next few days. You should come back and see me in a week just so we can check on how we're progressing and get your stitches out."

"We?" Jo said. "Why? Are you going to get stitches in your head in the next few hours? Because otherwise, this is all about me. We are not in this together."

The doctor looked a little shocked, then broke into a smile. "Okay, Ms. Weinstein. Come back in a week. How's that?"

Jo slid off the bed and slowly straightened up. "That's better," she said.

Maeve gave the doctor a sympathetic smile behind Jo's back, shrugging slightly. She noted that he was still chuckling to himself as they left the ER bay.

The hospital was a hotbed of activity on this Saturday afternoon. In the next room was an elderly man accompanied by a much younger woman, presumably his granddaughter. Jo, her tongue loosened by the painkillers she had been given prior to the first stitch to her head, hooked a thumb in the old man's direction as they exited the emergency room. "See that old guy? They gave him a catheter," she said.

Maeve looked over at the man, sleeping peacefully, his granddaughter flipping through a magazine.

Jo walked through the door that Maeve held open for her. "While he was awake." She put a hand to her head. "Get me the hell out of here. This place is the worst."

Maeve didn't tell her that it could have been much worse. Her own visit to a city emergency room when she was seven, her arm broken, was forever etched in her mind. That was the first time Jack had been accused of something he hadn't done (and would never do), explaining that his daughter, in the care of her cousin, had fallen off a swing. She was clumsy. An ER in a suburban hospital in a wealthy county paled in comparison with the one at the formerly named Misericordia Hospital, a place she had been taken by one of Jack's police officer colleagues after an "accident" on the playground. You wanted hell? That place made hell look like the Botanical Gardens.

Maeve pulled up in front of the fence that surrounded the little cottage that Jo lived in, a few steps away from the larger house where a mutual friend of theirs lived with her husband and four daughters. When Jo had had nowhere to turn,

Maria had offered the cottage, a supposedly short-term solution that was now in its sixth month. Jo put her hand on the door handle, starting to get out, but changed her mind.

"I'm coming in with you," Maeve said. The weight of what had happened was dawning anew on her, and she felt completely responsible for her friend's injury.

Jo protested, but only slightly, letting Maeve help her out of the passenger side of the Prius and hold her hand as they navigated the uneven bluestone treads that marked the way to the one-bedroom cottage. In the distance, over a beauti-fully manicured expanse of lawn, lay the Hudson, the sun sparkling on its surface. Maeve could see why Jo had lingered; what would be better than this little clapboard-sided cottage with its spectacular view?

Inside wasn't as charming as outside, but it was cozy. Maeve had been here only once—when Jo had moved in—and was surprised to see that not much had changed. Obviously, Jo had considered the situation temporary as well, and a testament to that—two unopened moving boxes—was pushed against the far wall under a big picture window that allowed her to take in the view every day. Jo had come away from the divorce with a large sectional sofa and her grandmother's bed frame, but not much else. She seemed to have filled in the gaps with finds at flea markets and antique stores; even though it was cheaper stuff than she had acquired when she was married and had a bit more disposable income, she had managed to pull together an eclectic look that spoke of her reverence for the past.

In the cottage, Jo caught sight of herself in a large mirror hanging by the door and gasped. She lowered her head, raised her eyes, and took off the bandage against Maeve's protestations, taking in the shaved patch at the top of her scalp, pink, raw, and held together with thick black stitches. "Shit." She quickly covered it again.

Maeve led her to the sofa and pulled over a large trunk, the one that served as the coffee table. She placed a pillow on it and told Jo to put her feet up. "Do you want tea? Ice water?" Maeve asked, going into the galley kitchen. "I think you can probably take another pill now so you can get some rest."

"It was a gun, wasn't it?" Jo asked from the other room.

In the split second she had to respond, Maeve considered lying, then realized that there was no point. Jo could sense a lie a mile away, which was how she knew, with barely a clue, that Eric had been cheating. "It was," Maeve finally said, almost relieved that the truth was out. She didn't know how Jo knew it was a gun and didn't want to ask. The sooner this conversation could come to an end, the better.

"Jack's?" Jo asked. "Or yours?"

"Jack's," Maeve said. "I don't know where to put it. I had to take it away when I moved him, and I haven't been able to think of a safe place to stow it."

"You moved him awhile ago," Jo said.

Maeve waited a beat, staring at her hands growing cold under the water running from the tap.

"So where's it been since then?"

"I had it at home, but I want to get it out of there," she said. That was almost true. She walked into the living room and handed Jo a glass of water. "You want a pill now or do you want to wait?"

"Will it make me forget everything that's happened today?" she asked.

Maeve gave her a little smile and shrugged. "Maybe. Probably."

"Then give me a pill," Jo said.

They sat in silence for a while, and when it appeared that Jo would soon be drifting off to sleep, Maeve unearthed an old quilt from the bedroom upstairs and covered her with it. "Don't come back to work until you're ready," she said, spreading the quilt over Jo's long body.

"I won't." Her eyes closed, and she let out a loud yawn. "What will you do without me?" she asked, only half-kidding.

"I think I'll manage," Maeve said, quickly

adding, "But only barely." She loved her friend and the company she provided in the store, but they both knew her skills as a counter person and part-time baker were a little lacking.

"As soon as I can think straight, I'll come back," Jo said, drifting off.

Maeve washed a few dishes in the sink and took inventory of what was in Jo's refrigerator, something that didn't take too long; she didn't have much. Since the bakery was unexpectedly closed for the day, she figured she'd take advantage of the extra time and stock Jo's pantry. Maybe she would swing by Buena del Sol and pick up Jack while she was at it; the old man loved wandering the aisles at the local supermarket, hectoring Maeve to buy him things that were definitely on his list of banned food items, like cheap domestic beer and crappy prepackaged cakes and sweets. The beer she could understand, but the Devil Dogs and Yodels were another story. With the stuff she turned out at the bakery, she couldn't comprehend why he would want mass-produced items, but there you had it; the guy had a taste for crap and there was nothing she could do about that.

Jo was muttering in the living room, her ramblings the product of a head wound accompanied by some excellent opioids. "Maybe you could kill Eric for me," she said, able to articulate her hatred for her ex-husband more than any other thought in her head. "Yeah, kill him. While you still have the gun."

Maeve opened her mouth to speak but didn't say anything in response. It wasn't as if the thought hadn't crossed her mind.

Chapter 17

After she left Jo, did a quick grocery shop without Jack, and returned to her friend's to put some items away, Maeve picked the girls up at home and brought them to Cal's. Maeve usually dropped the girls off and drove away, not wanting to spend any more time in the presence of her ex, his new wife, his third child, or the splendor that was the 1920s stone Tudor that Maeve had always worshipped from afar. She'd spent years hoping that one day she might know someone who lived there and that they would invite her in and give her a tour along with a glass of Chardonnay. Be careful what you wish for, the old adage went, and in this case it was entirely apropos. She had gotten the tour, but not the Chardonnay, and the whole experience had left her more than a little bereft. She had nearly been brought to tears when she saw the original and gorgeously maintained white subway tile in the bathroom that surrounded a cast-iron claw-foot tub situated in the perfect spot for a panoramic view of the river. Then there was the fireplace in the master bedroom, one of six in the entire house. She tried not to dwell on the fact that Cal slept in that bedroom with someone other than her, someone she had thought was a co-conspirator in the game of life but who had turned the tables on her and upended everything she knew about her world.

Heather, seated in the front seat after a heated negotiation with her sister, stormed off the minute Maeve stopped the car, slamming the door as hard as she could to make sure everyone within a hundred feet knew how angry she was at being grounded, this time for a new offense: a zero in math. Maeve looked in the rearview mirror and gave Rebecca a weak smile.

"She's such a bitch," Rebecca said in an uncharacteristic display of profane honesty.

Maeve bit back a response; she couldn't let on that she agreed with her oldest. It was days like this when she thought that she was lucky—as was Jack—that she had been an only child. "Good luck on the lit test on Monday," she said.

"Thanks," Rebecca said, leaning over the seat and giving her mother a hug from behind. "It's Chaucer. What could I possibly forget?" she asked. "It's only the hardest thing I've ever studied."

"From what I remember, no one in Chaucer has real names. So if you forget any characters, just make one up." She leaned into her daughter's

144

hug. "For instance, I would be the Baker. And you'd be the Good Student."

Rebecca pulled her backpack to her chest and slid across the seat. "And Heather?"

Maeve laughed. "I think we've already established that."

"The Bitchy Sister?"

Maeve touched her daughter's hair. "You said it, not me."

She blew a kiss as Rebecca walked up the sidewalk, then prepared to drive away; but Cal, running down the sidewalk toward her, made her hesitate. He had seen her see him, and that made her stop. Although he had broken the vows of their marriage, she would never want him to think her rude.

She rolled down the passenger-side window. "Remember. No party," she said, knowing he needed a reminder or three that Heather was grounded again. There were parties every weekend in Farringville, and Maeve's goal was to keep Heather away from as many as she could.

He brushed that off with a dismissive wave of his hand. "I got another call," he said. "Detective Poole?"

At the mention of his name, her blood ran cold and she couldn't figure out why. Was it that she didn't need a detective in her life right now—or ever—or was it the exceptional role-playing that they had both done at the speed-dating event, making it seem that Detective Poole was someone who was interested in her beyond the details of the case? She tried not to look unnerved, but she had known Cal a long time and if he was good at one thing, it was reading her face. He gave her a quizzical look, so she rearranged her features into something approximating neutral concern, thinking that this turn of events couldn't be good for Jack. Or her. "And?"

"And they want to talk to Jack again," Cal said, looking disappointed at his inability to dispatch this pesky problem regarding his former father-in-law. He splayed his hands on the car door, looking down. "I'm sorry, Maeve."

"They can't really think he had anything to do with this, can they?" she asked.

"They can," he said. From inside the house came the sound of a wailing baby or a second wife; Maeve couldn't tell.

"Can't they tell that Jack couldn't possibly have had anything to do with anything like this?" she asked.

"He could have, Maeve." Cal looked suitably nervous, and that brought Maeve no comfort at all.

"How could they?" She rested her head on the steering wheel. "He can't even remember what night book club is."

"Really? Do you really think he forgets all of those details?" Cal asked, not unkindly.

"What are you suggesting?" she asked. "That he's faking?"

He looked back at the house and then at her. "I have to go," he said, straightening up and walking back to the house, her question unanswered. Since he had retired, he had taken to wearing Bermuda shorts every day, and today was no exception, even though the weather was getting colder. As he walked away, the tail of his polo shirt falling past his backside, she saw a glimmer of the guy she had first met, the one who was funny and nice and destined for great things, at least in his own mind. He was the one she had fallen in love with; the one who would never hurt her, or so she had told herself.

She gripped the steering wheel for a few minutes, watching her knuckles turn white, wondering how easy it would be to find the one man Jack knew who had a car and sometimes even drove it. Maybe she could find Moriarty without finding Jack so that she could get some answers to some increasingly troubling questions. She looked at the clock on the dashboard and saw that it was a half hour before dinner would commence at Buena del Sol so the possibility existed that she could find him and get some answers. The day-old pumpkin bread in the back-seat, taken from the store and that Maeve had planned to eat for dinner, would be just the thing she needed to grease the wheels and get the old man talking. Because if there was one thing that she had learned from her visits to Jack at Buena del Sol and meeting his cronies, those guys loved them some good sweets since most of them were on a strict diet that denied them even the hint of sugar.

She knew it would be fruitless to call ahead. She didn't have a phone number for the old guy, and if her memory served, his problem was slurred speech—as well as a few missing teeth— and not dementia; but the speech issue, in and of itself, presented problems with a phone call. Armed with the pumpkin bread, tied with her trademark raffia, she made her way into the facility, noting with relief that Doreen, the simian-loving concierge, was gone for the evening. In her place was an officious-looking little woman with a name tag that said "Joy," a name that completely contra-dicted the look of disgust on her face at Maeve's approach.

"I would like to visit with Mr. Moriarty," Maeve said as politely as she could, hoping not to incur the wrath of the erroneously named Joy. Joy's hair was the color of a red plastic Solo cup with patches of white where she had missed with the dye, her eyebrows a shade somewhere between lavender and eggplant.

"Dinner starts in ten minutes," Joy said, resuming the important task of counting the number of visitors who had come by the facility that day.

"I'll be back in eight," Maeve said. She cut Joy some slack; she was old, she needed a good hairstylist, and she was having a bad day. Or life. It was hard to tell. Maeve put her hands together, pleading her case to Joy with only her eyes.

"And who should I say is calling?" Joy asked.

"Maeve Conlon," she said, her license out of her bag and into Joy's hand so as not to waste any more time. Buena del Sol—an "assisted-living facility for seniors who loved life"—was basically a jail. Joy took her time inputting all of the pertinent information into the computer, scanning Maeve's license, and looking at the old picture against Maeve's current face, something Doreen hadn't taken the time to do. Satisfied that Maeve was who she said she was, Joy made a phone call and was able to ascertain that Mr. Moriarty was in the garden out back, his court time just about to start. "Just dropping off a pumpkin bread." Maeve went through all of the possible problems that could bring. "It's lactose-free, sugar-free, and gluten-free." She thought that covered all of the bases even if it was a lie.

"That's good," Joy said. "Many of our residents have issues with their diets."

Maeve nodded enthusiastically. "I know."

Joy looked at her coolly. "Don't you think you should be going?" she said, looking pointedly at the clock.

Maeve took the hint and sprinted outside,

making her way around the side of the building. When she rounded the corner, she saw Jack, dressed up and looking handsome in spite of the mismatched shower sandals on his feet, squiring one of the younger and spryer residents toward the community room. It was nearly five, so Maeve guessed that he was taking a date to dinner, a thought that made her happy. She watched him usher the lady through the back doors of the facility and disappear into the large room on the other side of the doors, waiting a few moments before continuing her jog toward the tennis courts.

Mr. Moriarty was being soundly thumped by a spindly old fellow in crisp tennis whites, his shots going long and his serve looking as if it needed a serious refresher course from the tennis pro at the athletic club about a mile away. Moriarty wasn't a good loser and threw his racket on the ground like an AARP card–carrying John McEnroe, who Maeve supposed was probably carrying his own AARP card by now. His opponent took great delight in calling out the score every time a shot was mishit, and by the time Maeve arrived at the court, Mr. Moriarty was in a full-blown snit. She hoped he agreed that he needed a break, one filled with day-old pumpkin bread and a brief interrogation from her.

"Mr. Moriarty?" she called out from the other side of the fence.

"What?!" he called back. "Can't you see I'm in the middle of a match?" His speech had definitely improved since the last time she had seen him.

His opponent wasn't so sure. "You call this a match? It's like watching paint dry!"

Moriarty threw his racket to the ground, this time breaking the frame on one side, the strings twisting and becoming useless. "Why do I even bother?" he asked the sky, shaking a fist. "I'm done!"

"Why indeed?" his opponent called back. "That'll be twenty bucks, Moriarty. You forfeited the match. You can pay me after dinner." The man walked off the court and put his racket and balls into a large leather bag that looked as though it had seen its fair share of tennis matches. He exited the court at the far end, leaving Moriarty staring disconsolately at his broken racket.

Maeve opened the gate on her side of the court and entered cautiously. "Mr. Moriarty? I'm Maeve Conlon. Jack's daughter?" she said, holding the pumpkin bread in front of her like a peace offering to an ancient god. Come to think of it, the guy kind of looked like a statue from Easter Island, all flat-nosed from an earlier kerfuffle somewhere in the bowels of the Bronx, if she had to guess.

"Jack went to dinner. With that woman who's been sniffing around him. What's her name?" he asked, looking up. Maeve certainly didn't know but was intrigued. "Judy? Janie?" He walked over and stuffed his broken racket into his bag. "That for me?" he asked, looking at the pumpkin bread.

"It is," she said, handing it to him.

"What do you want?" he asked, getting suspicious. "My own daughter only comes here once a month and she certainly doesn't bring anything as good as a pumpkin bread. She does bring that chocolate pudding that doesn't have any milk in it," he said. "And that stuff stinks."

Maeve guessed right: lactose-intolerant. She was glad she'd gone with the pumpkin bread and not the cannoli. "I just wanted to know if you had been out with my father at all in the last several weeks. Maybe for a drive? To run some errands?"

He looked up at the sky again, searching his brain for the details. "I don't know, Ms. Conlon. I'm old. I don't remember what's going on from day to day," he admitted. "Although I don't have dementia. No sirree!" he said, making it clear to Maeve that being part of the forgetful crowd put one at Buena del Sol in a whole different category. "Except for my tennis. I remember that. Apparently, I stink. Every blessed day. Couldn't hit the side of a barn." He sat dejectedly in a chair at the edge of the court and put his head in his hands. He rubbed what used to be the bridge of his nose. "I don't know why I bother."

"I thought you looked pretty good," Maeve said. "That other guy was wiry. Big guys like you never have a chance against those little guys." She smiled. "Next time, challenge him to a game of basketball. He won't stand a chance."

Moriarty looked up and smiled. "You've got your old man's sense of humor."

She went over and crouched down in front of him. "Think, Mr. Moriarty. Did Jack ask you for a ride anywhere in the past few weeks? The last month? Anywhere?" she asked, trying to jog his memory.

He opened up the pumpkin bread and took a big sniff. "This smells great. I'm not sharing it with anyone."

Maeve waited. Moriarty ripped off a big piece and shoved it in his mouth, enjoying every bite of what to her was damaged goods, having been left over from the day before. She made a mental note to bring him a fresh one next time.

"Anywhere?" she asked again.

He pointed at her. "There was once. A few weeks ago. He asked me to drop him at the train station."

Her heart quickened and then skipped a beat.

"It was bingo night. Can't remember which one or how long ago," he said, tearing into the pumpkin bread again. "All's I know is that it maybe was a few weeks ago. And I won at bingo. So it must have been a Saturday."

Chapter 18

Maeve knew that Cal was a good lawyer and a good dad, but as a disciplinarian, she'd have better luck leaving her children in the care of Lindsay Lohan. He stunk at being the bearer of bad news in terms of what the girls could and could not do. It wasn't that he thought he should be the girls' friend, it was just that he now had so much on his plate with an overbearing and high-maintenance wife as well as a new baby that he found it hard to stick to the rules that he and Maeve had set up. It was armed with this knowledge, as well as experience with Heather, who could wear down the strictest parent with her debates and arguments, that Maeve found herself parked outside a house known for its raucous parties and visits from the local police, if the local blotter was accurate.

Across the street from the large contemporary, clear on the other side of town and a good distance from her own modestly sized home, she watched as the parents, notoriously lax, drove away, chatting amiably as they passed Maeve, slunk down in the seat of her car. Within minutes, several dozen cars appeared and kids piled out of each one like clowns from a circus car, the subcompacts seemingly holding more kids than the SUVs that pulled up. Maeve slid farther down in her seat and waited in the dark, trying to get a bead on whether or not her younger daughter had arrived with the rest of the partygoers.

What Heather didn't know, and never would if Maeve could help it, was that her mother had a fake Facebook page and Heather had accepted her "friend" request. As a result, Maeve knew more about Heather's life than her younger daughter could have imagined. She knew that Heather had missed the last few parties but was planning on getting to this one, come hell or high water. Kid had even invited her to the party, unwittingly, thinking that "McKenna O'Keefe" was a real person and would be interested in a party that boasted live music and a seemingly endless supply of booze. There would be some point where Heather might respect the lengths her mother had gone to protect her, after she realized she wasn't completely insane. Maybe when she had her own children and was trying to protect them. Maybe then she would see that Maeve, her worrying worn like a badge of honor, had done everything she possibly could to keep her girls safe.

She peeled open the brownie that she had packed herself as a snack, then took a loud slurp from the bottle of water that she kept in the holder between the seats. She was settling in. Heather would arrive, she was sure of that; it was just a matter of when.

The house, once dark inside, was now ablaze

with lights, music pouring out the open windows on the first floor. Although the house boasted a large lot, it did have neighbors on both sides, neighbors who—if the *Day Timer*'s blotter was to be believed—called the police with alarming regularity, usually on Saturday nights. Maeve wondered how long it would take for them to call this time, the sounds of a song with an incredibly heavy bass line already thumping away. If she lived next door to this family and had to endure this every weekend, she just might set a match to the house when its occupants were elsewhere.

After about forty minutes, Heather arrived in a car driven by the boy Maeve had seen her with at the soccer game, looking elated at the prospect of entering the house. Maeve's consternation with Cal grew as she watched Heather direct the driver of the car onto the long expanse of front lawn, helping him angle in between a Mercedes and a BMW as if she were directing a large jet into a bay at JFK. Once he was parked, the kid jumped out of the car and grabbed her around the waist, and the two of them ran into the house with nary a glance at the lone car parked across the street from the action.

Maeve ate her brownie, waiting thirty seconds before sending a text to her daughter. "Am across the street. You can either come out or I'll come in. Your choice." She closed her phone and waited. Just as she was about to get out of the car and march down the driveway to the house, Heather emerged, scanning the front of the house for a sign of her mother, eventually spotting the Prius under the streetlamp across the street. Maeve rolled the window down and, when Heather was close enough, said, "Get in."

Maeve had once read that the secret to good parenting was letting your kids believe that you were just a little crazy. So idle threats like "Do that again and you'll spend the next three days in your room" held water; they needed to know that if you asked them not to do something and they did it, they would be looking at the walls of their Laura Ashley bedroom for three solid days. With good enough acting skills, you could make the kids believe that you were capable of just about anything, the hammer of justice falling swiftly and cleanly, no debate warranted, no discussion necessary. She watched as Heather pondered just how crazy her mother was, wondering just how far she would go. She decided, in the end, to get in the car without saying a word and without a backward glance toward a party that was just about to break up anyway, if the sound of the siren in the distance was any indication.

"Where did you tell him you were going?" Maeve asked.

"Home," she said, plastering herself against the passenger-side door, a POW trapped with a crazy captor.

"Not your date. Your father," Maeve said. Kid had a one-track mind, and the track was herself.

Maeve snuck a glance and could see that Heather was ashamed by what she was about to admit. "Packing clothes for the Midnight Run in the city."

Maeve let out a sound that was a cross between a groan and a protest. "You can lie like that and not feel any kind of remorse?" she asked, even though she could tell that Heather had gone even further than she was comfortable with.

The police car passed them on the winding road, and Maeve waited at the one-car bridge to let another one pass. "I just wanted to go to the party," Heather said, wanting her mother to believe that that was a legitimate excuse for lying. Out of her mouth, it almost sounded reasonable. She was that good.

"Well, you know what?" Maeve asked, pulling onto the bridge, the car noiseless but making a racket as it went over the steel treads. "Now you're not going anywhere. For a long time."

She couldn't see the eye roll but knew that it had happened. Next to her was a fifteen-year-old the size of a twelve-year-old filled with enough piss and vinegar to make someone three times her age perpetually angry. "I hate you," Heather said, not under her breath enough for Maeve not to hear her.

Maeve had heard that sentiment expressed

before, but unlike before, this time she couldn't resist responding. "I don't like you very much right now either."

The sound that came out of Heather was a mixture of shock, hurt, and surprise. "You're not supposed to say that to your daughter. That's just mean."

A raised eyebrow in her direction was all Maeve could muster in response.

"I mean, really, like you can't say stuff like that. Do you want me to spend the rest of my life in therapy?"

Yes, I do, Maeve thought. Like the rest of us, I want you to spend your entire life thinking about how your actions affect others and talking, in therapy, about all of the times you almost gave your mother a heart attack and how if it weren't for her unconditional love and hypervigilance, you might not be here to complain about your father issues and low self-esteem. May that be the most her daughter ever had to complain about to someone she paid to listen to her. Maeve didn't utter another word until they were at Cal's. Heather jumped from the car before it was even in park, storming up the front steps to the Tudor and slamming the door behind her. Maeve stood on the steps, ringing the doorbell impatiently, waiting for someone to acknowledge that she was out front, in the dark, the temperature dropping to a point where soon she wouldn't be able to feel her toes.

Gabriela finally answered the door. "You're going to wake the baby," she said. She was dressed in a silk robe and, for some strange reason, high heels. Maeve had now been awake for seventeen hours and the stretch in her jeans was starting to let her down, the ass sagging, the hems drooping over the tops of the clogs she wore to the store to support her feet.

"Is Cal awake?" she asked.

Cal appeared behind his wife, his Bermuda shorts and polo shirt rumpled, his hair standing on end. Asleep on the couch. Maeve had seen this look many times and knew where he had been. Why his wife was dressed in a peignoir set with a come-hither look on her face didn't make any sense to Maeve, but she had other things on her mind and didn't want to waste her brainpower on figuring out why Gabriela did the things she did. As Gabriela stomped away in a pair of shoes that would have paid Maeve's electric bill for the month, Maeve took great delight in noticing the bald spot again.

Cal held up a hand to stop her from speaking. "It was the midnight run. That's why I let her out," he said.

"She didn't go to the midnight run packing meeting, Cal," Maeve said.

"I called the church and the youth minister said her name was on the list."

"Of course it was," Maeve said. "Because she's

smart." Unlike you, she held back. "She was at the party I told you she couldn't go to."

Cal stepped outside and closed the door behind him, leaving Gabriela to steam in her leopard silk robe in the massive foyer, the one that was bigger than Maeve's bedroom. "I checked this out before I let her go."

"Was I wrong, Cal? Do you want to be their friend? The good guy?" she asked. "I hate being the bad guy all the time. I hate being the one who has to monitor their every move."

"Then stop," he said.

"Excuse me?"

"Stop," he said. "Stop monitoring their every move. So she was at a party. So she lied. You think she's the first fifteen-year-old to tell a lie or three?"

Maeve stared up at him, incredulous.

"This is something we're never going to agree on," he said, shoving his hands deep into the pockets of his wrinkled Bermuda shorts. How he had gotten through law school and managed a successful career was starting to become a wonder to her. "I'll keep her home until you come back to get her," he said, turning to go into the house. He stopped before he got to the grand front door. With his back turned, he said, "To answer your question, no, I don't want to be their friend. But I do want to have an open enough relationship where they will talk to me

161

without being afraid. I don't want them to be afraid. Plain and simple."

"I—I don't want them to be afraid," she said, but she stammered, giving him the impression that there wasn't a lot of confidence behind the statement.

"You do," he said before he went inside. "You'd like nothing more."

She wasn't sure what that meant, but surely it was an indictment of her, a criticism of her parenting skills or, worse yet, her very being. Yes, she wanted to make them afraid. Bad things lurked out there and sometimes in innocuous, pleasant-looking packages. Sometimes those bad things—those bad people—told you things that you wanted to hear. She wanted them on their guard at all times so that they didn't get hurt. She wanted to protect them. That's all.

Nothing good happens at two a.m., Jack used to say, but there were other times, times when the sun shone bright, when bad things happened, too.

She stared at the door for a long time after Cal went back into the house. If he was stupid enough to be outsmarted by a fifteen-year-old who could lie like someone with a serious pathology, she had no idea how he was going to keep Jack out of jail.

Chapter 19

Getting Jack an alibi was proving to be harder than getting Jo to fall in love with Doug of the Dockers, as Maeve had come to think of him. Although Doug had shown tremendous care and concern for Jo after her accident with the pocketbook, as Maeve had come to think of it, Jo didn't seem very interested, so Maeve took every opportunity to remark upon how nice Doug seemed, how caring, how completely perfect for Jo.

Jo wasn't buying it.

She was feeling better just a few days after her collision with Maeve's purse and had not brought up the issue of the gun again, but she did ask for advice from her good friend about what to do about Doug. For once, Maeve thanked God for the self-absorption that took Jo away from the fire-arm in her purse and to the subject of her relationship.

"It's like he wants to take care of me," she said, disdain evident in her voice.

Maeve was cleaning the front counter, getting ready to close for the day. "And that's a bad thing?"

"Well, no," she started, clearly running out of gas with the thought. "I'm tired. Let's talk later. Doug is bringing me chicken soup."

"That's nice!" Maeve said, trying to fake-cheer her way into Jo's brain to let her know that the guy was a keeper. She wasn't feeling cheerful, and she couldn't understand why Jo couldn't see what she could: the guy was the real deal.

"Chicken soup is for a cold, not a head wound," she complained. In the background, Maeve could hear the television blaring. Obviously, Jo's headache had subsided, but that didn't mean Maeve could expect her back at work anytime soon. That conversation hadn't been broached yet, and Maeve suspected it would be awhile before she saw her friend again in a Comfort Zone apron.

Maeve couldn't argue with that, so she took another route. "Just accept it graciously. And stop overthinking things. The guy is nuts about you. What more could you want?"

"Passion. Chemistry. Lust."

"Oh, just those? Give it time," she said. "I'll talk to you later."

The parking lot out front of the store was empty as the clock crawled toward five. She went back to the shop so she could bake and keep up on things with Jo still recovering from her head wound. Maeve knew the plan she had concocted had a few flaws, but she was willing to give it a try. She hadn't talked to Jack in a few days, but she suspected that even if she did, and they revisited the conversation about where he had been several Saturdays past, he still wouldn't know, coming up with something about going to a dance class at Arthur Murray or going to his usual Saturday-night poker game with some of the boys from the precinct, two things that he hadn't been involved in in more than thirty years. Maeve turned the CLOSED sign over on the front door and headed out the back, leaving her apron next to the sink and taking her purse—which still held the gun—down from the reconstructed metal shelving unit that sat next to the kitchen door.

If the information she had gotten from Mr. Moriarty was correct, this would have been about the time that he had dropped Jack off at the train station on the night that Sean was killed. Who knew if the same ticket agent would even be at the window tonight? Did the schedules for the agents change at all? Was there a separate set of agents for weekends? She didn't know, but she figured it was worth a try to see if the agent was the same and if he remembered Jack from that night. Or others. When it came right down to it, Maeve wasn't sure of the exact number of times Jack had gotten loose and where he had gone. He might have ridden the train a half-dozen times for all she knew.

She had a picture of Jack on her phone, and when it was her turn to approach the ticket window, after listening to the sad story of a woman who had gotten on the wrong train and now couldn't figure out how to get back to Tarrytown, she held up her phone and asked the agent if he had seen this man in the not-too-distant past. The agent, a middle-aged guy with an impressive paunch straining behind the striped shirt and blue buttons of his uniform shirt, gave the picture a much longer gander than Maeve would have thought necessary.

"No."

"Were you here a little over three weeks ago? On a Saturday?" she asked.

"Lady, I'm here every Saturday. Every Monday, too. Come to think of it, I'm here practically every damn day, so if I saw this guy, I would remember."

"But that doesn't mean he didn't take the train," she said, more as a question to herself than to the agent.

He threw his head toward a bank of machines at the far side of the station. "He could have used the ticket machines over there. I never would have noticed," he said, looking over her head pointedly at the line of people forming behind her. "Now, if you don't mind?"

She walked away, going over to check out the bank of ticket machines. They seemed easy enough to use, very intuitive, but would Jack have been able to figure them out? She had given him a small laptop computer so that he could e-mail with the girls, but even that had seemed beyond his abilities technologically. She poked at the screen dejectedly, wondering if Mr. Moriarty had remembered correctly or if he was as confused as her father, "misremembering" things and making up facts to suit the situation.

"I was wondering the same thing," a deep voice to her left said.

She knew to whom the voice belonged, not needing to turn and look at the speaker. "Detective Poole."

"Ms. Conlon."

She finally turned and looked at him, ending her mindless poking at the ticket machine screen. "Just picking up a schedule," she said.

"Or figuring out how your father could have gotten to the Bronx on his own pins," he said. He was sitting on one of the metal benches along the same wall that held the ticket machines, his legs crossed, a folded *New York Times* on his lap. He looked like a regular commuter waiting for the train to take him to Grand Central, just an ordinary guy killing some time by catching up on the news. At this time of day, there were a fair number of people in the station, and he didn't look out of place, his rumpled corduroy pants and tweed blazer a credible uniform for a guy on his way to work, even in the late afternoon.

"So you're following me now?" she asked, frozen in the spot at the ticket machine.

"Not exactly," he said. "You probably won't believe me when I tell you this, but I came by the store to buy more cupcakes."

"You're right," she said. "I don't believe you."

He shrugged. "Suit yourself," he said, getting up. "The ticket agent doesn't remember seeing your father." He smiled sadly. "But as he told you, and he told me, that doesn't mean he didn't take the train."

"There's no way my father could have figured out how to use this machine," she said, poking angrily at the screen welcoming her to Metro-North. "You don't know him like I do," she said.

"That's true, Ms. Conlon," he said, the formality coming back into their relationship. "But maybe he's a little more technologically savvy than you think?"

She waited. Maybe he had some news to impart, something that he was holding back for maxi-mum dramatic effect. She clutched her bag closer to her chest, trying not to clutch it so tight as to give away the outline of the gun resting in its dark, messy depths. But there was nothing. Just conjecture. Was Jack better at the computer than she had thought? Was Poole's silence suggesting that?

She looked out over the tracks below to the river beyond them. "And even if he had gotten to the Bronx," she said, spinning her defense as she stood there, "how would he have gotten from the station to the park?"

Poole was not impressed with her reasoning. "Cab?" he said. He smiled that sad smile he had.

"I also understand that your father does quite a lot of walking, too. He's in good shape for an old guy."

Maeve couldn't let it go. "Then how did he get Sean to meet him?"

Poole was cryptic. "Maybe you should ask him that."

"When are you talking to him again?" she asked.

"Tomorrow," he said.

She watched as a group of kids, all clad in Rangers' hockey jerseys, headed down the stairs toward the platform to wait for the next train to the city, their voices melding together into one rich sound, the sound of pure excitement. "He didn't do it," she said quietly. She wasn't sure how many times she'd feel obliged to say that but would just keep repeating it until someone understood and left him alone.

"Where are your father's guns, Ms. Conlon? The ones from his days on the PD?"

It should have been a question that she expected, but she was caught off guard. One had been sold years ago, while the other was still in the bottom of her purse. Regardless, she wasn't giving a direct answer to the question. "I'm not exactly sure, Detective. Did you ask my father?"

"Of course," he said, his attention diverted by the sound of an Amtrak train steaming into the station. "As you might expect, he can't remem-

169

ber." He studied her face. "A lot of ex-cops at Buena del Sol."

"A lot of ex-cops in the area," she said.

"A lot of them probably keep their guns." He smiled. "I know I would."

"Really?"

"Yep, tough habit to break, I imagine," he said. "Once you've been armed. In control."

She knew what he was insinuating—Jack had access to firearms even if he didn't still have his own guns—but she played dumb, figuring that was the best course of action, given the circumstances.

Poole stayed silent, too, waiting for the response that wouldn't come.

They waited until the commuters who had come in on the train from Penn Station had streamed by, the cacophony of their voices dying out after a few long minutes.

"Off the record, Detective?" Maeve asked.

He considered that for a moment. "Off the record."

"Focus your attention elsewhere. On other cases. On other people whose killers deserve to be caught," she said, relaxing her grip on the bag, the Doppler effect of the kids' voices fading into the background. "Because Sean Donovan? He wasn't a very nice person."

He walked away; it was clear he didn't know the proper response to that statement. She had said too much and nothing at all.

But that didn't change the fact that she knew that Jack was slowly moving from person of interest to prime suspect, and there was likely nothing she could do about it.

Chapter 20

With no one to cover for her during the morning rush and Jack probably having forgotten that he was meeting with detectives again today, she called Cal. They hadn't spoken since Saturday and their argument on his front steps, and she hoped that he had cooled off enough to have a calm conversation with her about Jack's interrogation.

The niceties aside, she cut to the chase as she poured a cup of coffee for a jittery commuter who was itching to get out the door so much so that rather than take his change, he left her a dollar seventy-five tip. That's how it was with commuters: they were always running behind and could barely wait for their order to be filled, never mind wait for their change. She often made out like a bandit on particularly busy mornings because most people didn't leave themselves enough time to catch their trains but wouldn't sacrifice a hot scone and a delicious cup of coffee on their way to work. "Can you go to Buena del Sol a few minutes early and make sure that he looks okay?" she asked, harkening back to the image of him in two different socks at Sean's ash scattering. Or the shower sandals on Saturday when he was on his way to dinner. When Cal said he would, she turned away from the counter so that the three people milling in the front part of the store wouldn't hear what she had to say. "And thanks, Cal. I really can't thank you enough," she said, swallowing her pride and trying to sound as sincere as possible.

"You're welcome."

She waited until everyone was out of the store to get to the real reason she had called. "You don't possibly think that they consider Jack a serious suspect?" she asked, something she had asked him before and something that she thought about constantly. In her mind, it just didn't make any sense, but she wasn't a detective trying to close a case, so she was self-aware enough to realize that she might be just a wee bit biased.

"I don't know," Cal said. In the background, she heard the baby crying and hoped his mother could attend to him so Cal could tell her what she wanted to hear. "I have to prepare you for this, Maeve. They may hold him if they feel like they have enough on him."

The jingling of the bell atop the front door was the only thing that kept her from going to her knees. She grabbed hold of the edge of the counter, smiling at the woman who had walked through the door for her usual order of a chocolate-chip scone and a large coffee, half-caf/half-decaf, light, and sweet. Maeve had the order ready, knowing that she came in every morning at the same time, and handed her the bag. The woman mouthed to Maeve, "Thank you. Everything okay?"

Maeve asked Cal to hold. "Everything's fine," she said.

"You're as white as a ghost," the woman said, handing Maeve exact change and giving her a curious look before leaving.

Maeve went back to her phone call. "They wouldn't possibly put an eighty-year-old man in jail," she said.

"They would," Cal said. "Jack is looking more and more like someone who either had a hand in this or knows more than he's letting on. I'm thinking we should have him evaluated by a psychiatrist, Maeve."

"What?"

"A psychiatrist. Do you remember Vinnie the Chin?" he asked.

She wasn't sure she'd heard him correctly.

"Guy was in the Mob. Big case a few years back. Wore his robe to court every day trying to get the jury to think he was crazy," Cal said. "He was crazy. Crazy like a fox. It almost worked."

"Are you saying that the police don't think Jack is really suffering from dementia?" she asked.

"What I am saying, Maeve, is that we need to cover all of our bases."

The words hung in the space between them as she held the phone to her head, not hearing the sounds of cars driving by or the blare of the train whistle signaling the arrival of the Poughkeepsie train and the departure of the one to Grand Central. Outside, the parking lot was beginning to fill up again, and in a few seconds, she would have a store full of people clamoring for coffee, crumb cake, and muffins. "Keep me posted, okay?" she said, words that sounded less fraught than they should have, given the situation.

She wondered if Detective Poole had found Mr. Moriarty yet, or his connection to Jack. He was the only guy Jack knew who had driving privileges, and she had been able to suss him out by spending only a minute or two thinking about it. Had Poole and his colleagues figured out Moriarty's link to this yet?

As she waited on the myriad customers who came in that morning, some regulars, some just passing by on their way south on the adjacent highway, she wondered if Jack had it in him to kill anyone and if the NYPD saw something in him that she didn't see herself. Did he give off the impression that he was cold-blooded enough to kill someone in a park, at night, and walk off, with no one the wiser? She kept returning to the same fact, and that was that an eighty-year-old with Jack's failing faculties could not have pulled off something so sinister and so perfect. They would have to know that. Anyone with half a brain would know that.

Things settled into a quiet hum after the commuter traffic departed, and that was when Maeve caught up on her baking. Today, after putting three dozen cupcakes into the oven to bake and knowing she had exactly fourteen minutes until they needed to be pulled out, she opened the kitchen door so she could hear any foot traffic coming into the store and waited in the kitchen, a plan hatching in her head that was beautiful in its simplicity but maybe a little harder to execute than it seemed at first blush. She drummed her fingers on the countertop until the buzzer on the oven went off and she pulled the cupcakes out, putting them in a metal rack by the refrigerator to cool.

She went into the store and turned the OPEN sign to CLOSED. "Back in fifteen minutes," she scrawled on a Post-it note before going out the back door, locking everything up tight, and heading the few short blocks to her house.

The kids would be at school for another four hours, but she didn't need that much time. She went directly up to Heather's room, the one with the door with the scuff mark on it from the time Maeve had gotten so angry at her younger daughter that she had kicked it open, leaving a mark that was wide and black and didn't adequately do her ire justice at the time. She had been mad enough—but not big enough—to break the door in two. Sure, she could have painted over it, but she liked Heather to see it every time she entered her room, thinking that maybe she had just had the worst luck in the world to be born to a mother with an insane streak.

Maeve pushed open the door and went to work. For the first time ever, she was happy that Heather was a pack rat, saving every scrap of paper, every memento, and every McDonald's Happy Meal toy she had ever come into contact with. They had had countless arguments about the state of her room, Maeve pointing to tidy Rebecca's room as proof that just because you were a teenage girl you didn't have to be a slob. The room had a distinct odor, one borne of decaying food stuck on plates under the bed, dirty clothes piled in the corner intermingled with the clean ones, and a variety of potions and sprays and creams that adorned the dresser top and were half-empty, their contents dripping down the sides of their canisters. One whole wall was covered with concert posters—Arcade Fire, Death Cab for Cutie, Adele—and Maeve wondered why she had bothered to spend close to eight hundred dollars getting the room painted a special-order shade of lilac to please her Oscar Madison of a kid. Maeve held her breath and looked at the mirror over the dresser, the one that held assorted ticket stubs and programs from the various sporting events and Broadway shows that her daughter had been to, searching for the ticket to the Yankees game that had serendipitously taken place the same night that Sean Donovan had met his Maker. Heather had gone with a friend from school, an outing that Maeve had approved because the parents were taking the girls on the train and would be with them the whole time. The family had also invited Rebecca, a nice touch. She scanned each and every piece of paper she came across, coming up empty.

This was not like her daughter. Maeve stood in the middle of the room, her hands on her hips, trying to get into the mind-set of a fifteen-year-old with an attitude. She pulled open the top dresser drawer, the one where Heather kept her underwear, and riffled through an assortment of tangled bras and panties, a few mateless socks, and, not surprisingly, a bag of joints, three in all, which Maeve stuck in her pocket.

This yoga thing wasn't doing anything to calm her down. Maybe marijuana was the ticket.

Underneath an athletic sock that had seen better days, a hole in the big toe area and a brown spot on the bottom, was the golden ticket, so to speak, a stub from the game. Something exciting in Yankees history had happened that night, but Maeve couldn't recall what it was; all she knew was that she needed that stub and now she had it.

Finding the stub had been the easy part. Convincing Jack that it was his would be more challenging, but not impossible.

She hoped he had forgotten that he was a Mets' fan.

Chapter 21

When she thought about it, Maeve realized she wasn't a pothead and never would be. But she knew someone who was. She threw the bag of joints on the trunk in front of Jo's sofa and watched her friend's eyes grow wide. Maeve didn't mention that between the gun and the joints, she was a walking class A or B misdemeanor; her knowledge of the penal code in New York wasn't comprehensive enough to know which it might be.

"Help yourself," Maeve said. "They're all yours."

"Do I want to know where you got them?" Jo asked, reaching for the bag.

"Nope."

"Thank you," she said, pocketing the bag. "If this is your way of enticing me back to work, you really don't know much about smoking pot. Once you smoke a joint this size, you don't really care that you have a job—if, that is, you remember you have a job."

"I don't know a lot about smoking pot and I'm going to keep it that way," Maeve said. "How's the head?"

Jo instinctively fingered the bald spot where the stitches held her scalp together. "Better. Hey, will you take me to get my stitches out on Saturday?"

It was the least she could do. "Of course. Maybe we can do dinner afterwards?" When Jo didn't respond, she added, "My treat?"

"Sounds good," Jo said. "Do you want something to drink?" she asked. "Eat?"

Maeve looked at her watch. "Can't. I have to go see Jack," she said. "But Saturday, definitely, okay?" She leaned over and kissed Jo's head, the part where there was still hair and no stitches. The quick glance she got at the wound showed that it was healing nicely despite still looking angry and red.

Earlier that day, after their visit to the police station, Cal had dropped Jack off at Buena del Sol and come straight to the store. The store should have been busier than it was at that time of day, but the lack of customers allowed them to talk for a long time. Cal looked more concerned than Maeve was anticipating, something that troubled her. He wasn't quite so flippant about this visit as he had been with the last one, and he had sounded concerned before they had gone. From the look on his face when he walked in the store, Maeve finishing up at the counter with a customer, she knew that things were about to get more com-plicated.

"Can we go in the back?" he asked, not wanting to have the conversation in the front of the store, with the chance that someone could walk in. Behind the counter, he made himself a cup of coffee and grabbed a muffin from the glass case.

Maeve grabbed a stool and pulled it up to the big table in the back. Cal stood, taking the wrapper off his muffin and eating a few bites before he began to tell her the saga of their visit.

"Did Jack go all Vinnie the Chin on them?" Maeve asked, sounding as though she were making light of the situation, when in actuality she knew just how bad this could be.

"And then some," Cal said. "At one point he's telling them exactly where he was and what he was doing on the night Sean was killed, down to what he ate for breakfast, lunch, and dinner, and then he's saying that he can't remember what the year is. Does that sound normal to you?"

"Normal for my dad."

"Do you have any idea why they might be looking at Jack for this murder, of all things?"

Her first thought was: Because he wanted to protect me. But then she realized that he was far too late for that, and would know it, even in his state of mind. Unless he was giving it one last shot.

Cal knew she was holding back. "You need to tell me everything, Maeve."

"There's nothing to tell," she said, trying to sound definitive but ending up defiant. "There's nothing. Nothing at all. Sean was my cousin and Jack's nephew and that's it. Jack had no reason to want to see him dead." She laughed, but it was sad. "As a matter of fact, I don't think Jack even knows that he's dead."

"Oh, he knows he's dead," Cal said. "He thinks he succumbed to Dutch elm disease. Now why would he think that?"

"He's just pulling your leg, Cal. He doesn't really think that." But she wasn't sure. Between protesting that he read the paper daily and knew what was going on and asking all his questions regarding Sean's demise, she wasn't sure what he thought exactly, what in his mind was real and what wasn't. It also depended on when you asked him, and Maeve wasn't quite sure why that was. "They're done with him, right?"

Cal shrugged. "That's anyone's guess. I can't help feeling that they're using him," he said.

Maeve got a chill but refused to shiver, holding herself perfectly erect. "Using him?"

Cal shrugged again. "Forget it. It's nothing. I don't think they're serious about him, but I'm not entirely sure and that's what's bothering me." He took another swig of his coffee. "Listen, I'm sorry about the other night." When she didn't respond, he added more detail; he had let her down on numerous occasions, so he was going to have to be more specific. "Heather? The party?"

"Oh, that," Maeve said, reaching into her jeans pocket and pulling out the bag of joints. "And we now have this."

Cal wasn't as shocked as Maeve would have expected. A simple "Oh" was all she got.

" 'Oh'?" she repeated.

He quickly rearranged his features into something approximating concern and horror. "We have to deal with that."

"And this is why, Cal," Maeve said deliberately, so that there was no misinterpreting her feelings on the subject, "we have to crack down on Heather. She's headed for trouble, and I'm not content to sit back and watch."

He pulled out a small pad and a pen from his jacket pocket. "Give me her schedule for the next few weeks."

"There is no schedule," Maeve said. She thought that was obvious. "When she's with me, she stays home. When she's with you, she stays home. It's as simple as that."

She wasn't sure what he wrote down, but he jotted something on the pad. For a supposedly smart guy, he was pretty dense sometimes.

She thought about their conversation as she drove away from Jo's, now three joints lighter but still troubled by Jack's repeated questioning by the police. She headed straight for Buena del

Sol, where she hoped she could catch Jack before he went to dinner, if only to check what he was wearing.

Doreen was manning the front desk again and had her faithful companion, Caesar, in tow. She gave Maeve a big smile, one that Maeve tried to return but was so forced, it made her cheeks hurt. "Jack Conlon?" she asked.

"Is he expecting you?" Doreen asked.

"No. I'm his daughter. I'm just dropping in." Hadn't they been through this before? Maeve looked around the lobby of the facility and noted that a lot of residents had guests this afternoon. It was when the lobby and the surrounding grounds were empty that she felt Jack was in the wrong place, thinking that this was where family members stuck their elderly relatives to die. But today it was full of life and everyone seemed happy, even those who were being pushed in wheelchairs or getting around with the help of walkers. Still, she felt impatient and nervous and had to get to Jack's room to execute her plan.

Doreen looked at her sadly. "Mr. Conlon isn't answering the phone in his apartment, nor the page I sent out," she said after a few minutes. She looked at Maeve expectantly.

Maeve felt that old flutter of fear, the one that started in her throat and slowly worked its way down to her stomach. "He's not?"

"Nope," she said, checking her log. "And it

appears that he didn't sign out on any of the excursion buses."

So, no trip to the grocery store, no outing to Woodbury Common with the rest of the more ambulatory residents, no excursion to Mohegan Sun. Jack was on a walkabout. Maeve beat it back to her car without saying good-bye to Doreen or her stuffed simian companion and headed back the way she came, this time sticking to the roads closest to the river so she could spot him easily.

The road along the river, however, was empty of pedestrians, a fact that relieved Maeve in one way—the road was not suitable for walkers—but concerned her overall. Where was he? She took a chance that he had gotten to his favorite destination before she had arrived at the facility, so she headed to the walking path along the water, hoping that she could spot him easily. This late in the day on a weekday found the river walk almost empty, a few people taking dogs out for a pre-dinner walk, one or two kids riding bikes under the watchful eyes of parents, one woman pushing a jogging stroller. She scanned the thin crowd for a sign of her father, jogging along the path in a pair of clogs wholly unsuitable for running, and had reached a bend in a path before she spotted him.

He was sitting on a bench that was positioned above a cluster of rocks at the water's edge, gentle waves lapping at the outcropping. His eyes were closed, his face turned up to the last rays of the sun, seemingly oblivious to anyone around him. It wasn't until Maeve touched his arm— momentarily afraid that she had found him too late, postcoronary—that he jerked awake, his vision clearing after a few seconds, a smile lighting his face as he realized who was sitting on the bench next to him. Rather than look at him, she turned and faced the water.

"Went a-wanderin' again, Dad?"

"Figured I was owed a wandering after the morning that I had," he said.

"And what kind of morning was that?" she asked.

He folded his arms across his chest. "Now there's a question you don't need to ask."

Which was his way of telling her either that he couldn't remember or that he remembered every last detail of his questioning and didn't want to talk about it.

"The thing I don't understand is why they care so much that that little puke was killed. He had it coming," Jack said, remembering enough about Sean—she wasn't sure what—that his anger toward him came bubbling back up to the surface, something Maeve hadn't seen in a long time. "I always told you that anyone who hurt my little girl would come to no good," he said cryptically. She didn't know what he thought he knew or what he remembered.

She felt another shiver go up her spine. She was shivering a lot lately. "What does that mean, Dad?"

"It means nothing. It means I don't remember. Something bad happened. . . ." He closed his eyes again. "It means I don't know why they're looking at an eighty-year-old man with a bad memory for a murder. How in God's name would I have gotten myself to the Bronx?"

His frustration seemed to be clearing his mind, his take on the situation more on point than at any other time. She thought about the ticket stub in her pocket, wondering how she was going to get it into his wallet or his apartment at the facility.

"You didn't hurt Sean, Dad," she said, even though she didn't think he was unsure of that point.

"I hope I didn't," he said. "But frankly, I don't care if I did or if they ever catch who did. He was bad." After a few seconds, he looked at her worriedly. "You didn't do it, did you?"

She laughed. "Now why would you think that, Dad?"

He shook his head and stared out at the mountains on the other side of the river. "I don't think that. I think any one of us in the family had motive. Kid stole money from my brother Brian, you know."

"I didn't know that."

"Wrecked his mother's car, too." He closed his eyes as if to stop the memories that at other times he reached for. "You don't think they're going to put me in jail, do you, Maeve?"

She tried not to let her heartbreak show on her face. "No, Dad, I don't."

He tried to laugh it off, but she could hear genuine concern there, right below the glimmer of bravado. "Because I don't think I would make it. I mean, I'm still built like a guy half my age . . . ," he started.

"Yes, well, if you keep up these daily three-mile walks, you'll be built like a guy a third of your age," she said. "Dad, you've got to stay put at Buena del Sol."

He snorted dismissively. "It's landlocked. You know how I hate that."

"So, I'll come get you and we can walk the river after I close the shop. How about that?"

"Sounds fine. Won't happen, but it sounds fine," he said. "You'll get too busy with the girls or you'll stay open late to do a cooking class, and the next thing you know, it will be winter and I won't have seen the outside of Buena del Sol in four months." When he saw that she was getting upset, though not necessarily disputing his prediction, he patted her knee. "Forget it. I don't want to make you feel bad. But you already do enough to make sure I've got it good. I'll try not to mess up."

She pointed toward the end of the walk, the spot where the path ended and a mosaic-tile oval made people turn around and start back toward the parking lot. "Race you to the end?" she asked.

He looked at her shoes. "With you in clogs? You're on," he said, bolting up from the bench and starting a slow trot toward the end of the walk. For an old guy, he was surprisingly fast, and Maeve had to hoof it to keep up. When she reached him she was out of breath, but he wasn't so he slowed down. They jogged the rest of the way and part of the way back, Maeve begging him to stop halfway; they walked to the car slowly, allowing her to catch her breath.

As they reached the parking lot, Jack had a question for her. "Who do you think killed Sean, Maeve?" he asked.

"Like you, Dad, I don't care," she said. She punched the keypad and opened the doors. "Hop in."

Back at Buena del Sol, he escorted her in past Doreen—today, "dumber than a box of rocks," according to Jack—to his apartment on the second level of the facility. It had been a few weeks since Maeve had been in the apartment, and she was happy to see that it was clean and that Jack had enough of the food items that he liked—cheese, some diet soda, and a couple of cartons of yogurt—so that she didn't have to make a trip to the grocery store. When he excused himself to use the bathroom that was attached to his bedroom, she looked around the apartment to see the best place to stick the ticket stub so that it would be alternately noticed and unnoticed. She decided to stick it under a magnet that held an image of Rebecca on the soccer field, one of the "extras" that Maeve had purchased when team pictures had been ordered. She stuck it under the powerful magnet and stepped back, admiring her handiwork. It was now right there, proof that Jack had been at the Yankees game and not in Van Cortlandt Park the night that Sean had been killed.

When Jack came out, she gave him a kiss. "You look tired. No more marathon walks for a while, okay?"

He gave her his usual snappy salute. "Yes, sir."

"I'm not kidding, Dad," she said.

"I'm not either," he said. "I am kind of tired," he admitted. She was nearly out the door when he called her name. "What am I going to do if the police call me again?"

"I have a feeling they're done with you, Dad," she said. "I wouldn't worry about it."

He looked around the apartment as if he were memorizing every knickknack, the placement of all the furniture. "Because I'm not really sure I didn't murder him," he said. "It's not like I didn't think about it once or twice."

"Why did you think about it, Dad?"

He looked at her, but he had already forgotten. "About what, honey?"

"About Sean. Hurting him."

"Bad seed, that kid. Didn't you think so?" He shook his head. "I feel like I wanted to hurt him."

She rubbed her arm instinctively, the one that had been shattered and which had required that she be taken by one of Jack's cronies to the emergency room, Jack not wanting to waste the time waiting for an ambulance. "I think we all thought about it, Dad." She rubbed the arm until the skin was hot. "At least once or twice."

Maybe more.

Chapter 22

Jo's doctor was thrilled with the progress she had made and impressed with his handiwork. Jo was not quite as enamored with the way her head looked and let him know.

"Is my hair going to grow back? Will I have a scar? Should I stay home from work longer? Are you single?" she asked, the last question slipping out amid the other, more salient concerns that she had regarding her accident and the overall well-being of her head.

The guy was game, answering each question in the order it had been asked. "Yes. Probably. Need to return soon. Yes."

A smile spread across Jo's face as she realized that she had gotten the answers she wanted, the scar notwithstanding; the hair would probably cover that. "Okay!" she said, brighter and lighter than she had been in a week.

"And you can return to work," he added.

At that news, she didn't look quite so thrilled, but she went with it. "But no heavy lifting, right?"

DR. NEWMAN—Maeve finally got a look at the name tag that had been hidden under his lab coat—smiled. "You can do all the heavy lifting you want."

"But I shouldn't work quite so many hours as I usually do, right?" she asked.

"That depends," he said, writing a few notes down on his chart. "How many hours do you normally work in a week?"

"Fifty," she said at the same time that Maeve said:

"Twenty-five."

He looked confused. "You can work anywhere between twenty-five and fifty hours a week. You're fine, Ms. Weinstein. Go about your daily life and put this little bump in the road behind you. Okay?"

Jo looked disappointed, clearly not ready or willing to resume her role as Maeve's halfhearted helpmate in the store. According to Dr. Newman, she was definitely able. "Okay," she finally said, relenting. She pointed to Maeve. "She's my boss, so what she says goes, anyway."

Maeve resisted the urge to laugh. That was never the case, and she had the extra logged hours to prove it.

"Take care, Ms. Weinstein," Dr. Newman said, sending them on their way. When Maeve turned around, he was holding his clipboard at his side, a smile spreading across his face.

They walked down the hall toward the front door, passing the nurses' station, where a man in a baseball hat, his back turned, was filling out paperwork while a nurse helped him find the proper spaces to fill out his personal information. Next to the nurses' station was another section of the emergency room, and from inside one of the bays came the sound of a child crying, a woman's voice uttering soothing words. As Maeve passed the man, almost in slow motion, he turned and looked at her, the look on his face causing her to suppress a gasp and force herself to keep walking.

"Mr. Lorenzo?" the nurse at the station said. "We need your insurance card. We need an X-ray of your daughter's arm."

But he was fixated on Maeve, and as she watched the color creep up from the collar of his T-shirt and onto his stubbly jowls, she grabbed hold of Jo's arm and moved her forward quickly. Jo was too busy taking inventory of every sick person in every slot of the ER, noting who had someone accompanying them and who was alone, chattering away to Maeve about the state of health care in the United States and why she was voting for some fringe candidate in the next presidential election.

"Mr. Lorenzo?" the nurse called, trying to get his attention.

Maeve dragged her eyes away and fixated on the tiled floor in front of them. In the slot where the child had been crying was Tina Lorenzo, begging her daughter to be quiet so as not to disturb the other patients. The little girl was in too much pain, though, and Maeve could hear it in her voice as a low, moaning sob that was replaced by a high-pitched cry that even got Jo's attention.

"Poor kid," Jo said. "Wonder what happened to her."

He finally broke her arm, Maeve thought. That's what happened to her.

Chapter 23

When things had gotten bad, just before the end had come, Maeve had told Cal that they needed to remember why they had once loved each other. All he had done was stare back at her blankly; it was then that she knew he had already forgotten and would never remember.

Maybe that's why Jack's slow decline into

complete dementia was presenting such an emotional challenge for her. At some point, he too would forget why he had once loved her, seeing in front of him a petite, trim woman with a mess of blond waves, concern and uncon- ditional love etched forever on her face. Beyond the fact that he would forget her sooner or later, some things that he had forgotten he would never remember, no matter how hard he tried.

Like the details of her mother's death.

The shoebox that sat between her legs on the floor was filled with reminders of when things were good, with a few pieces of memorabilia from when things weren't. A photo of her as a baby, reaching out to someone, maybe the person with the camera, while sitting on her mother's knee. A grainy photograph of Jack and Claire on the steps of St. Augustine's on their wedding day, Jack in a white dinner jacket and her mother in a dress that was shorter in the front than in the back, the bodice covered with a delicate organza that was probably yellowed and moth-eaten now, the dress in a box in Maeve's attic for safekeeping. A ticket stub from Maeve's first Broadway show— *Cats*—and the playbook, the front page ripped slightly but otherwise in good shape.

Her mother's obituary was also in there, copied from the original that Jack kept in a book on a shelf in his apartment, along with another copy of the page from the *Daily News* that had reported the hit-and-run of a young mother in the Bronx, on her way to the grocery store for a quart of milk and a pack of cigarettes for her husband, a faded picture of her mother's beautiful face alongside a story that said the police had no leads on who may have hit Claire Conlon but that they would keep investigating.

It hadn't done any good. Maeve had never heard anything to suggest that they had found the person who had killed her mother, spilling the contents of her purse along the avenue, people returning things that had blown away for weeks to come. The first was a lipstick, the second was a prayer missal. The last, as Maeve remembered it, was her kindergarten picture, her tiny teeth all still intact, a light in her eyes that she lost soon after. They were all in the box.

Her mother had died, in the street, alone. That was what happened when you told, Sean had said to her a few years later, right after he had put his hands on her in that way for the first time.

That was what happened when you told.

She said she was never going to tell, but he didn't believe her. That's what made her mother's death even more tragic to her, her brain not fully realizing the impact of what had happened at the time.

She carried it with her, though, and thought that the moment, etched in her memory, of her mother leaving the house, was the one that stayed with her and reappeared the most, more than anything else that had happened, the accidents, the tears, the suppressed memories, the silent indictments. She wondered how much of her life had been dictated by that one moment.

"Be back soon," Claire had said, something she had no idea would turn out to be false, a lie she never intended to tell. She did what she always did before they parted, kissing her daughter's head, forehead, nose, and cheek before going out the front door, the screen making its usual racket when it slammed shut behind her. "Be back soon," her mother would always say.

Maeve was watching *Soupy Sales*. She wouldn't move until her mother came back; that was their deal. She sat in that same position for a long, long time until her legs ached and her feet got sweaty in her Keds. When someone had finally come for her, it was Claire's brother, Declan, Sean's father. He had lifted her up and her legs were still crossed, cramped into a position that told what a good girl she had been. She had never moved, just as her mother had asked.

The officer who had investigated the case had been a guy named Pollizzi; his first name was Peter, but everyone called him "Pepe." Back in those days, a lot of cops worked in the same precinct as their neighborhood, so Pepe was both a neighbor and a guy who patrolled their safe streets. At one time, he and Jack had been partnered, but while Jack wanted to stay on the beat, Pepe had higher aspirations, becoming a detective in the squad. To Maeve, he was like a big, burly bear, but a kind one. Kind of like Winnie-the-Pooh grown up and in human form. Soft, but obviously very strong, his hands were rough, the nails big and square. He always wore a gold watch and a pinkie ring, something that Maeve found fascinating, even at a young age. His aftershave lingered in her nose long after he left. When she thought about him now, the word *dandy* popped into her head.

He had come by the house a lot after Claire died, and not just to ask questions. He sat with Jack, he drank with Jack, he brought Maeve toys. He insisted that she call him Pepe, because that was his nickname and that's what Jack called him. Maeve had never been allowed to call adults by their given names or their nicknames, so she felt that Jack allowing her to address Pepe as such was the beginning of a new chapter in their lives, one where things would be looser, more casual. Everything had changed, and nothing that she knew would ever be the same. Claire's death had seen to that. So had Sean Donovan.

She wondered what had happened to Pepe Pollizzi. After a few years, he stopped coming around. Jack told her that he had moved to the Jersey Shore, a place that Jack would never drive to, even if it was to "see the pope," as he had said at the time. Too far. Too much traffic in the summer, too dead in the winter. But Maeve wondered if there was more to it than that. She wondered if seeing Pepe opened the wound all over again, the wound in which Claire was still dead, her killer still out there somewhere driving a red car, according to witnesses, and living a full life.

Several times before he moved and they never saw him again, Maeve had tried to speak the words to Pepe, the ones that got stuck in her throat every time. "You know who has a red car?" she would start but never finish. "My cousin Sean." Why could no one see that but her? She would never tell because she knew what happened to people who told. They ended up with their body laid out on the avenue, the contents of their purse blowing across the street and into the alleys behind the stores, dead because a little girl wanted someone—anyone—to know that every day she got hurt and died a little bit inside.

When Maeve was done going through the box and picking at wounds that had never fully healed, she went to the computer and searched for information on how to report child abuse cases in her county. An 800 number was listed on the page she found. The woman at the other end of the phone sounded tired, phones ringing incessantly in the background. Maeve wondered if the agency took calls only on suspected child abuse or if where this woman worked housed other agencies that dealt with other types of problems.

"I suspect a person in my town is mistreating his daughter," she said, feeling better about things now that she was actually making the call. But her feeling of doing something important, something to help the little girl who loved her cupcakes, was short-lived.

"What makes you think this child is being abused?" the woman asked.

"I just saw her at the hospital and I think she broke her arm." She wasn't sure that that was even the injury, and the question in her tone was enough to lose the interest of the woman at the other end of the phone.

"And you know that this situation is a result of child abuse?"

"Well, not for certain, but I think it is."

The woman paused, and in that pause resided an unuttered sigh. "Why is that?"

"Because he beats his wife, too."

The sigh burst forth over the line. Either this woman was having a really bad day or Maeve was sounding like a crazy person with delusions. Wasn't it this agency's job to take these kinds of accusations seriously? What was it about the way Maeve was delivering this information that made her sound less than credible? She thought the best course of action would be to start again. "I saw his wife and she had a black eye. She looks like she is being battered. The little girl, she's four, was just in the hospital and I think her arm was broken. Don't ask me how or why I know, but I just do. And I'm worried about her."

The woman responded better this time; Maeve didn't know why. "If the child is in the hospital with a suspicious injury, she will be questioned first by medical staff and then by a caseworker from our agency if the medical staff thinks there is reason to suspect abuse." She delivered this information in a matter-of-fact voice, one that softened when she asked the next question. "Why are you so sure about this?"

Maeve considered beating around the bush a little bit more but realized that it wouldn't help her help Tiffany or Tina. "I was abused." After it was out, she thought that while the chance existed that it may give her credibility, it might also have the reverse effect, making it seem as though she saw abuse around every corner. She wanted to reassure the woman that it didn't but that she did have a honed sense of when someone was being mistreated. Or had survived the same, her mind flashing on Rodney Poole for some reason, although she wasn't sure why.

"Ma'am, I wish I could send a caseworker out based on your feelings, but without an incident to go on, I'm afraid that that's just not possible. Let's hope that you're wrong, but if you're not, that someone at the hospital felt the need to investigate further. I'm sorry. That's the best I can do."

Maeve opened her mouth to speak, but begging this woman to believe her didn't seem like a viable option. Besides, the woman, the product of an overworked, underfunded, and ill-staffed agency that had too many children to protect and not enough resources, was gone. She looked at the phone for a few seconds, wondering what she would do next.

She got up and put on her sweater, getting ready to go out. It was one of those days that had been warm while the sun was out but had turned cold now that it was dark. She didn't need much beyond her still ugly, still gun-toting purse and a little determination.

Cal had been right: she had needed a hobby. Now she had one and it felt good.

Chapter 24

That night, she sat in front of the Lorenzos, waiting to see what he would do, if anything. Like her, was he restless? Did he need to go out? Did he have someone to meet? As she sat there, in the dark cocoon that was the Prius, she watched.

And waited.

Eventually, he did leave. The only wrinkle was that she wasn't sure where he was going on the nights he pulled out of his driveway, if he was headed to another assignation with the mouthy and ethically challenged Julie Morelli or somewhere else. The other problem was that she never knew when he'd leave, so that made for a lot of boring nights, but she took the opportunity to catch up on the papers she hadn't read, the magazines that contained recipes she wanted to try. She was nothing if not a multitasker. Too bad she hadn't been paying attention to Rebecca when she had tried to teach her mother to knit; by now, Maeve would have been able to knit an afghan to cover most of the top floor of her house.

She prided herself on being relatively smart, but that night, after some soul-searching in the dark at home in her bed, she realized that what she had done earlier that evening had been beyond stupid. Following Michael Lorenzo to the bar on the corner, a place she had never seen him go, and pulling up a bar stool next to him was not her style or a testament to her sharp intelligence. While she was there, though, the sights and sounds of Mookie's offering enough cover for their conversation, it seemed like the best idea she had ever had, if only to see the look of shock on his face as she ordered a glass of cheap Chardonnay and a plate of wings.

"Fancy meeting you here," she said, taking a sip of the wine and holding back a grimace. Mookie's was known for a lot of things, but a good house wine wasn't one of them. Maybe that's why the wings were so spicy; they drowned out the flavor of bad hooch.

He didn't turn to look at her, focusing his attention on the hockey game that was playing on the television suspended over the bar. "I don't remember inviting you out to talk."

"You didn't," she said, her heart racing. Although she had committed to what she was doing, it still wasn't comfortable. "How's your daughter?"

"Still none of your business," he said, signaling the bartender for another beer.

"She must be in a lot of pain," she said, having a nodding acquaintance with the discomfort that followed an arm breaking.

"She's fine," he said. He slid a ten-dollar bill in the bartender's direction after his beer was delivered. "You know what harassment is, right?"

"I do."

"Then you should know that one call to the local police and I could probably get you locked up."

"For sitting next to you at a bar?" she asked.

"For that and for finding me at the dam and for all of the other times you've sat outside my house in your crappy little car," he said, still not looking at her.

"Gosh, I have no idea what you're talking about," she said. "But since we're on the subject, do you really think you want the police nosing around in whatever goes on between us? What-ever goes on in your house?"

He dragged his eyes away from the game and looked at her. "You don't want to go there. I told you that already. It's none of your business."

"Is that from a script?" she asked. "Because that's what you keep saying. It is my business. You're hurting your wife and that little girl."

"Stay out of it."

She shrugged. "Okay," she said. Suddenly, the wings she had ordered didn't seem all that appetizing. She leaned over and grabbed Lorenzo's knee as hard as she could. "Listen to me. Do not touch that little girl again."

She could tell that he was trying hard not to show that it hurt. "Stay out of what you don't know," he said through gritted teeth.

She squeezed harder. "I will not stand by idly and watch you abuse her. Know that." She released her hand and watched as he used every fiber of his being not to reach down and massage what was sure to be a red, bruised area.

"And what gives you the right?" he sputtered finally. "What makes you think you're right about any of this?"

She thought for a moment. How to put this? She went with the easiest answer. "If I was wrong, you would have told me why. But you have no excuse. No reason."

"Maybe I don't want to give you a reason."

The bartender put her wings in front of her, and Maeve pushed them in front of Lorenzo. "I don't have an appetite anymore. Here." She pulled a twenty out of her purse and left it on the counter. She noticed that his hand was now on the knee that she had squeezed. "Think about what I said," she said, smiling, not in the business of threatening someone, regardless of whether or not they were in a public place like Mookie's, where she knew every waitress and most of the bartenders.

"Or what?" he said, not content to leave well enough alone.

She stopped, her hand on the back of his stool. "Or nothing," she said, which was a lie. She already had a recipe all planned out, but surprise was its main ingredient.

Chapter 25

Heather probably wouldn't be talking to her, something that Maeve was used to, post-grounding. When Maeve got home after work on Monday, though, Heather was chattier than usual, telling her mother that Jack had called and wanted a call back and giving her details about her day at school, down to how delicious the wonderful lunch her mother had packed for her was and which she admitted she had enjoyed heartily.

She knows the joints are gone, Maeve thought,

and held back a smile. Nothing to get her kid talking about the mundane, the stuff Maeve loved, more than having had her mother beat her at her own game. There would be a new hiding spot, but Maeve would find that, too. The look on Heather's face, when she wasn't busy chattering away about the yoga class she was now taking to fulfill her PE requirement, asking her mother what her favorite pose was, was one that said it all: "Well played, Mother. Well played."

They had a conundrum, however. Heather couldn't bring up the missing ticket stub—the one thing that indicated to her that her mother had been riffling through her drawers—without Maeve bringing up the joints, and Maeve couldn't bring up the joints without Heather bringing up the missing stub. Because even though the kid was a pig, she knew where her stuff was. It appeared to Maeve that they wouldn't speak of either, but the satisfaction that she took from appropriating three sizable joints without her daughter being able to ask about them could not be expressed in words.

"Did you eat?" Maeve asked. "I didn't go shopping today, but I could make you an omelet." She looked around, not seeing any sign of her older daughter. "Where's your sister?"

"Where is she ever?" Heather asked, rolling her eyes. "Library."

In Rebecca's case, there was no reason not to believe that she was really at her favorite hangout—the Farringville Library—her desire to get out of Farringville so great that she used every extra moment that she had to study so that she could go to the college of her choice. Maeve never reminded her that Vassar wasn't that far from the little village where they lived, but to Rebecca, it signified freedom and a way out of a life she saw as one-note and going nowhere. Maeve respected that. It was Heather she worried about, Heather who once proclaimed that she "would never leave" and seemed to run with a crowd who felt exactly the same way. All Maeve needed was to raise a "townie."

Maeve cracked a couple of eggs into a bowl and heated a frying pan while she whisked them together with a splash of water. "Do me a favor and dial Grandpa's number, would you?" she asked Heather, who was deep in thought over a page of history homework that required her to glance back and forth between a huge textbook that must have been a delight to lug home and a notebook beside it. Heather handed her the phone just as she poured the eggs into the pan. Jack answered on the second ring, not giving her a chance to identify herself; his caller ID had already done that.

"Well, I'm off the hook!" he said.

"You are?" Maeve asked. "About what?"

"Sean. The Dutch elm disease," he said. She couldn't tell if he was kidding or not, but to make herself feel better, she went with the idea that he was. "I was at the Yankee game."

She looked over at Heather guiltily, her head still tucked in her history book. "You were?"

"I was," he said. "I must have gotten a bug up my ass about it. I guess I thought I would go down and see the game. Moriarty must have driven me to the train station." He chuckled. "Or I walked. There's always that possibility."

"When did you remember this, Dad?" she asked.

"When I found the ticket stub on my refrigerator door," he said. "It was right there, the entire time. Don't know how I missed it."

"I don't either, Dad," she said, feeling discomfort form in her stomach, a mushy ball of deceit seasoned with guilt. Even though she knew that getting her father an alibi was the right thing to do, at the moment, it seemed unseemly and ill conceived.

"Tell that dunderhead of an ex of yours that it's all fine now. I've got proof of where I was."

"Dunderhead?" That was a new one on her.

"Yes, dunderhead. I would have been better off being represented by Atticus Finch, and he isn't even real." He let off a few obscenities, letting Maeve think that he had known all along just how much trouble he could have been in without an alibi to call his own. "Sweating, pulling at his collar, he might as well have said, 'Hang 'em high, coppers. Old coot is dirty.' "

Maeve had to smile at his diatribe in spite of the fact that she had thought Cal had been the man for the job, at least in the short term. "He was a corporate lawyer, Dad. He might have been a bit out of his league if this went any further, but I think for what you needed, he was fine."

"I don't think they were really serious about me," he said.

That was a pretty astute observation, one that coincided with the dunderhead's assessment. "No?"

"No. Jeez, even if I wanted to kill the kid," he said, referring to the middle-aged Sean, who to Jack would remain always, in his mind, young. "I just don't have the energy anymore to pull off that kind of caper."

She wanted to tell him that murder was more than a caper but let him go on.

"He was a bad seed," he said, not the first time she had heard it. "I hate to say it, Maeve, but I'm not entirely sorry that he's gone. I don't remember why exactly, but I'm not sorry."

"Just don't ever tell anyone else that, Dad. Please."

"I may be forgetful, but I'm not an idiot," he said, making it known that he hated when she adopted a parental tone with him. He dropped his voice to a whisper. "Heck, maybe I did kill him. Now wouldn't that be a kick in the head?"

She was silent.

"Maybe during the seventh-inning stretch," he said, laughing.

"This isn't a time to be joking," she said, watching as the eggs burned around the edges, the smell jolting her out of the state she was in. She put the phone in the crook of her neck, knowing that she would regret that, a pinched nerve in her neck her chronic ache, and tried to fold the omelet over once. "Dad, I have to go. I'll call Cal and let him know about the stub."

Heather's interest was piqued. "Stub?"

Maeve focused her attention on the frying pan. "Yes. Stub. Grandpa was cleaning out some drawers and came across something he thought he had lost." She waited to see if Heather would bring up the missing stub from her dresser, but she didn't.

It didn't take her long to change the topic. "Can I have cheddar?" she asked.

"You can have whatever you want," Maeve said, realizing that she couldn't broach the subject of the joints with Heather now that she had overheard the conversation with Jack. Instead of what she had planned—a maternal checkmate, because there is nothing that mothers love more than dropping the hammer unexpectedly—she had a stalemate, which was far less gratifying.

Maeve handed her the plate, disappointed that her "say no to drugs" speech would have to be shelved for the evening. "Toast?" she asked.

Chapter 26

The next time she saw Rodney Poole, he brought his partner along for the ride. Maeve didn't know why, but she didn't think Detective Colletti found her as charming or talented as Poole did, even though she seemed to be enjoying the chocolate cupcake that Maeve handed her as soon as they were introduced. Jo, who was now back at work and bringing her special brand of laziness to her job, was trying desperately not to be alarmed by the presence of two cops in the store, but at the same time, she couldn't drag herself away from the action. She wiped the same spot on the counter over and over, her eyes alternating between the two detectives and Maeve.

Poole knew the lay of the land, indicating that they should go back into the kitchen. Detective Colletti finished her cupcake, eyeing the remaining ones in the glass-fronted case. Maeve put an assortment on a plate and led them into the kitchen area, offering them stools to pull up and putting the cupcakes between them.

"Coffee?" she asked.

"This isn't a social call," Colletti said, even though she was pulling the wrapper off her second cupcake. "But I'll take one. Light and sweet."

While Poole always looked sad, Colletti looked

angry, making them an interesting pairing. She was a big woman, taller than Jo and about fifty pounds heavier. Today, she was packed into a pair of dark-washed jeans and a leather bomber jacket, giving her the appearance of a modern-day Amelia Earhart, right down to her expensive aviator sunglasses, the ones pushed up on her head and holding back a cascade of black curly hair. Maeve felt small and a little weak in her presence, but at this point she had nothing to fear from a woman who wanted to eat cupcakes and drink coffee. She went into the front of the store, avoiding Jo's gaze, and poured two cups of coffee, making Detective Colletti's the way she wanted and Poole's the way she knew he liked it.

Poole took out his pad and a pen and flipped through some pages. "So we heard from your father's lawyer and we understand that Mr. Conlon may have an alibi for the night in question?"

Phrasing the sentence in the form of a question, he didn't sound all that convinced.

"Yankee game?" he said, looking up at Maeve.

"So it would seem. Something big happened that night, but I wouldn't know what that was. I'm a Mets' fan," she said, attempting humor to cut the tension. "Once he remembered, he seemed very excited about having been there."

Poole took a turn at questioning that Maeve didn't expect, but she tried not to let it show.

"And where were you that night, Ms. Conlon?"

"Home. Alone." She held his gaze to convince him that that was the truth. Why would she lie about that? It would have been much easier to come up with an alibi that he could investigate and never disprove.

"Watch TV?" he asked.

"Probably. What day of the week was it again?" she asked.

"Saturday."

"*Cupcake Wars* followed by *Chopped*," she said. "The guy who owned the dive bar in New Paltz won." She immediately regretted that last statement, thinking that she was laying it on a little thick.

"You have a good memory," Colletti said in between mouthfuls of chocolate cupcake.

"I watch a lot of Food Network," Maeve said, giving a little shrug. Nobody said what they were all thinking, which was that she could have watched it after the fact. The detectives didn't say anything and she didn't offer anything further, but she knew what they were thinking because she was thinking exactly the same thing. "I watch a lot of Food Network," she said weakly, her voice barely a whisper.

Colletti turned to Poole. "Would it be bad if I got a dozen cupcakes before we left?" she asked.

"You have to pay for them," Poole said.

"I don't have any money," she said, holding out

her hand. "I didn't bring my wallet." Curiously, Poole pulled out a worn leather wallet and handed her two twenties. This seemed to be a common occurrence between the two of them, and neither looked remotely uncomfortable with the trans-action.

Maeve was kind of stuck in place, and it wasn't until the detective waved her newfound wealth in the air that she asked her what kind of cupcakes she'd like. When she went into the store, Jo was standing at the far end of the counter, holding a box in her hand, ready to fill the order. Jo had her usual deer-caught-in-the-headlights look, the one she got when she was nervous. Detective Poole obviously made her anxious, a feeling that he didn't engender in Maeve.

"All chocolate with chocolate icing," Maeve said.

"Are they still interested in Jack?" Jo asked in her usual loud stage whisper.

"You tell me. You were listening at the door," Maeve said.

Jo rubbed the top of her head self-consciously, something she had taken to doing since the stitches had come out. "You?"

"I guess we'll find out," Maeve said, helping Jo put cupcakes in the box.

"Why are you so calm?" Jo asked, affixing a Comfort Zone sticker to the top of the box.

"Because I didn't do it," Maeve said. "The truth will set you free and all."

She could feel Jo's eyes on her back when she went into the kitchen. "Will that be all, Detectives?" she asked, handing Colletti the box of cupcakes.

Poole snapped his notebook shut. "For now," he said. The sadness in his eyes had been replaced by something else, something she couldn't identify. Maybe it was consternation at being partnered with a woman who never had cash. Or the fact that he had lost his person of interest once Jack had unearthed the ticket stub from the Yankees game.

She kept her eyes on him and not on the purse on the shelf by the door, the one that still held the gun. Today she would figure that out, she promised herself. Right after she made a birthday cake for fifty.

"You know," Poole said right before he left, "we could find out who your father was sitting with at the game and ask them if he was actually there."

Colletti stood to the side, nodding enthusiastically. That proposition would keep her from eating cupcakes, something she seemed intent on doing the minute she and her partner left the store.

"You should probably do that," Maeve said, sounding more confident than she felt. Her eyes never left Poole's.

He looked as though he had something else to say, but then the weariness that seemed to engulf him from time to time returned. "So," he started, not sure where he was going anymore if his inability to form words was any indication, "we'll be seeing you."

Maeve nodded. For some reason, she wouldn't mind that.

Chapter 27

Jo had opened and closed the store for Maeve countless times, but every time she did, Maeve had to go over the alarm code, the way to deal with orders, and the closing routine. Since it was Halloween, she had parked Heather at the store with Jo after school, Jo being a better disciplinarian than Cal and a person Heather actually respected. Maeve didn't know if Heather had plans, but since making mischief was her specialty, Maeve thought it wise to keep her occupied on the most mischief-prone day of the year. Maybe it was their unspoken, mutual love of pot that bonded them, but Jo had conversations with Heather that Maeve could never picture herself having with her daughter, and for that reason alone, she was glad that Jo was in her life. She certainly didn't make her workday any easier.

"Where are you going again?" Heather asked, reluctantly pulling a Comfort Zone apron over her head, careful not to mess her perfectly styled, flat-ironed locks.

"The Jersey Shore," Maeve said, handing Jo the keys to the store. "This should be a pretty straightforward day. All of the orders have been paid for."

"What do we do if someone wants a cake?" Jo asked.

"Send them to Homebake," Maeve said.

"The competition?" Jo gasped, putting her hand to her heart.

"Yep. Or you could actually bake," Maeve said, swiping some lipstick across her mouth while looking into the chrome of the toaster on the counter. She gave her hair a finger comb. "I'll be gone all afternoon."

Jo followed her into the kitchen. "Tell me again what you're doing?"

"I told you," Maeve said, grabbing her purse from the shelf. "I'm visiting a friend."

Jo eyed her suspiciously. "Who's the friend? I didn't know you had a friend down the shore."

"He's an old friend. From the neighborhood. He's sick," she said, and that wasn't a lie. When she had finally tracked down Pepe Pollizzi, he had been happy to hear from her, telling her that he didn't get too many visitors this late into the fall, especially now that his own kids had moved to Florida and he was pretty much housebound, his oxygen tank keeping him from being footloose and fancy free.

He had asked her to bring Jack, but she had

lied and said that Jack wasn't feeling well and couldn't make the trip. She had a feeling, she didn't know why, that even if she asked Jack, he wouldn't want to go along for the ride. Something nibbled at the edge of her brain, a memory that was white-washed and faded but that spoke to a falling-out, some kind of disagreement between Jack and Pepe. She couldn't summon it, as hard as she tried, but it was there, either begging her to remember or imploring her to forget. She couldn't decide which it was.

When Pepe asked her why she was coming, she was brief. "I just want to know about my mother," she said, a statement to which he had no response, the only sound on the other end of the phone the *whoosh* of his oxygen.

Jo looked happier to be spending the afternoon alone with Heather than Heather did at the prospect. Heather leaned disconsolately against the shelf behind the counter, picking at a cuticle that seemed to demand her full attention. With Rebecca at soccer practice, Heather was the next best thing to a co-worker for Jo, but that was stretching it.

She left the store, grateful for an afternoon away from work, a box of cupcakes and an applesauce cake in a bag to be given to Pepe. She didn't know if he was on a restricted diet, but she had come to learn that nobody honored their diet when cupcakes and buttercream were involved.

The ride down the Garden State was smooth and Maeve made better time than she'd hoped, arriving at four, her goal to leave shortly after five. Pepe didn't sound like the man she remembered, and she wondered just how much time he would have to give her. When he opened the door to his tidy apartment in an over-fifty-five community off a main drag, she was surprised to see that he looked very much like the man whose younger face she could still conjure up after all these years, tall, tan, and fit, but now with a yellow cast to his tan, the result of a lack of oxygen, which now came in a large can and went everywhere with him. He smiled widely when he saw her, telling her she looked just the same as she did when she was little.

"Maybe that's because I'm still little?" she joked, putting her small hand in his big one, feeling his rough fingers close over her own.

He led her into a small living room that held a matched set of furniture, sofa, love seat, chair, and ottoman, the chair seeming to be his go-to spot if the worn seat was any indication. She took a spot on the couch, noticing that he had put out some coffee in a stainless-steel urn as well as some packaged cookies on a plate. She placed the bag of treats that she had brought from the store on the coffee table and told him to save them for later.

"Help yourself to some coffee," he said. "And if you wouldn't mind, pour me a cup, too?" He leaned back in the chair and closed his eyes for a few seconds, taking in some deep breaths of the oxygen, the air going into a clear tube that sat beneath his nostrils. "I hope you don't smoke, Maeve. It's a terrible thing. I never imagined that this is how I would end up, but I guess I did it to myself."

"I don't smoke," she said, handing him a cup of coffee. "I eat too many sweets, though. I'm sure that will come back to haunt me."

"Not like this," he said, pointing to the tubes. "Not like this . . . ," he repeated, trailing off.

She didn't have a lot of time; she could see that. She cut right to the chase. "I wanted to talk to you about my mother, Pepe."

"You mentioned that," he said.

She looked around the room, not sure where to start. Her eyes landed on a picture of Pepe's wife, black and white and posed, taken years earlier. It had a prominent place on the mantel, placed purposely front and center, the kids and the grandkids taking a backseat to this photograph of a gorgeous, dark-haired woman whose image was the focal point of the entire room.

"Jeannette," he said.

"She's beautiful."

"I wish she had stayed longer," he said.

She waited, not wanting to bring the conversation back to her mother until he was done reminiscing.

"Probably how you and Jack felt about Claire," he said.

She nodded.

"That was a terrible thing that happened to your mother," he said. "How was . . ." He trailed off.

"How was what?" she asked.

"Your life. After she was gone."

Talk about complicated. Pepe wore his sadness like an old bathrobe, and it emanated from every pore on his body. She held back. She didn't want to tell him how it really was, or how he could never imagine what he had left behind once he and Jack stopped talking. "It was good. My dad took very good care of me."

"I hope so," he said, but he didn't sound convinced.

"He did," she said. "It was just the two of us, but that was enough."

"Jeannette didn't think that Jack was up to the job of being both a mother and a father to you," Pepe said. "I didn't agree, but that's a mother for you."

"He did a great job," Maeve said, even though in the back of her mind, she sometimes felt he could have done more.

"She wanted you to come live with us," he said, an old, sick man with nothing left to hide and more to say. "Jack wouldn't hear of it. Told her that your family was all around and that that's all you needed. Your family. They would take care of you."

Maeve looked at Pepe, wondering what her life would have been like living with this big bear of a man and his wife. What it would have been like to have brothers and sisters, even if they weren't her blood. What it would have been like to have been loved by someone other than her overworked and exhausted father, someone who tried desperately to give her the best life possible but who hadn't been able to achieve that goal.

"Did they take care of you?" Pepe repeated to Maeve, who was lost in the fantasy of being part of a large Italian family where there was no Sean. No pain.

"My family?" She thought about that for a moment. "In the best way that they could," she said, not willing to place blame.

"That sounds like 'no.' "

She shrugged. "It was a long time ago, Pepe." She let out a little laugh, but it could have easily been a sob. "I turned out all right."

The air in the apartment was charged with the things that neither of them wanted to say, but with so little time, for the man who was at the end, and for Maeve, who needed to return home, they left a lot unsaid. Pepe did say that Jeannette's persistence in hounding Jack for the right to raise his motherless daughter was the wedge that drove the two men apart, something that explained

Pepe's sudden absence in Maeve's life and Jack's reluctance to ever see him again. Jack was nothing if not proud, and pride had ended more than one relationship he had had in his lifetime.

It was after a silence, uncomfortable and laden with unanswered questions, that Pepe cut to the chase.

"What do you want to know?" he asked.

"Who did it? Who hit her?" she asked, knowing that there was a good chance he still didn't know the answer. Or had forgotten.

"Oh," he said sadly. "Is that why you came down here?" He shifted slightly in his chair, disappointed that the trip down memory lane wasn't going as he expected. "I thought maybe you wanted to know what she was like. How she acted."

"That, too," Maeve said, although that wasn't the purpose of her visit. She remembered every single thing about her mother, down to the way she cut her food: knife in right hand, fork in left, more refined and continental than any other woman she knew. She remembered how she always wore a full slip under her dresses and how she rarely wore pants. She thought back to how her mother always kissed her good night after tucking her in tight, running back one more time to give her an extra one before leaving Maeve's room.

Pepe's head fell to his chest while she thought about the woman she had known for only a short time but whose absence had such a profound effect on her. If Claire had lived, Maeve was sure, she wouldn't have been as vulnerable. She would have been protected.

Maeve cleared her throat, hoping to stir the old man from his slumber. She worried that she wouldn't get Pepe's observations on the case before he drifted off to sleep, which even after a few minutes of their together seemed like a distinct possibility.

"The wives were good friends," he said, looking over at the picture of the late Jeannette. "Jeannette was devastated when Claire died."

Maeve had little recollection of Pepe's wife, the photo of her bringing back a distant memory, but something that she couldn't grab hold of completely.

"We didn't see a lot of you after that. Jack kind of kept to himself. I think seeing me and Jeannette together reminded him of what he had lost," Pepe said. "And he was furious that we would even broach the subject of taking you in as our own." He took a deep draw of oxygen and kept going. "I kept coming around for a little while, though. I liked to keep Jack in the loop on what was going on with the case."

She waited.

"But we really had nothing," he said, again looking sad and exhausted. "Someone hit your poor mom and we never found out who it was."

To Maeve, etched on his lined face were years of disappointment for that and other unsolved cases.

"It was a red car," Maeve said, harkening back to a sentence she said over and over when she was small, as if that would help someone figure out the person behind the crime.

He nodded. "Yes. It was red. Lots of red cars out there. Even then."

She couldn't bring herself to say it, even though it was what she was told, what she believed all these years. It was as if telling—the most grievous crime, according to Sean—would bring him back and allow him to do the bad things that he purported to do every day that he was alive and in her life. The things he did to her while he was in her life.

Pepe was getting tired and his head fell slowly toward his chest again. They had been together less than twenty minutes and she had no way of knowing if she would ever see him again, but she couldn't bring herself to indict the one person she thought might be guilty of murdering her mother. Turned out she didn't have to. Before he fell asleep, Pepe let out a small laugh.

"Funny thing was Jack always thought he knew who did it," he said, raising a shaking hand to adjust his oxygen. "And he said if he could prove it, he would kill him."

She didn't need to ask who it was. She already knew.

Chapter 28

She was exhausted by the time she got home, the emotional weight of her visit with Pepe, a man she was sure would be deceased in a few short months, bearing down on her with such intensity that she could feel the approach of a blinding headache. She turned off the lights in the hope of dissuading little ghosts and goblins from ringing her bell in their quest for candy. The Pollizzis had wanted her as their own, something that she found perplexing and that she knew would have sent Jack into a blind rage. The implication that he couldn't raise her on his own would have been a blow to any parent, but to one who loved his daughter as much as Jack loved Maeve, it must have been exponentially harder. He was proud; he loved his daughter. To think that anyone wouldn't trust that love explained a lot about how he had raised her, trying to keep her close while relying on family members to pick up the slack, a decision that turned out to be the worst one he had made.

She stopped by Cal's to say good night to the girls. She put on a happy face, the one that she had perfected throughout the years, as Cal came outside to brief her on the plans for the evening and the next day.

Maeve got out of the car and leaned against the passenger-side door, trying to look relaxed when all she felt inside was a roiling pot of emotion. Cal cut right to the chase.

"I think Heather is running with the wrong crowd," he said, concern etched into his handsome features, a storm brewing behind his eyes. Around them, the street flooded with costumed children and their protective parents, happy voices filling the air.

"I think Heather *is* the wrong crowd," Maeve said, annoyed that he was late to the party, as usual. "You can only blame things on other people's kids for so long, Cal, until you have to look at yourself and your parenting style." She corrected herself. "Parenting styles." No need to leave herself out of this; in some ways, she was as much to blame for Heather's slide into juvenile delinquency, what with the fervor she had devoted to clearing her father's name of her cousin's murder and the amount of space that took up in her already crowded brain. "So it took finding the pot to get you to this point?"

He got that weird look on his face again and in the space of a few seconds turned a red she had never seen. Cal didn't blush, but at this moment in time, he was sporting a severe flush.

"What?" she said, looking for a sign of what could have made him so uncomfortable.

"Nothing." He turned and looked at the house

as if it were a safe haven from the impending storm that was his ex-wife's anger.

Finally, it hit her. "It was yours."

"I have a chronic pain in my back!" he said, backing up a little. She didn't know what her face looked like, but if he was backing up, it must not have been good.

"And I have a chronic pain in my ass, but you don't hear me complaining about it all the time," she said, "or getting high to deal with it." She looked up at the sky, hoping for answers to all of the questions that she had. "It's called lumbago, Cal, and it affects every single person over the age of forty."

"Lumbago?"

"Yes. Lower back pain."

"Sounds like something Jack made up," he said, the word rolling around on his tongue. "Lumbago?"

She snapped her fingers in front of her face. "Can we focus on the matter at hand?" she asked. "The one that doesn't have anything to do with your middling health problems and your organic solutions?"

His face turned dark. "They are not 'middling,'" he said. His hands went to his lower back as proof that he suffered more than any man should.

"Okay, so you keep pot in your house where your teenaged daughters can find it. Check that: one teenaged daughter." Rebecca wouldn't look for it, nor would she do anything with it if she did find it. "That needs to stop," she said, her mind going to the gun in her purse. At least she didn't keep it in her house; she just toted it on her errands around town and had it within reach at the store. *What kind of message does that send?* she thought, thinking of glass houses and such but keeping her peccadilloes to herself. *What kind of woman tracks a wife and child abuser like prey, following him to assignations and plopping down next to him when he's out for a beer? A woman with a sense of justice,* she told herself, but she couldn't quite make the argument convincing, even to herself.

"Where do you suggest I keep it?" he asked, reflecting, a second too late, that that probably wasn't a good question to ask the mother of his first two children, who was about as angry as he'd ever seen her. "I'll stop. I'll stick to traditional remedies."

"Yes, I've heard there are these people called 'chiropractors' whose only job practically is to cure lower back pain. You may want to see if you can find one," she said. "As a matter of fact, I think our mayor moonlights as one."

He put a hand up to stop her. "Enough. I get it. I'm sorry. Is that what you want to hear?" he asked.

Yes, it was, as a matter of fact. But not for the pot; that was minor compared to everything else. She wanted apologies for the myriad other offenses that he had committed since they had met twenty years previous. She was smart enough, however, to know she would never get them.

When she left, they were on fairly good terms again but wary of each other, he of her anger and she of his bad judgment. They had never even gotten into the discussion about where Heather might have come across a significant amount of marijuana in his house; Maeve didn't want to know how easy it was to find things in Cal's new abode. Even if the pot had been hidden well, one intrepid fifteen-year-old had found it and taken it with her—for what purpose, however, was still the question. Smoking? Selling? A combination of both? It made her realize that she had to keep the gun in her possession. Heather probably wouldn't touch the gun if she found it, too afraid, hopefully, but Maeve couldn't take that chance.

Chapter 29

Jo was sprawled across the counter, the *Day Timer*'s blotter—the source for all things local and illegal—front and center. "What was the name of the people who had the birthday party here a few weeks back? The one with the dad who was a real ass? The Ed Hardy model?"

Maeve made a grand show of pretending to

forget. "Loretto?" she said, wondering how Jo thought it was okay that she was loading the beverage case while Jo took a break, coffee and all, not a thought given to helping her supposed boss.

"Was it Lorenzo?" Jo asked, leaning in close to the paper, her arms folded under her chest. "Says here that the police were called to the house. 'Domestic dispute.' "

Maeve hesitated and then continued putting cans of seltzer into the refrigerated case. "Really?" she said. "When?"

Jo scanned the paper. "Last Saturday night."

Maeve dropped a can of soda on the floor and watched it roll under the counter. "Last Saturday?"

Jo looked up from the paper, unconcerned about the can rolling around by her feet. "Yeah. Why?"

Maeve decided to go with the truth insofar as it wouldn't indict her entirely. "I saw him at Mookie's. I was picking up some wings."

"And what? He didn't look like he was going to go home and beat the stuffing out of his wife?" Jo asked.

"Is that what it says?" Maeve asked, returning to the mindless task of stocking the soda case, her mind on Mrs. Lorenzo and the poor little girl who lived in that house.

"In so many words," Jo said. "Blah blah blah, police called, wife refused to file a complaint . . ."

"Then who called the police?"

"Neighbor." Jo folded up the paper. "Funny. Guy didn't look like an abuser."

Maeve's grip tightened around the can in her hand. "And what does an abuser look like?"

Jo straightened up, tossing the paper into a recycling bin by the kitchen door. If Maeve's tone had come through in her question, Jo hadn't picked up on it. "I don't know. Sinister? Evil? That guy was just your garden-variety schlub as far as I could tell."

Maeve slammed the case shut and picked up the empty carton on the floor. "See, that's the thing, Jo. They look just like the people we love," she said. And sometimes, she wanted to add, they start out as people we love absolutely before they turn on us. Jo had been through enough, though, and Maeve didn't need to remind her that sometimes we were wrong when choosing whom to love.

Jo's apron was off and she was halfway through the kitchen door when she asked if they were all through for the day, her assumption being that they were.

"Go ahead," Maeve said. "I'll lock up."

Jo hesitated, her back turned. "Eric's getting married."

Maeve wasn't sure what the appropriate response should be, so she stayed silent.

"Yeah. Married. To the woman he was texting

the whole time I was in the hospital. After my surgery. During my chemo. The one he moved into my house last week."

"I'm sorry, Jo."

She let out a rueful laugh. "Don't be sorry. I've got Doug, king of the Dockers. And maybe you can open up my head again and I can get a second date with Dr. Newman." She rested a hand on her head. "She's pretty and she has big boobs."

"They always do, Jo." Maeve surveyed the sodas, stacked neatly, in the refrigerator. "When is he getting married?"

"A couple of Saturdays from now," she said. "I went to get my bike out of the garage and saw a discarded invitation in the mail. They're apparently doing an outdoorsy sort of thing in the backyard with a tent and shit." She gave a little laugh. "I'm praying for rain or snow."

"Find out when it is and we'll go away," Maeve said, wondering, the instant it came out of her mouth, how she would make that happen. With only one other employee besides herself, taking that employee away would mean that the store would be closed for the better part of two days.

Jo waved the suggestion off. "And close the store? That's not going to happen. We'll stay here and work, and maybe when the day is done, you'll come over and we'll smoke the other joints, if I haven't smoked them by then."

"How about a cheap bottle of Chardonnay?"

Maeve suggested. "The big bottle? The one with the kangaroo on the front?"

"You're on," Jo said. "We'll tie one on. Should be great," she said, disappearing behind the kitchen door. Maeve heard the back door slam shut behind her. Jo had a date with Doug and needed sufficient time to primp, according to her.

She wondered why Jo had waited the entire day to tell her about Eric's marriage but didn't spend a lot of time on it; Jo did things her own way and in her own time. Maeve unearthed the paper from the recycling bin and turned to the blotter, knowing that at best, the details would be sketchy, and at worst, nonexistent. As she scanned the feature, glossing over the numerous rabid raccoon sightings, she determined that it was somewhere in between. The most interesting part, however, was that the neighbor who had phoned in the complaint was none other than Marcy Gerson, the mom whose presence at soccer games one could not ignore, her cheering so intense that Maeve always opted for a bleacher seat as far away as possible from the loudest woman she had ever encountered. Reading the blotter, though, she had a newfound respect for her even if she knew Marcy would probably sue the editor of the paper for printing her name. At least she was trying to let someone know what was going on in the house. That, or the disturbance had kept her awake, something that would not be tolerated in a suburban neighborhood.

Tomorrow's game was home after a spate of away matches. Maeve knew where she'd be sitting.

Maeve locked the front door of the store and went into the kitchen. The presence of someone other than Jo brought her up short.

Rodney Poole was sitting at the end of the table, close to the back door, her purse right next to his left elbow. "I hope you don't mind," he said. "Your co-worker let me in. I wasn't trying to be rude."

She stayed at the far end of the table. "You weren't trying, but you were," she said. "Rude, that is." She threw her apron toward her purse, the balled-up fabric falling right on top of it, just where she wanted it to land. "I thought we were done with this," she said.

He raised an eyebrow and she wondered what she had seen in him that night when they had been fake speed dating. "This?"

"Yes, this. My father. Sean's murder. The whole thing." She put her hands on the counter to steady herself. "It's over. You don't have a suspect in my eighty-year-old father, so you need to look elsewhere."

He took that all in, his expression never changing.

"And speed dating, Detective? What in God's name was that all about?" she asked.

"Your cousin was a complex man," he said, really not an answer to her question.

"That's one way of putting it," she said.

"And there's more to this story than you're letting on," he said. "But I just can't figure out what it is."

"And there's more to your story than you're letting on," she countered.

"I told you before. There is a connection between your cousin and someone who participated in speed dating. That's all I can say." He pulled out his notebook. "Now. Why don't we spend a little bit of time talking about your relationship with your cousin?" he asked.

"We were not close," she said slowly so that there was no way he could misinterpret her intention. "He was older and doing his own thing for the whole time my father and I lived in the neighborhood."

"You were neighbors, correct?"

"Yes. We were neighbors. That's it. We were not close," she repeated. Slow your breath, she told herself, modulate your voice; don't give anything away. "You know who you should talk to, Detective?" she asked. "His wife. The one who probably didn't know that he was speed dating, if that's what was going on. Or the one who knew what he was doing and wanted to kill him for it." She was on a roll. "Or maybe one of his business partners. Surely there's someone there with an ax to grind."

Rather than look annoyed, as she thought he should have, Poole looked amused. "Thank you," he said, jotting some notes down in his notebook. "Those are avenues we never would have thought of. What was the first one again? Interview the wife?"

She smiled in spite of the fact that she was sitting with a homicide detective, a man who was within arm's reach of the gun in her purse. "Would you like a cupcake, Detective?" she asked, figuring that in the time it took her to plate a cupcake, she would be able to regain her emotional equilibrium.

"Sure," he said, taking out his wallet.

"It's on me," she said, going back out to the front of the store, plating two chocolate cupcakes, and bringing them back into the kitchen. "I don't have any coffee left," she said, watching him slowly take the wrapper from the cake, an action that reminded her of how flirtatious he had been at the speed-dating event and how a little shiver of excitement had traveled up her spine at hearing his description of a date. Even though she felt as though her childhood had made her better at reading people, she wondered if she had misread him, if she had missed the signs that he had just been toying with her. She didn't think so, but that playfulness, that familiarity, was long gone; their relationship now centered around murder, cup-cakes, and the occasional cup of coffee.

"Your father told us that he hated Sean. That once he beat Sean so hard that he broke his nose?"

Maeve stopped what she was doing, then put the cupcake that she had been unwrapping for herself onto the table and pushed it away. "I didn't know that," she said quietly, and it was the truth. "Did he tell you that?"

Rodney nodded, the information not deterring him from taking a big bite of what had seemed to become his favorite dessert.

"Did he say why?"

"He says he can't remember."

"He probably can't."

"I'm not so sure," he said, and finished his cupcake. "Boy, I wish you still had some coffee."

She smiled slightly, feeling a little sick to her stomach. "Where does this leave us, Detective?"

"I'm not so sure on that one, either," he said, getting up. Again, she was struck by his solitary performance, his solo investigation into Sean's death. His partner had made just that one appearance, that one time. She wondered what that meant, if anything at all.

Detective Poole had taken an interest in her, and she wasn't sure what was at the heart of that interest. Either way, professional or personal, it was starting to make her uncomfortable.

Chapter 30

Doug of the Dockers seemed to be ingratiating himself with Jo. Maeve wasn't sure what he had done, but after their third official date—the visits to Jo's while she was recuperating did not really count in Maeve's or her friend's mind—Jo's emotions seemed to take a very positive turn when it came to the man who was doing everything in his power to make her like him.

Maeve was trying to get out of the store, on her way to Rebecca's soccer game; she didn't want to be late. Although she knew there would be a wide berth around Marcy Gerson and the sound of her perpetual screaming, she wanted to make sure she could sidle up to her unimpeded by other mothers in the stands. Cal would also try to get there, but he was always late, always bogged down with the menial tasks that every woman in town did with grace and ease but which seemed to present obstacles for him that were almost insurmountable now that he had an infant again.

Jo was still recounting the story of the date, something she had started at eight o'clock in the morning but which didn't have a natural or linear trajectory, work continually getting in the way of a straight retelling. Maeve had lost the thread of the story, not really sure where they were but knowing she would have to leave without hearing the end. "Cut to the chase, Jo," she said, stripping off her apron and finger combing her hair, then applying lip gloss using her favorite reflective surface, the toaster, to make sure it looked okay. "I've got to get to Rebecca's game." In the store, she heard the bell over the door jingle, indicating a new customer. She looked pointedly at Jo.

"I'm going," she said, her sense of urgency when dealing with patrons not matching Maeve's. Her exclamation when she entered the front of the store was far more jovial than Maeve had ever heard, and it took her a few seconds to process the name that she had heard Jo call out.

Jack.

Jack, Maeve's nondriving, wandering, ready-to-be-evicted, losing-his-marbles father. Maeve steeled herself for the inevitable confrontation, pushing through the swinging doors into the front of the store.

"Dad," she said, half question, half statement.

"Mavy!" he said, digging into a piece of cheesecake that Jo had served him. She was pouring him a large cup of coffee and making it to his specifications: lots of cream, even more sugar. "Gorgeous day. Went for a little walk."

"Four miles is more than a 'little walk,' Dad," she pointed out. She took the cup of coffee from Jo's hand and poured it down the sink. "No more sugar," she said.

"I'm a—," he started.

"Grown man," she finished. "I know. We've been through this." Jo, sensing a negative turn in the conversation, went back into the kitchen to hide. "We've also been through the fact that you should not be leaving the facility without letting someone know."

"I let Moriarty know," he said, forking in a huge piece of cheesecake. "He's someone."

Maeve wondered how to play this. If she got angry, he would get angry in turn and they would get nowhere. She didn't have time to get him back to the facility and make the start of the game, so she decided that the easiest thing to do would be to bring him along for the ride. "Dad, I'm going to Rebecca's game. Do you want to come? We can have dinner after that and then I'll take you back." She pulled the plate of cheesecake away from him and tossed it in the garbage.

"I'll go. I love Rebecca's games," he said, and by the way he said it, Maeve was sure that he didn't know what sport she played but that didn't matter.

"Let me call Mrs. Harrison first," she said, concocting her story before she picked up the phone. The gods were with her, and she got Charlene's voice mail. "Oh, hi, Mrs. Harrison, it's Maeve Conlon. I realized, with alarm, that I forgot to sign my dad out when I picked him up today, but he's with me and he's safe. I'll have him back after dinner," she said, keeping an eye on Jack, who gave her a toothy grin and an enthusiastic thumbs-up.

"Good job," he said after she hung up. "Where'd you learn to lie like that?"

"Oh, Dad," she said, leading him through the kitchen to the parking lot, "I've had lots of practice."

On the way over in the car, Jack kept up a running commentary about his fellow "inmates," as he called them, at Buena del Sol. In her mind, she kept going back to Poole's assertion that Jack had beaten Sean at one point—she didn't know when—and wondered what that meant. It was on the tip of her tongue to ask her father, but she knew he wouldn't remember. And even if he thought he did, it might not be for the real reason.

She thought back to a phrase that came out of Watergate—what did he know and when did he know it? She felt certain that at no point during her time in Sean's care did her father suspect what was happening. She was clumsy. That was the story that everyone told, that everyone believed. Jack worked day and night to keep her comfortable; she knew that, and she loved him for that. But had he finally learned at some point of this horrible aspect of his daughter's childhood and executed some ham-fisted revenge?

She let it go. It was water under the bridge. And she had to move on.

Marcy Gerson was sitting at the top of the bleachers as always, all the better for the masses to hear her screams of agony and ecstasy during the game. It was times like this, when they had to hoof it somewhere, that Maeve was grateful Jack was as nimble and agile as he was, his illicit walks through the village keeping him robust and healthy. They climbed to the top of the bleachers and settled in next to Marcy, who was surprised to see anyone take a seat near her, let alone Maeve, who often sat by herself until Cal arrived and inserted himself into her personal space.

"Well, look what the cat dragged in," Marcy said, smoothing down her tailored jeans, the ones that purported to hold everything in while lifting one's buttocks. Maeve figured she'd have to host a lot more than kids' birthday parties to afford them; unfortunately, her wholesale business was still in its infancy. "What's going on, Miss Maeve?" she asked.

Maeve pointed to Jack. "Marcy, do you know my dad, Jack?"

Jack held out his hand. "*Enchanté*," he said, ever the gentleman.

Marcy giggled like a schoolgirl; old Jack could still turn on the charm. "Nice to meet you, Jack." She turned back to Maeve. "What brings you up here in the cheap seats?"

Jack looked at his daughter, sensing that their

visit, and their placement, had a purpose. "Yes. What does bring us up to the cheap seats?" He crossed his legs and gave her a wry smile while waiting for her answer.

It astounded Maeve that it never failed: when she needed Jack to be checked out, he was incredibly checked in. She shot him a look that basically told him to shut his pie hole. "Well, I just had to engage in some idle gossip," Maeve said, going for the truth.

Marcy put a hand over her mouth in embarrassment. "The blotter," she said. "With the amount of money I give to the Policemen's Benevolent Association in this town, you'd think they'd have the common courtesy to keep my name out of these things."

Maeve tried to make a face that reflected both the awe she felt at Marcy's generosity and the indignation she felt on her behalf for seeing her name in the police blotter. By the look on Jack's face, she guessed that she had failed miserably at both.

Marcy leaned in, dropping her voice to a whisper. "What goes on over there is beyond crazy."

Maeve assumed "over there" meant the Lorenzos', but Marcy was off on another tangent within seconds, this one having to do with the response time of the village PD, men and women, she asserted, who couldn't get "real police jobs."

"I think I like you," Jack said, considering himself retired from a "real police job."

Maeve wanted information, but it seemed that Marcy only had eyes for what was going on on the field, where MIRANDA!!! was setting up mid-field, Rebecca across from her on the far side. Maeve decided to give her a little prod before the game started. "So what goes on next door?"

Marcy rolled her eyes. "You don't want to know."

Yes, I do, Maeve thought, but she could tell she wasn't going to get anywhere. Marcy took a lipstick out of her pocketbook and applied it expertly, even without the benefit of Maeve's toaster. The game started and they turned their attention to the field. The Farringville girls scored two goals almost immediately, which sent Marcy into paroxysms of glee. It didn't help that Miranda scored the second goal and looked to be on her way to scoring the third when the whistle for the first quarter was blown and she lost her last chance for glory.

Maeve tried to reopen the conversation during half time. "So your neighbors. Lots of problems there?"

Marcy was loud, but she wasn't stupid. She put a hand on her hip and gave Maeve a look that shot a frisson of terror through her; she didn't want to get on Marcy's bad side after seeing that look. She wondered what was behind it. "Why are you so interested in my neighbors?"

Maeve decided to come clean. "They had a birthday party at the bakery for their little girl and I felt like something was 'off' with them."

"Yeah, something's off," she said, turning her attention back to the field. "They fight like cats and dogs."

Maeve already knew that, but she wasn't sure what she was looking for. Maybe she was more interested in hearing how the children fit into the cycle of abuse or what, if anything, Mrs. Lorenzo did to protect them. But the subject was closed if Marcy's body language was any indication. The last thing anyone wanted in this village was to have their name printed in the blotter, and Maeve knew that. She had touched a nerve and needed to let it go before she turned Marcy off completely.

Maeve had almost forgotten about Jack and realized with alarm that he wasn't by her side any longer. She scanned the small crowd that had assembled, not seeing him in the stands. Finally she spotted him by the fence at the edge of the field, talking animatedly to Rebecca, who had left the sidelines to greet her grandfather. Maeve excused herself, but Marcy didn't seem to care; she'd taken up a new conversation with a person on her right whom Maeve didn't know, discussing Miranda's college application essay topic, which was, not surprisingly, soccer.

Original.

Maeve headed down the bleacher steps and reached Jack just as his impassioned plea for Rebecca's team to adjust to a man-to-man defense was coming to a close. Rather than the glassy-eyed look she usually got when talking to adults, Rebecca seemed rapt, hanging on his every word. She barely gave her mother a glance before running back out to the field. Maeve was accustomed to that kind of treatment. With her girls, she was on a need-to-know and speak-only-when-spoken-to basis. Rebecca was the better of the two, but even she had her limits, and apparently they included not talking to her mother in public.

"Man-to-man defense, Dad?" Maeve asked. "These days, we prefer to call it person-to-person."

"Why are you so interested in that insufferable woman's neighbors?" Jack asked, hanging over the fence that separated the spectators from the players, his eyes never leaving the field.

I'll tell him everything, she thought, right here, right now, and I won't leave anything out. He'll forget by dinnertime anyway. He'll tell me why he beat Sean, why he broke his nose. I'll tell him that I wouldn't be able to live with myself if I knew that another little girl was being hurt and I had done nothing to stop it. She stared at his wide-open face, the one with the blue eyes that looked like hers, now guileless and filled with an innocence that stemmed from a lack of memories, the ones that made her own eyes look so sad. Something made her hesitate, though, and that's when she saw that he remembered something, though he couldn't put his finger on exactly what it was, judging from the look on his face. She decided that that's the way she wanted to leave it, a distant memory for a guy who had done his best with nobody to help him do it.

They were in the midst of the fourth quarter, still standing by the fence, when Jack announced he had to "see a man about a horse." Maeve threw a thumb over her shoulder, telling him that the Porta Potties were right beyond the entrance to the field and that after he used the facilities, he should come right back. No wandering. No walking about. It was just void and return.

He gave her his patented salute and took off, climbing the steep hill toward the entrance. She watched him enter the portable john and then turned back to watch the game, which was not quite the runaway it had seemed it was going to be in the first half.

Five minutes passed and then ten, and her exasperation turned to worry as she saw not one but two people who weren't Jack exit the big blue structure and return to the game. She looked around, but as she knew would be the case, he was nowhere to be found. She started up the hill herself, feeling her calves burn as she raced toward the entrance, her heart starting to pound.

If she found him, she would kill him.

But she knew that was just her worry talking. She wouldn't kill him. She wouldn't even reprimand him. He didn't know where he was or that he was supposed to return to her or why he was at a soccer field at a school unfamiliar to him. A lump lodged in her throat and stayed there. She wondered how far he had gotten.

She crested the hill and turned the corner toward the parking lot, people jockeying for spots so that they could see whatever sporting event was taking place at a distant field. To her left was a playground that she knew was right outside the kindergarten wing of the elementary school that the fields surrounded, and from it, she could hear voices, including one like hers and one her dad's.

Jack was sitting on a bench beside Tina Lorenzo. The baby was on her lap, sucking enthusiastically from a bottle of juice while Tiffany dallied on the jungle gym, the arm in the sling holding her back from playing with reckless abandon. They were the only family in the playground, and Tina was talking animatedly to Jack, who was listening eagerly. It looked as though they were old friends.

Maeve approached cautiously; she wasn't sure why. As she got closer, she heard Jack bellow, "And there she is now!"

Tina looked at her and smiled tentatively.

Tiffany jumped off the jungle gym and ran toward her.

"Do you have any cupcakes?" she asked.

"Dad, I was worried," she said after saying hello to Tina and telling Tiffany that no, she didn't have any cupcakes. "I thought you were going to come right back."

"Right back where?" he asked, the smile on his face masking his uncertainty.

She waved it off. "It doesn't matter. The soccer game is almost over," she said.

"I was walking along and I saw this little girl. Doesn't she look just like you did when you were little, Maeve?" he asked, beaming at the little girl, her face bringing back some memory from Maeve's childhood that made him happy. "When I saw her, I thought to myself, Why, it's my little Mavy! But then I remembered that you're old now." He slapped his knee and let out a big guffaw. "I mean, not old like me, but older than this little beauty." He gave Tina Lorenzo a winning grin, and she was charmed. "I'm seventy-three years old," he said, flexing his bicep. "I bet you find that hard to believe."

Tina smiled genuinely, not the look of someone who was humoring an old man. Jack's openness had that effect on people.

Tiffany pulled at the hem of Maeve's shirt. "This is where I'm going to go to school next year," she said.

"Kindergarten?" Maeve asked.

She smiled and Maeve could see two teeth missing from her bottom row.

"Kindergarten was the best year of my life," Maeve said, and it was the truth. She still had her mother, and the torture hadn't started yet.

"You look just like my Maeve," Jack said again. "The spitting image." He got that faraway look in his eyes, the one that told Maeve he was thinking about the past. It was the look of someone grasping for the string at the end of a kite, just out of reach. He looked at his daughter and smiled. "Just like you."

Chapter 31

New day, new recipe.

Take a dash of nosiness, a sprinkle of annoyance, a cup of concern, and a layer of consternation, and bake for an hour. When you're done, you've got a woman who should mind her own business instead of sticking her nose where others would not dare to tread.

Maeve had missed the dam. Seems that she and Michael Lorenzo both had Saturdays free, but for different reasons. That was the night her daughters went to their father's house and one of the nights that Lorenzo exited the giant house in the new part of town to meet Julie Morelli, she of the big and apparently talented mouth, in the vacant parking lot adjacent to one of the county's man-made wonders. Maeve wondered why it was Saturday and wondered if Julie had divorced the Mute or vice versa. It seemed too serendipitous to think that Maeve could continue her stealth missions on one of the only nights that she ever had free, but there you had it. Sometimes life hands you the lemonade first instead of the lemons.

She didn't know why, but her mother was on her mind more and more. She'd thought that once Sean was dead she would have some peace; that she would stop thinking about her all the time. But the opposite was true. The red car, the contents of the purse strewn across the avenue, the lifeless body sprawled on the double yellow line . . . the thoughts stayed in her head, fighting for prominence in the little space she had left to think and feel. She had compiled the images from bits and pieces of conversations overheard throughout the years, snippets she had read in newspapers that had been left around, which had created what she was sure were imperfect memories of what had happened and what other people had seen. She slid down in her seat and closed her eyes, hoping to get rid of the tattered remnants of the thoughts of her mother, a person who, in Maeve's mind, was rapidly becoming both larger than life and a distant memory all at the same time.

What was she accomplishing by sitting in the dark, a light rain falling once again, watching a man she had little knowledge of beyond what she had witnessed at the birthday party and the two nights she had confronted him? She wasn't sure. Was it to let him know that someone was watching, even though she tried to stay as hidden as possible? Or was it to make sure that he was evil, as she suspected? A lot of men cheated on their wives, but his adultery just added to the specter of his menace and increased the sleazy factor tenfold. She went farther down in her seat and ruminated on the practical logistics of this tryst. Was Julie Morelli so hard up for a roll in the hay that she was content doing it in a mini-van with an incredibly disgusting guy? Maeve shuddered to think that she would ever get to that point, happy that although it wasn't necessarily her choice, she was now a practiced celibate who hadn't really had a sexual thought in close to three years.

Except for the night of the speed-dating event.

Like the memory of her mother, which was faulty and skewed, her lingering impression of Detective Poole was not what it should have been, based on his occupation and the frumpiness that he since had exhibited in the execution of his job. That night, the night in which she had tried to steer romance in the direction of her lovelorn friend, he was someone different, someone who had a heartbeat underneath his pilled sweater and rumpled sport coat.

She wondered why he had let that—the heartbeat—show itself to her. Maybe the save-your-marriage baby hadn't been as successful as he had hoped.

As the rain fell, Maeve watched the minivan from the safety of her Prius, which she realized was starting to smell like Rebecca's soccer togs, the ones she left in the backseat after Maeve drove her home from the game yesterday and that wouldn't be removed until Maeve had had enough of the odor of pungent teenage girl. Julie did what she did every other night when her interlude with Lorenzo was done. She got out of the minivan, climbed back in her sports car, and began talking on her phone, the time it took to execute whatever sexual task she had been charged with using up precious minutes when she could have been talking. Maeve waited until Julie drove past before starting the Prius, deciding that this was not the night to be confronting Michael Lorenzo.

Lorenzo, however, had other ideas.

Although she was at the far end of the parking lot and as hidden as one could be in the open air of a village park, he had spotted her. She wasn't sure when or how, but he knew she was there; maybe his conscience had alerted him to the fact that what he was doing was wrong. Now someone besides Julie Morelli—a woman whose moral compass could be considered faulty at best—knew what he was doing with his spare time. Maeve saw him striding across the lot, his destination clear, so she began to accelerate, slowly at first and then flooring it when it became apparent that Michael Lorenzo was going to chase her on foot and that he had a baseball bat.

He was screaming at her, but she could discern only the curse words, of which there were many. She drove in toward him, hoping to scare him as he charged her like an angry bull, veering to the right at the last second to avoid the baseball bat coming down on her windshield and shattering it. As she drove past, he caught her right taillight with the bat and smashed it, the pieces scattering around the parking lot. She hit a large pothole and winced as the Prius listed to one side, half of it seemingly being swallowed up by the hole. She looked in her rearview window and saw him bent over at the waist, the exertion of chasing her sensible hybrid catching up with him. The bat was resting across his knees.

She angled out of the parking lot and up the ramp toward the main road, the only thing stopping her hands from shaking being her grip on the steering wheel. She decided, for safety's sake, to take a detour through the back roads of the village just in case Lorenzo had gotten his wits about him and had plans to follow her home. She took a right and headed toward another town, making a quick left just before she got to the edge of the village proper and wended her way through the windy road that anchored her little burg on one side. When she realized she was hyperventilating, she pulled off onto a small dirt road where only two houses were set, turned off the car, and rested her head on the steering wheel.

For perhaps the hundredth time that month, she asked herself what she was doing, but she still didn't have an answer. Tonight's escapade underscored that she was way out of her league and things were getting to a point where she could get hurt if she kept it up. She needed to mind her own business. She needed to stay home and attend to her own affairs, the ones of a noncarnal nature. It was time to hang up her avenging angel persona and go back to the business of being a mother and a daughter.

But still. Something inside her had snapped, she felt, and she was using these nocturnal recon missions to fuel something inside of her, although she wasn't attuned enough to her feelings to know what it was. Sean had seen to it that she'd never really be able to figure out what she thought, what was true, and what was a lie. She hadn't been able to trust her feelings—her gut—for as long as she could remember.

Until now.

Her gut was telling her that what she was doing was not only right but necessary. Crucial.

Important. She was making sure, in her own small way, that someone who was preying on the weak would be taught a lesson. She wasn't sure what that lesson was, but she would figure it out in time.

She had rubbed the skin on her arm raw without realizing it, her sleeve pushed up over her elbow and the scar where the bone had poked out all those years before. These days, an arm broken like hers would have been set and then subjected to weeks of painful physical therapy, but back then the plaster cast was fitted, worn, and then sawn off a few weeks later. She pulled the sleeve down and lifted her head off the steering wheel. In front of her car was the mother of one of Heather's classmates, a nice woman she had served pizza with at a basketball game two seasons ago and who rarely frequented the shop. She was holding a garbage bag and was ready to throw it into the shed at the foot of her driveway, the heft of it making the muscles in her bony arm stand out in a kind of strange, fleshy bas-relief. Instead of throwing the bag away and going back into the house, she stared at Maeve through the rain-slicked windshield of the Prius. Maeve saw her mouth her name.

She left the bag by the shed and started toward the car, her first name escaping Maeve's memory even as she racked her brain to try to summon it. Maeve rolled down the window of the car.

"Hi!" she said cheerfully to cover her overall panic at what had transpired at the dam and her inability to come up with the woman's name.

"Maeve?" the woman asked.

Jane.

Joanna.

Jessica.

Jolene? That wasn't it. "Hi," Maeve repeated. "I was just going. I realized I had forgotten something and was going to turn around."

"You've been here for a while," the woman said. "I noticed you about fifteen minutes ago. Is everything all right?" The rain, now heavier than earlier, was soaking her blond bob, and Maeve felt bad at seeing it go from perfectly coiffed to sodden and droopy.

"I'm fine," Maeve said. "Just forgot something."

The woman put a hand over her head as if that would protect her head from the pelting rain. "It's funny seeing you, because you know what I forgot?" she said, laughing. "I forgot to place an order for a cake next weekend."

Maeve waited. She knew what was coming. The woman would give her an elaborate set of directions for what she wanted and never follow up with a phone call. She'd end up with a Batman cake instead of a bat mitzvah cake, or something equally ludicrous, and whisper all around town that Maeve was losing her edge. Instead of telling her to call her in the store, because she knew she wouldn't, Maeve rustled around in her purse for a pen and a piece of paper, her fingers grazing the cool metal of the gun, the one that clearly wasn't safe being stashed in a cheap knockoff with ripped lining but which inexplicably stayed in her possession at all times. "Shoot." No pun intended, she thought.

The order was elaborate, and the woman—Judy?—didn't seem to mind that the rain was soaking her through to the bone. She was relieved that Maeve had happened upon her driveway to do her mental inventory and seemed to forget that it was a little unusual and a lot strange that a local businessperson and mother was sitting alone on a back road at nearly ten at night, her car running, her windshield wipers slapping at a driving rain.

"And make sure the ganache doesn't drip onto the cake round," she said.

Maeve wrote that down, as if that would ever happen. "Okay . . ." Janelle? "Saturday? What time?"

"Three."

"You got it," she said, and put the paper back into her purse.

The woman didn't back away from the car. "Are you sure you're okay?"

Maeve appreciated her concern and was even a little touched. Jody! It was Jody. Now she could call her by name. "Thank you, Jody, but I'm fine. Jody."

"Because if you aren't feeling well, I can order the cake from someone else," she said.

I just got chased by a bat-wielding adulterer and now I'm taking cake orders in the rain, she thought. "I'm fine," she said. "No chocolate ganache on the cake round. Got it."

"And I really don't want to spend more than fifty dollars."

The cake she wanted cost sixty-five and she let Jody know, but the woman wasn't budging. She remembered that Jody was a dental hygienist in a local office. Maeve wondered if she could bargain down her next cleaning. Maeve let out a little laugh; it was the price of doing business in a small town and she let it go, telling Jody the cake would be fifty dollars.

What a kick in the pants. In the span of a half hour she had gone from defending her life to defending her prices.

Jody wandered off, her garbage now stowed in its cedar shed, her cake ordered for the weekend. Maeve put the car in drive and headed home, still sticking to the back roads. She had never been so anxious to get back to an empty house.

Chapter 32

Julie Morelli came into the store right before yoga the next day and the sound of her voice made Maeve freeze, the coffee that she was dispensing into a mug for herself sloshing over the top and onto the counter. She grabbed a dish towel and wiped up what she could; the stream that was running onto the floor would have to wait.

She hadn't seen Julie socially in a while. The visits to the dam had been her only sightings of the leggy yoga devotee, and in Maeve's mind, those didn't really count. She was glad she had stopped going to yoga because she had decided that she hated it. All of that relaxing and meditating was just another opportunity for her to be alone with her thoughts, and if there was one thing she had figured out, it was that that was no place to be. She felt a little guilty because that hour in yoga had constituted the only exercise she got for the week, especially after having promised Jack that she would take him for walks at the river. But she realized he was right and that they would never go. That promise had already been broken, and it didn't look as though she'd be able to follow through anytime soon.

Julie's yoga pants were giving her camel toe,

and Maeve used every ounce of energy she had to draw her eyes to Julie's face. Julie perused the items in the case while Maeve continued to clean up the mess she'd made. Lorenzo was well aware of Maeve's presence at the dam, but she didn't know if he had let Julie in on the fact that she was spying on them. Julie seemed to be her usual self-involved self, mussing her hair after looking at her reflection in the bakery case and talking to herself, because besides Maeve, there wasn't anyone else to talk to and Maeve was otherwise occupied. She finally stood and threw the dish towel into the sink on the counter and asked Julie if she could help her. Jo was nowhere to be found.

"What's fresher, the scones or the muffins?" Julie asked, pursing her lips.

Maeve had an unsettling image of Julie and Lorenzo in a carnal clinch in his minivan. Her stomach did a little lurch. "Made them both at the same time this morning."

She smiled at Maeve. "I'll take one of each." She leaned over the counter, much more comfortable in Maeve's presence than Maeve was in hers. "So, Maeve, I haven't seen you at yoga."

Maeve got a paper bag and picked out a scone and a muffin for Julie. "I found that it stresses me out."

Julie let out a loud laugh. "Seriously? You are so funny, Maeve."

She wasn't sure why that was funny, but she let

out a dutiful laugh as she handed Julie the bag. "How are the kids, Julie? Your husband?"

"Great!" she said. "Everyone's great. Especially Frank. He's great."

Methinks she doth protest too much, Maeve thought. "Really."

"Yes, really," Julie said. "Doing great at work, loving life, spending time on the golf course. What could be better?"

Maybe not being married to you? "Nothing," Maeve said. "Nothing could be better. That'll be four dollars, please."

Julie handed her a five and winked. "Keep the change," she said.

My silence costs more than a dollar, Maeve thought as she shoved the bill into the cash register, her back turned to the counter. She wanted to ask Julie if she knew she was sleeping with a man who smacked his wife around and broke his little girl's arm, but the jingling bell over the door signaled that she had left the store. Her departure coincided with Jo's arrival from the kitchen.

"Is she gone?" Jo asked, a little breathless. Gossip. She had some, obviously. She had assumed her gossip voice (a barely audible whisper) and gossip face (complete incredulity). She watched as Julie navigated her sports car out of the parking lot before she spilled the beans. "I heard she's having an affair."

Maeve slammed the register shut. "Really?"

"Yes." Jo came closer to Maeve, the better to spread whatever details she had heard. Maeve had to give her credit: although she was single and didn't have children in the school system—two prerequisites to getting good information in the village—she really had her finger on the pulse of what went on in Farringville. "I ran into—"

Maeve held up a hand. "Stop. I don't care." She handed Jo an empty basket, the one where the muffins had been until Julie had bought the last one. "What Julie Morelli does with her spare time is not my concern." She sounded so convincing, she almost believed herself.

Jo looked disappointed. "Fine. Want to read the blotter aloud?" she asked, going around the counter to pluck the village newspaper from the rack by the door.

She didn't. She headed out the back door and into the parking lot. If she smoked, this would be the time she would light up, but that was one habit she had never gotten, sticking to garden-variety oral fixations such as eating and nail biting. There was a bench next to the door, and she sat down, staring up at a gray sky that threatened more rain and did nothing to alleviate her foul mood. Jo's bike, parked next to her Prius, was listing to one side, the basket on the front starting to rust a little, giving her the idea that she should buy Jo a new basket and have semihandy

Cal put it on, just a little something to continue to assuage the guilt she felt for the head wound.

The broken taillight on her Prius would need to get repaired. Add that to the list of things that needed to get done but would be pushed aside in favor of other things. Most of the cops in town were customers, so if she got pulled over, she would be sure to turn on the charm to get out of a summons. She wasn't averse to a little bribery in the form of scones and coffee, either.

Jo was calling to her from inside the store, her voice insistent and a little shrill. Something was wrong. She jumped up and went inside, expecting Jo to be attempting to tackle an order she couldn't handle or dealing with an unhappy customer, memories of the Batman cake flooding her consciousness. When she got inside, Jo was holding the cordless phone at arm's length, the look on her face a mixture of distress and panic.

"It's Jack," she said.

The acid in Maeve's stomach heated up so that it felt like hot lava roiling around inside of her; her palms went slick with sweat. She took the phone from Jo. "Dad?"

"Oh, Mavy, I did it this time." The din in the background was muddled, as if he were holding the phone too close to his head.

"Did what, Dad?"

"I got myself arrested."

She wasn't sure she'd heard him right.

"You heard me. Arrested."

She didn't want him to say too much over the phone and told him so. "So you're at the Farringville police station?" she asked. She could be there in less than five minutes even if she hit the one light in the center of town.

"No. The Fiftieth." She heard a catch in his voice. "It's murder, Maeve. They think I murdered Sean."

Chapter 33

Maeve racked her brain on the drive down, trying to recall who she knew in town who was a lawyer, and a sharklike one at that. It was Farringville, though; everyone was either in publishing or an architect. She didn't need a book edited, and she wasn't in a position to build onto her house. She also knew that Cal wasn't up to the challenge of defending her father, his corporate legal instincts having served them not so well thus far. She had asked Jo to call him to get a recommendation; maybe he knew someone better up to the task. And if he gave Jo any guff, he'd get an earful. Cal got on the girl's last nerve, and she wasn't afraid to tell him.

In the meantime, she sped down the highway, hoping to get to her father before he got a twenty-five-year-old legal aid lawyer and ended up "in the system," somewhere that was no place for an eighty-year-old who was completely innocent.

She had been to this precinct once, right after her twelfth birthday, though she'd never been inside. Rather, she had stood on the sidewalk in front of the putty-colored building, staring at the front door, wondering where the courage she had mustered earlier had gone. She was finally going to tell someone what she had endured for so many years in front of so many eyes, hoping that someone would finally see the truth and set her free. But the thought of her mother—the image of her mother—sprawled across the avenue, her belong-ings lost to the wind, stayed in her mind. If she told, who knew what would happen? Who knew what he would do next? So she stood until the shift change and Jack had emerged, thinking that his little girl had come to meet him after his workday to beg him to take her to dinner at her favorite pub or to ask for money. She did neither and he did both, walking her down to the pub on the corner, pressing a ten in her hand because of her excellent report card, telling her that it didn't matter that he hadn't had time to change, because when you had a girl as perfect as Maeve, you took her out and spoiled her.

To him, she was that perfect. But in reality, she was damaged goods.

She double-parked on the block next to the precinct, not caring if the Prius got towed. It was more likely she would get a summons for the broken taillight, but she would deal with that if it happened. Maybe after she gave Rodney Poole a piece of her mind, giving him hell for arresting an eighty-year-old man with encroaching Alzheimer's, he would fix the ticket. In the event the car got towed, they'd take the train home or to some-where Jack wasn't suspected of murder.

Inside, the precinct was a beehive of activity, if a beehive comprised a cadre of cranky cops shuttling a group of unruly prisoners to and fro in front of a large desk that held a sergeant and a few assistant types who were answering phones and working on computers. She asked the desk sergeant where she could find Detective Rodney Poole or Jack Conlon.

"The old guy?" the man asked, and Maeve wasn't sure if he meant Poole or Jack, so she nodded. He threw his head to the right. "Up the stairs. Detective squad."

She raced up the stairs, taking them two at a time, dodging a guy in handcuffs who apparently had decided to engage in a sit-down strike on the second landing, giving grief to the female uniformed cop imploring him to get up. She didn't look much older than Rebecca or much more street savvy. She was practically crying at the effort of getting this guy either up or down. Maeve reached the top of the stairs and raced through the first opening. She saw Jack at the far end of the room, Poole at a desk beside him, staring wearily at him while Jack spun a tale, the details of which reached Maeve, a good twenty feet away.

"And that's how we did it back then," Jack said, concluding a lengthy and long-winded story, if Poole's expression was any indication. Jack looked up, and for a fleeting instant, Maeve was convinced he didn't know who she was. After a few long seconds, he broke into a grin. "This is my daughter, Detective. Maeve Conlon."

Maeve clutched her purse to her chest and regarded Poole; keeping the gun in her purse was a boneheaded misstep. "I understand you've arrested my father?"

"He hasn't been arrested, Ms. Conlon." Poole stood. "We had a few remaining questions to ask your father."

"Oh, good!" Jack said. "I really don't look my best today. A mug shot would look like hell."

"Does he need a lawyer?" she asked, not entirely sure how this worked.

"Do you think he needs a lawyer?" Poole responded.

Jack watched the exchange with interest. "I do not need a lawyer. What I need is a ham sandwich and a beer."

Maeve put her hand on his shoulder. She'd get him the sandwich, but not the beer; by the time they got to lunch, he would have forgotten and would probably want Chinese takeout and a cream soda. "In a minute, Dad."

"We just had a few inconsistencies in his story that we wanted to check out," Poole said cryptically.

Maeve arched an eyebrow. Inconsistencies. That was rich. He was interrogating a guy with progressive mental degeneration and he was surprised by inconsistencies. He was screwing with her and she knew it. "Detective Poole, my father and I are happy to answer any questions you may have regarding Sean's untimely passing, but this is getting ridiculous. He's been dead over a month, you've questioned my father a number of times, and frankly, neither of us have time for this anymore."

"We don't?" Jack asked.

"I get the sense that you really don't care if Mr. Donovan's murderer is ever caught," Poole said.

The din in the background faded, and it felt as if everyone were waiting for her answer. Poole already knew the answer to that question, so she didn't feel compelled to prove him right. She kept her mouth shut, her purse clutched to her chest as if she were an old lady guarding her Social Security check and coupons, and stared at Poole. "Can we go?" she finally asked.

He waved a hand toward the door. "Yes. You can go."

Jack jumped up from the chair. "You don't have

to ask me twice." As he passed his daughter, his back turned to Poole, he gave her a little wink.

"Did you even give him a chance to call a lawyer?" she asked after Jack made his way across the open expanse of the squad room.

"We did. But," Poole said, flipping through his notebook, "your father said, and I'm quoting, 'I'd rather take my chances with a new law school graduate than that idiot ex-husband of my daughter's.' " He flipped the notebook shut. "We took that as a 'no.' "

That sounded just like something Jack would say. Maeve stood, rooted to the ground. "This is ridiculous, Detective. He's an old man. How in God's name could he have killed a man who was twice his size and half his age?"

"Very easily, Ms. Conlon. He could have shot him and walked away. It was a dark park, at night, with no one around. From what I gather from Mrs. Harrison at Buena del Sol, your father has a bit of a wandering jones. She told us that when we picked him up."

Maeve resisted the urge to smile at the expression she had used many times herself.

"And as I have mentioned before, the person who did this knew enough to make the crime scene virtually unreadable."

"Anyone with cable TV and a remote could do that, Detective."

"How so?"

"There are about a hundred true-crime, fake-crime, police procedural, and other types of shows that could give anyone a step-by-step guide to killing someone and getting away with it," she said. "Seriously. You need to stop this."

"The police generally don't like being told what to do." Poole seemed undeterred in his focus on Jack. "Get him a lawyer, Ms. Conlon. A real one. One who hasn't done mergers and acquisitions and isn't emotionally invested in you or your father and who doesn't look terrified by the thought of representing the old guy," he said. "That would be my best advice to you." He sat back down at his desk and flipped open a file.

The air in the room had shifted, and rather than feeling relieved that she was bringing her father home this time, she was more worried than before. Would they do this again? Would they keep him for a longer time, the next time they brought him in? She stared down at Poole for a few moments, his head bent over some photographs of Sean's crime scene, in full view, she suspected, for her benefit.

Poole spoke without looking up. "Why don't you tell me the truth, Ms. Conlon?"

Her breaking point had arrived. She leaned in close to him, the images that appeared in the photographs burning into her consciousness. "What do you want to know, Detective? That he broke my tooth? My arm? That it got worse than that and continued, in plain sight, until he left?" she asked. "That nobody did anything to stop it? Because being Irish," she said, laughing a little, "means never seeing what's right in front of your face, and even when you do, ignoring it for fear of bringing trouble to the family? Is that what you want to know, Detective?" She leaned in closer. "I have stories that would curl your hair. But the truth of the matter is, my father did not kill Sean Donovan."

Poole stared at her, never blinking, her emotion so thick, it was as if he were afraid to do anything that would break her train of thought. The look on his face told her that he was afraid she would continue and give him details he didn't want to hear. Or that she'd stop, relieving him of the reason he might hate Sean Donovan, too, even though he was charged with finding his killer.

She straightened up, immediately regretting her outburst even though she'd been whispering. No one else had heard it, the buzz around the station house continuing apace. "That's the truth, Detective. All of it. What else do you need to know?"

When he spoke, his voice was hoarse. "Why we're not looking at you."

"If you're not," she said, "you'd be an idiot."

She turned slowly and started for the door, noticing that Jack had a new audience, someone who seemed a little more enamored with the old guy's stories of life in the Fiftieth back in the day, someone who was listening intently, his hands thrust deep into the pockets of his nondescript, conservative Dockers. She came up short, stopping by another detective's desk, putting her hand on the corner to steady herself.

Doug's shield was in full view, hanging on a chain around his neck, swinging a little when he threw his head back and laughed at something that Jack said. After a few seconds, he excused himself and walked out the door and down the hallway, never having seen Maeve, leaving her to wonder if he knew that she was the one who had come to get her father.

Jack beckoned to her from the doorway. "Let's get out of here," he said.

She moved forward, her legs filled with lead. Between the crime scene photos, her revelation to Poole, and the Doug of the Dockers sighting, she felt as if she were living in some alternate universe where up was down, black was white, and old men got sent to jail for crimes they wished they had committed but hadn't.

Chapter 34

Maeve's plan was to stay in the kitchen after she got back to the store, making it easier to be with Jo but not actually have to talk to her. She gave Jo a quick update on Jack's potential incarceration, leaving out the part where she had revealed to Rodney Poole the one thing she wanted no one to know and making light of the fact that the detectives thought someone like Jack could commit murder. Jo was suitably horrified and said she had never reached Cal but had left a message with Gabriela, whom she delighted in calling the "überbitch."

Maeve prayed that the afternoon would be busy, but not for monetary reasons. The busier the front of the store, the more unlikely it was that Jo could hang around the kitchen and shoot the breeze with her. Although she had been keeping secrets all her life, she knew the one about Doug was written all over her face, and Jo was perceptive, particularly when it came to Maeve. Jo would know something was up, and although she wouldn't know exactly what it was, with a little hard work and pointed questioning, she would get the truth from Maeve in no time. She was that good.

Maeve stood in the kitchen, looking at her hands, wondering what they were supposed to do now. She had dropped Jack off after a quick lunch, immediately missing the chatter that he had kept up in the car for the entire ride home, thinking of the time when she wouldn't hear his voice, or if she did, it would be the voice of someone completely without cognition. From the front of the store, she heard Jo talking to a customer, laughing uproariously, and selling the hell out of a large chocolate cake that was a few hours away from being discarded, its freshness rapidly fading like the afternoon light. Maeve picked up a knife and plunged it into the butcher-block countertop next to her prep area, taking satisfaction in the deep groove that was left when she pulled it out. "Goddammit," she whispered to herself. "Goddammit to hell."

She put the knife in the sink and pulled out the stand mixer, preparing to make a bread dough. It was a new recipe, but one that she knew by heart, having committed the ingredients to memory one night while sitting in front of Michael Lorenzo's house, a copy of the latest *Bon Appétit* on her lap, a flashlight illuminating the words on the glossy pages of the magazine. She went over to the metal rack by the back door and pulled down some flour, noticing Jo's bag, which was new, and a paper bag from the local hardware store. Peeking inside, she found a can of red spray paint, still sealed shut, and a sales slip indicating it had been purchased that day. She took it out and shook it, hearing the little ball rattling around inside the can. Interesting. She wondered what house project Jo was undertaking, if any at all. She put it back in the bag and replaced it next to Jo's purse moments before Jo burst through the kitchen door, the giant chocolate cake in her hands.

"Mrs. Lorenzo's outside. She wants to know if you'd write 'Happy Birthday, Michael' on this cake," Jo said. Jo had lousy handwriting and was an even worse speller, so simple decorating tasks were beyond her skill set. She picked up a pastry bag with a small tip and pointed it at Maeve. "You're on, sister."

Maeve looked at her blankly.

"You remember them. The sad mother and the cute little girl from the birthday party a while back?" Jo wiggled the pastry bag under Maeve's nose. "Writing on cakes? That thing you do?" Jo left the bag on the counter. "Poor kid. Fell off a swing or something. Her arm is in a sling."

Maeve touched her own arm, rubbing tiny circles on her skin.

"Hey, are you still upset about Jack? The police?" Jo asked, getting another pastry bag, one that made blue flowers around the border of the cake, and placing it in front of Maeve. "They're playing games, Maeve. There's nobody in their right mind who could think that your dad, despite being the stud that he is, could kill your cousin. No one."

"Well, the NYPD would have you think differently."

"If they are that stupid, I give thanks that I'm dating a boring accountant. At least the guy is smart," she said.

Maeve felt her stomach clench and she took a few deep breaths until the pain subsided.

Jo looked at her expectantly. "The writing? 'Happy Birthday'?" she said.

Maeve picked up the smaller pastry bag and wrote the words Jo had requested, flawlessly, across the top of the iced cake. When she was done, she took the other bag and created florets all around the outside of the cake, top and bottom.

"Steadiest hand in the West," Jo said, picking up the cake and going through the swinging door backward.

Maeve followed her back into the store, where Mrs. Lorenzo was kneeling beside a stroller that held the baby, Tiffany holding on to one of the handles with her good hand. The other hand hung down limply from the blue sling that her broken arm rested in, and when she turned at the sound of Jo's reentry, Maeve froze, noticing a fresh and florid-looking bruise blooming on her cheek. She found her voice, but it was weak, asking Tiffany if she wanted a cookie.

Her face lit up and she attempted a smile, one that didn't quite take given that the smile turned into a wince. She nodded and Maeve handed her a chocolate-chip cookie, one of the larger ones that sat on a white ceramic tray in the case.

"What happened to your face, honey?" Jo asked.

Tiffany opened her mouth to speak, but Tina did the answering. "She fell," she said. "At the playground."

Tiffany turned and focused her attention on the baby, breaking off half of the cookie and placing it on her lap. Her sister had fallen asleep but would have a chunk of cookie to drool over after she awoke. That simple act of kindness from the four-year-old caused Maeve to take a step back. There was something deep in that child that still had a capacity for love, and that, to Maeve, was breathtaking.

Jo made a face that made the child laugh. "You have to be super careful at the playground!" she said in a funny voice, making Tiffany laugh harder, even though it appeared that it hurt; she put her hand to her cheek protectively.

Maeve got a box for the cake and tried to find her voice again. Although she felt sorry for Tina's plight, the fact that things were trickling down to the innocent little girl was making her blood boil. She was sure that the child's new bruise was a result of her father's violence; for some reason, beyond not acting to prevent what he was doing, Maeve couldn't see Tina perpetrating any aggression toward her children. Coupled with her trip to the police station, she felt as if she would snap in two. Instead, she focused on assembling the box and gently putting the cake inside. Why didn't anyone see what she saw? Why wasn't somebody doing something to stop it? Thoughts rolled around in her head like pinballs, careening from one side to the other, but there were no answers available to her. The child wasn't in school yet, so she didn't have the benefit of some eagle-eyed school nurse, suspicious and interested only in protecting her little charges while diagnosing head lice cases and taking tempera-tures. And Maeve didn't know if she had any friends with mothers who could spot the signs of abuse and who would care enough—the way Marcy Gerson did—to alert someone to the trouble. It was a small town, and one of its hallmarks was that everyone let everyone else live the life they chose, to the point where nobody was really watching out for anyone else, so disaffected had they all become. It was different from the way Maeve was raised, where people thought they were sticking their necks out, but only for the wrong reasons, giving Jack grief when Maeve wore knee socks instead of anklets for her elementary school graduation, or forgetting to fill out the paperwork to get her confirmed, something that came back to haunt her when she attempted to marry in the church. Maybe nobody went out of their way to interfere when it was heavy-duty, when someone was being beaten, abused, or worse, and that was something that Maeve just found wrong.

The wet pushed at the backs of her eyes, threatening to spill onto the box and leaving a stain that no one would recognize as tears but her. She swallowed hard, feeling exhausted and almost crushed until she looked over and noticed the little girl staring at her, attempting that same lopsided smile that seemed to cause her pain.

Maybe she had given Jo too much credit for her perceptiveness, because her friend didn't seem to notice that Maeve was frozen, her voice choked and her body language indicating that she wanted to be anywhere but in the same room with this sad little family. Maeve pushed the box toward Tina. "That'll be fifty even," she said.

Tina plucked three twenties from her wallet and handed them to Maeve. "Thank you. I'm so glad you had a cake. I don't know what would have happened if I had forgotten my husband's birthday," she said without a trace of irony.

Maeve gave her a tight smile. "I can only imagine."

Chapter 35

The best thing to do, she decided, was to invite Jo to dinner that night. Although it was Sunday and not a night when the girls would be elsewhere, the minute dinner was done, they would vanish, going off to their rooms to do whatever it was that they did behind closed doors. Like a good, watchful parent, Maeve had never gotten them their own computers, preferring to keep the one desktop in an open area where she could keep an eye on what they were doing while listening to them fight about whose turn it was to use the machine. That night, neither seemed to have any homework, so after checking her personal e-mail and downloading a recipe for Ina Garten's flourless chocolate cake so she could compare it with her own, she shut off the computer and went back into the kitchen to start dinner. Jo was expected in fifteen minutes, just enough time to start frying up some chicken cutlets and boiling water for pasta. It was also just enough time to rehearse her speech in her head, the one where she implored Jo not to ask Doug to do her taxes come spring. Something told her that he wouldn't be much help.

She was pouring herself a glass of wine when Jo came through the front door, hanging her jean jacket on the newel post at the bottom of the stairs. "Chicken and pasta?" she asked. "I walked and I'm starving."

Maeve cooked the same thing five nights a week. "You got it. Wine?" she asked, taking a glass from the cabinet over the sink.

"You know it," Jo said, flinging herself into a chair by the kitchen table. "I'm hoping you don't need me to set the table. I'm beat."

"From what?" Maeve asked before remembering that Jo thought she was the hardest-working woman in America. But this time, it was different. Jo flushed a deep red. "From what?" Maeve repeated.

"Listen, if I tell you something, can you keep a secret?"

If you only knew, Maeve thought.

"I did something bad." She crossed her arms and lowered her head to avoid Maeve's gaze. "Don't look at me like that."

Maeve poured Jo an extra-large helping of wine and placed it in front of her. "Here. Liquid courage."

Jo raised her head and took a large swig, emptying her wineglass by half. She cocked an ear, listening for the girls, presumably, but Maeve assured her that they were in their rooms and would stay there until the dinner bell rang. "I went to Eric's last night and did something bad."

Maeve drew her mouth down in a grimace that was almost painful to execute. "Jo . . ."

"I didn't tell you this because you've been going through so much, but do you know that he had the nerve to call me and tell me that a check for me had been delivered to the house?" She finished the wine and held out her glass. "It was from my mother. No matter how many times I give her the address at the cottage, she sends all my mail to the house. He wouldn't bring it to me at the store."

Maeve leaned back against the counter, the only sound coming from her side of the kitchen the chicken cutlets frying in the pan.

"So I went last night. He didn't answer the door, so I let myself in with my key. I was just going to go in and grab it, but I couldn't help myself. I went inside, and he and that . . ."

" 'That slut'?"

"Right. He and that slut were in the hot tub. You know, the one that I spent my grandmother's inheritance on so that he could soak his aching back?"

Another one with an aching back. Maeve wondered if he knew what lumbago meant and how two Advil could solve the problem.

Jo looked straight at Maeve. "I'm not proud of the next part."

Maeve turned her back and flipped the cutlets, figuring that without eye contact, Jo would let her know what had transpired.

"I went into the house. When I got into the kitchen, I took one last look at what Grandma Sylvia's ten grand to me had bought. That's when I noticed that they were naked."

Maeve turned back around and poured another healthy serving of wine into Jo's glass. If all else failed, she'd drive Jo home and let her pick up her car in the morning.

"I locked all of the doors and left."

"Meaning?" Maeve asked.

"That they were locked outside without clothes," Jo said a tad triumphantly. She let a smile form on her lips. "I'm really hoping that makes it into the blotter next week."

The sound that came out of Maeve was the first real laugh she had uttered in months. Once she started, she couldn't stop, the laughing eventually allowing the tears that she had been holding back to burst forth in a moist torrent. The sound was so loud, so uncharacteristically boisterous, that it brought the girls from their rooms, the sounds of their feet stampeding down the stairs indicating to Maeve that she needed to get herself together. She wiped her eyes on the dish towel, trying to turn the sobs back into guffaws and doing a passable job. The girls seemed none the wiser.

Rebecca looked particularly offended that her mother was laughing; something about her mother engaging in frivolity made her uncomfortable. Maeve chalked it up to teenage hormones. Rebecca poured herself a glass of milk, leaving it to her sister to ask what was going on.

Jo laughed it off. "You know your mother. One bad pie crust story after another. I don't know why you two don't find her as funny as I do." She held her glass out for more wine.

Maeve wasn't sure if getting Jo drunk was a good idea or not, but she finished off the bottle that had been opened and pulled another one down from the wine rack on top of the refrigerator. Heather, inexplicably, had begun setting the table. Ever since the party incident and her subsequent grounding, she had been on her best behavior, something Maeve suspected had to do with the tearful phone calls that Maeve had overheard between her and the boy she was dating, the one Maeve was going to kill—no joke—if there was any hint of sexual activity that went on beyond petting. Heather wanted out of her room and into his arms, and since she had served almost her entire sentence and had not had an infraction during that time, Maeve had no choice but to let her out.

Maeve put a platter of chicken, a bowl of pasta, and another one of salad on the table and everyone dug in. As she expected, the girls ate their food at warp speed, loaded their plates in the dishwasher, and asked to be excused. Jo was on her third helping of food when Maeve cleared her throat, preparing to start the conversation about Doug.

"What?" Jo said, lifting the salad tongs out of the bowl with a giant helping of salad dangling forth. "Too much?"

"No," Maeve said. "Eat as much as you want." She shifted in her chair. "How's Doug?"

Jo was in the midst of shoving a forkful of pasta into her mouth when she stopped. "You know what? He's great." She put the pasta in her mouth and chewed loudly. "Better than great. I don't know, it's like we reached some kind of new level in our relationship and I can see things really going somewhere."

"Did you tell him what you did to Eric?" Maeve asked.

"God, no," Jo said. "He's really straitlaced and wouldn't find that funny. It's like he's the good manners police or something."

Maeve hoped that her flinch hadn't registered with Jo. He was some kind of police, but it didn't have anything to do with good manners.

"And he says he wants to get to know you better," Jo said. "You gotta love a guy who wants to get to know your best friend better, right?" She put her fork down and grew serious. "I think he's a good guy, Maeve. Not like Eric. He seems to want to make me happy, and I wasn't entirely sure that I would ever find someone who would feel that way about me."

Maeve hoped her smile looked more sincere than it was. She rubbed her back against the chair in the hope that she could wipe away the sweat rolling down her spine. "And he's an accountant?" she asked.

"You know he is," Jo said, her eyes narrowing. "What gives? You've got a weird look on your face." The weird look didn't stop her from spearing more chicken onto her fork and helping herself to more pasta, but she looked at Maeve after she had filled her plate again. "You still think he's a good guy for me, right?"

"Do you feel like you know him?"

Jo thought about this as she ate. "I think so." Finally, she pushed her plate away and touched her stomach. "I think that's enough."

Maeve picked up her plate and put it by the dishwasher. "You sure?"

"I'm sure," she said, standing up and stretching.

Maeve scraped the leftovers on Jo's plate into the garbage and, without turning around, whispered her confession into the trash can. "He's a cop."

Jo was in midstretch. "What?"

Maeve turned around and put the plate on the counter. "He's a cop. Doug."

Jo let her hands fall to her sides. "I thought you just said, 'He's a cop.' Tell me you didn't just say, 'He's a cop.' "

Maeve tried to make a joke, but it came off poorly. "You might want to get rid of the pot."

Jo wasn't amused.

Maeve leaned back against the counter and didn't say another word, watching the realization of what she had said dawn on Jo's face. Surprise went to disbelief and culminated in anger. "I'm sorry," Maeve said finally. It was all that she had.

"You're sorry?" Jo asked. "Does this have something to do with your goddamned cousin and his freaking murder? Is that what this is about?" She sat heavily in the chair. "Because that would explain why he keeps asking me about you and Jack and your relationship and just how crazy Jack is and how you keep it all together. And where you go most nights." She looked at Maeve, her eyes shiny with tears. "That would explain all of that." She stood, unsteady on her feet. "Is that it?"

Maeve leaned back against the counter and

looked at a spot above Jo's head. "Probably."

"Does he even like pot roast?" she asked.

It was all Maeve could do not to laugh, but she realized that Jo wasn't kidding. "I think he does."

Jo looked down at the table. "Does he love me?" she asked. When Maeve didn't answer, she looked up, her voice coming out shrill and hurt. "Does he love me?"

"I couldn't possibly know," Maeve said.

"So what do I tell him when he inevitably asks me if I think Jack killed Sean?" she asked. She choked back a sob. "Because that's what this is all about. It's never been about me." She sank back into her chair. "It never is."

"I'm sorry," was all Maeve could think to say.

Jo took a napkin out of the ceramic holder on the table; Rebecca had made it in the third grade, and it had somehow survived intact over hundreds of family dinners. Now, because it was dangerously close to the edge of the table, Jo's forceful extraction of the napkin sent it crashing to the floor. She wiped her eyes and blew her nose, ignoring the shattered pottery beneath her feet. "God, I hate you so much right now," she said.

"I had no idea, Jo. Not a clue," Maeve protested, but it was too late. Jo needed someone to blame, and she was "it."

"So what do I tell him?" Jo asked again.

"Do you think my father is capable of murder?" Maeve asked.

"I don't know what your father is capable of. Sometimes he's fine. Other times he's not." Her glare was harsh and unforgiving. "I wonder if your father even has dementia or if this is just some ruse—"

"So you do," Maeve said quietly, stopping Jo's rant. "You do think that he is capable of murder."

Jo stood. She didn't answer, opting instead to head toward the front door, brushing past Maeve in the narrow kitchen. When Maeve offered to drive her home, she held up a hand. "No. Thanks. I'll walk."

"It's two miles, Jo," Maeve said, looking out the kitchen window. "And it's dark now." She heard the screen door slam and Jo's footsteps as she made time on the porch stairs. By the time Maeve got to the front door, she was gone, no sign of her on the street.

Chapter 36

Maeve woke up the next morning with a headache, her pajama pants riding down over her backside, the waistline finally having given way sometime during the night. She pulled at a loose thread and the stitching at the top of the pants unraveled.

Unravel, she thought. That's a good word. That describes exactly what is going on in my life, she thought as she rolled over and looked at the clock. Five fifteen. She was late.

The girls were old enough to get themselves off to school and actually preferred that she not be there to harass them before they left. She was cutting it close, though, getting into the bathroom just ten minutes ahead of when Rebecca would expect it to be hers for a half hour or so. So she took the quickest shower she could, jumped into a pair of jeans and a T-shirt, and headed to work, hoping she could get a few things in the oven before she opened officially at six.

Jo was due in at ten, and Maeve wondered what it would be like once she arrived, if she came in at all. Maeve had tossed and turned all night, thinking about how hurt Jo must have felt upon learning the news of Doug's real occupation; but she still felt she had done the right thing. Jo needed to know, and hopefully, she would come to that conclusion on her own, without prompting or pleading from Maeve.

Maeve went to the store feeling lower and more dejected than she had felt in a long time. The feeling that things truly were unraveling even overrode any elation she felt when she listened to a voice mail message telling her that the wholesaler wanted a weekly delivery of twenty cases of cookies and ten of brownies. It was news that normally would have made a dance of joy the correct response; instead, she burst into tears, the emotional weight of the past weeks, coupled with the feelings she normally carried, pushing her to the breaking point. She couldn't remember the last time she had cried, and the never-ending store of tears that poured forth did not ebb. She rested her head on the counter while her body shook and let it out, thinking that when it was over, she would close off again, not wanting to feel like this ever again.

She hastily threw together some muffin batter —banana nut—and put a batch in the oven. Behind her, the screen door to the kitchen slammed and she pulled herself together, ready to face her best friend, someone she hoped would remember all of the years that they had loved each other, supported each other, and been there for each other when no one else had. She wiped her eyes on her apron and turned around to find Cal standing there, absent the baby who usually hung on his front. Of course it was Cal, she thought; it was too early for Jo. And if there was one person she didn't want to see her in her current state, it was him, but there you had it. Never around when you needed him and always there when you didn't.

"You okay?" he asked, his look a combination of concern and fear.

"I'm fine," she said. "The wholesaler called. They want a huge weekly standing order." She smiled. "I've made it, Cal. Almost," she added, not wanting to jinx it. She told him the specifics of the order and how much she would profit every month from the consistent income. She didn't tell him that she was stressed out just thinking about what filling this order would entail and how she would have to hire new people, something she was loath to do. She liked that it was just her and Jo, even though some days the schedule and the execution of orders was crushing. Having other people around would upset the order of their little operation and bring her the responsibility of dealing with actual employees.

He gave her a quick, awkward hug, still not sure what the dissolution of their marriage meant in terms of physical contact. "That's fantastic news."

She looked at the clock that hung over the sink and then back at him. "What are you doing here? It's just after six."

"We're out of coffee." He stood there expectantly, waiting for her to serve him, she guessed.

"It's not ready yet," she said. Getting up late had put her behind schedule, and she hoped her tardiness wouldn't make the morning more stressful than it promised to be after her conflict with Jo. "If you wait ten minutes, it will be ready." An image of Gabriela in some kind of peignoir-type getup flashed through her mind. She was probably reading *Women's Wear Daily* while the baby screamed with a soggy diaper as Cal ran off to get coffee.

"So what's going on?" he asked. "Heather been behaving?"

"Oddly enough, yes," Maeve said, choosing to ignore the question about what was happening. What wasn't happening? "Seems she's flying right, at least for the time being."

"How's Jack?"

"I'd joke and say, 'Out on bail,' but there's a ring of truth to that."

He stood straighter, looking at her to see if she was joking.

"He was questioned again."

"Again? Why didn't you call me?" he asked, because if she had learned anything during their marriage, it was all about him, all the time, which was what made his new marriage so confounding.

"Didn't need to," she said, walking over to the oven and taking out a tray of banana-nut muffins, the tops golden brown, the insides, she knew from years of experience, moist and bursting with cinnamon. She pulled one gingerly out of the muffin tin and handed it to Cal. "It's hot. Be careful," she said, thinking that was advice she should have given him before he had walked down the aisle again. He was waiting for her to explain. "They're not serious about him, Cal. We knew that."

She went out to the front of the store and grabbed two cups, filling them with the coffee that wasn't quite ready but would have to do in a pinch. She left them black, bringing them back into the kitchen and handing them to him. "They're on the house."

"What makes you so sure?" he asked, returning to their original conversation. He hadn't moved an inch since he had come into the kitchen, the muffin still in front of him in its wrapper, steam rising from the top. "Did someone say something to you?"

"I had a conversation with Detective Poole."

He blanched. "Bad idea." Spoken like a true lawyer. Even one who specialized in mergers and acquisitions.

She busied herself making more muffin batter, steeling herself for the inevitable lecture, which, when it came, was lengthy, filled with all sorts of legalese and insinuations that what she said could and would be used against her in a court of law. "You done?" she asked.

He sputtered for a few seconds, not sure what to do with an ex-wife who wasn't remotely similar to the woman he had married years before. "You seem to be the only person not concerned with what happened to your cousin."

"That's because I know what happened to my cousin," she said, licking the batter from the spatula before throwing it into the sink. The noise startled Cal, who clearly couldn't function at that hour of the morning without a jolt of caffeine. "He called a hooker or went on Craigslist or found someone on the street. She—or he—killed him. I don't know if it was over money or one or the other's performance or if things just turned violent for another reason. And he's dead."

Delivered in a matter-of-fact tone, it seemed very cut and dried and perfectly logical to her, but to Cal, it was different. He looked as if he had seen a ghost when she was done.

"Guy was scum, Cal. There's no reason to be upset unless my father continues to be involved. He's the only one I care about right now." She opened the oven, the blast of hot air putting a flush in her cheeks. "But he's not involved anymore. It's over. Trust me."

"He had kids," Cal whispered, as if that were a reason to mourn the loss of Sean Donovan. "A wife."

"They're better off without him." She pulled another tin off the shelf. "You always fancied yourself the sensitive one, Cal. Maybe you were right."

He reached in his pocket and pulled out his wallet.

"I told you. On the house," she said.

He riffled through the wallet and pulled out a card; he left it beside his uneaten muffin. After he left, planting a brief, soft kiss on her cheek, something that was completely at odds with his earlier hug, she picked it up.

She should have taken his money, because the last thing she needed was a therapist.

Chapter 37

Maeve and Jo went forty-eight hours speaking only about baked goods, work schedules, and the weather. By Wednesday, Maeve had had enough and put the BE BACK SOON! sign, the one with a cupcake serving as the dot of the exclamation point, on the door, then dragged Jo back into the kitchen for a talk.

"This can't go on," she said, noting that Jo was looking anywhere but directly at her. She grabbed her friend's face and pulled it toward her, not caring how rough she was being.

"Hey!" Jo protested, trying to release herself from Maeve's grip. "Stop it."

"You're mad at me. I know that. But there's nothing I can do to change what happened." She let go of Jo's face, noticing the red fingerprints that had bloomed under her cheekbones. "For what it's worth, I think Doug is crazy about you. Cop or not. And I had no idea that he wasn't who he said he was."

Jo crossed her arms over her chest, blinking back tears.

"You've got to admit, nobody's got a meet-cute like yours." Maeve pulled herself up onto the counter. "And if it hadn't been for this case, he never would have been speed dating. You never would have met him."

Jo's expression told her that was small consolation. "Was the murderer there maybe?" she asked. "Was that it?"

Maeve shrugged and made one last attempt to smooth things over, leaving the sarcasm aside. "I'm sorry, Jo. I never would have thought that you would have gotten dragged into this. It's my fault, and while I can't do anything to change that, I want you to know how sorry I am."

Jo found her voice. "You've changed. Since Sean died. You're different."

"Happier?" Maeve asked.

"No. Not happier," Jo said, the tears rolling down her cheeks. "Why weren't you sad? Why didn't you ever cry?" she asked. It was clear that Doug's questions about Maeve had infiltrated her subconscious, making her suspicious of her best friend.

"I did," Maeve lied. "When I was home."

"I don't think you did," Jo said.

Maeve tried to be honest. "You know we weren't that close."

Jo considered that. No one, at this point in Maeve's life, knew her better than her co-worker and friend. "It doesn't really matter to me how you felt about him. But I want to know why it changed you."

The BE BACK SOON! sign was rapidly becoming

false advertising; the conversation they were about to have would take far longer than either would have predicted. Maeve looked at Jo and wondered what would be the point of revisiting the past. It was gone, and so was Sean, and although it might make her feel better for a while, it would be a burden to Jo, one that she didn't need.

"There's more to this story," Jo said.

Maeve closed her eyes and nodded. "There is. But I'm not sure you want to know." She opened her eyes but turned her head away so that Jo couldn't look directly at her. "I don't know if I can even say it."

"Tell me everything."

Maeve was anxious to get it out and then go back to work, but she knew it wouldn't be that easy. She started with the first day, two days after her sixth birthday, the day that he had knocked her off the curb and she had skinned her knee on the edge of the sewer grate; it was her earliest memory. She told about her cracked tooth and her broken arm and how he would pinch her hard where nobody would see or whisper things in her ear that she wasn't supposed to tell and how it was one day when she realized that the hurt that she thought was only on the outside was now becoming a piece of her heart, the thing that made up her soul. "And when he stopped beating me, or hurting me in that way that he had that made it look like I was just clumsy, he started molesting me." She rubbed her arm. "I was ten."

Jo's mouth hung open, a gasp trapped in her throat.

"He was my babysitter. He was saving money for a new record player," Maeve said, laughing a little. "Remember record players?" she asked.

Jo nodded, silent.

"Well, that's what he wanted. So Jack paid him a dollar an hour to take care of me. He took me to the Bronx Zoo and he took me to Arthur Avenue and he even took me to the Botanical Gardens. My big, handsome cousin. The one the girls all liked. And it was times like those when I wasn't sure if what had happened was actually true or if I had made it up in my own mind." She wrapped her arms tight around her body, her one hand caressing the spot where her arm had broken. "I hadn't, though. I hadn't made it up. It was all true," she said, her voice barely a whisper.

"Why didn't anyone help you?" Jo asked, her sadness turning to anger, her tears coming fast and furious. "Why didn't you tell?"

As Jo cried, Maeve told her how she'd wanted to tell but didn't and why. Jo looked sick when Maeve got to the part about Claire. "He killed my mother, Jo. And he would have killed Jack." Her mind went to her sweet, lovely father, the man who had tried so hard to give his girl the best life she could have but had failed. "And I couldn't lose him. Not after I had lost my mother."

"Jack failed you, Maeve," Jo said, and while there was truth in that statement, it was nothing Maeve ever wanted to pin on the man she loved the most.

"I can think that, but you can never say it," Maeve said. He had failed her, but he just didn't know that he had. Working day tours, night tours, overtime and then some, he worked as hard as he could to give her the best life he had imagined for her. The private school in New York City, the tuition at the CIA ready and available when she was accepted, he thought he had done all the right things. Sure, she had been a latchkey kid far earlier than the term had even been coined, but she was the best little girl in the world, as he always said, and would never get into any trouble. But what he didn't know was that when he needed help, he had left her in the care of a sadist, someone who wore the costume of a big, strong, loving cousin; someone who would never let anything happen to Jack's perfect daughter, the daughter who would never tell.

She was almost a hundred percent sure that he never knew what had happened, and even if he had learned something along the way, he had long forgotten it by now. Still, every once in a while she caught him looking at her, and in those looks was a sadness that said, "I know something about you; I just don't know what it is."

Jo was looking at her differently, and Maeve wasn't sure she liked what she saw. "Is this going to change us?" Maeve asked.

Jo was distraught, and in the center of that swirl of emotion, Maeve saw fear. "So either one of you could have done it. No one would blame you."

Maeve touched Jo's shoulder. "But we didn't. It was disgusting and salacious and all those things that the tabloids love about a murder. He was meeting a hooker, Jo. And he died."

She could see Jo trying to work that out in her head. It was something that anyone would have a hard time believing, but she hoped her friend knew her well enough to believe her. To believe the truth about Jack.

Now that she was done, she was less upset than Jo and less upset than she'd thought she would be. The telling wasn't as she'd always imagined it would be—emotional and fraught with myriad emotions—but delivered in a flat, almost detached style that belied just how terrible it had been. The years had made the story almost foreign to her, as if it had happened to someone else in a very different time. The horror that crossed Jo's face, her tears something that Maeve envied because they showed that she could feel, indicated that even with the most level and dispassionate recitation of the heinous acts that had been perpetrated against her, her childhood self, it was still the worst thing that anyone could hear. Her tears that morning had come from being overwhelmed, not sad. There was a difference.

Jo started toward her, her arms outstretched. "Don't," Maeve said, holding out her hand. She clasped an empty muffin tin to her chest for protection. "Just . . . don't."

Jo's hands returned to her sides, limp, her fingers playing with stray threads on the sides of her overalls.

"You can never tell," Maeve said, uttering the words that Sean once said to her.

Jo raised an eyebrow; she didn't understand.

"Doug. You can't tell him." The last thing she needed was for Doug to know. Yes, she had told Rodney. But for some reason, she knew he understood in a way that Doug never would.

"So he'll rot in hell," Jo finally said, thinking about Sean Donovan.

"If there's a God," Maeve said.

"There's a God," Jo said, "and she's a woman. And she hates ugly." Jo's anger turned on Maeve. "You should have—"

Maeve stopped her. "Told? Tell that to my six-year-old self, my eight-year-old self, Jo. Tell a scared little girl that the cruel teenager who threatens her every day with violence to her or the people she loves should be told on. I couldn't do it." She could feel heat rising in her chest. "Don't tell me what you think I should have done. If you want to go there," she said, giving Jo a pointed look, "we'll go there. I have a lot to say on the subject of Eric and what you should have done."

Jo was ready to unleash a defense but thought better of it, closing her mouth, her lips set in a grim line that let Maeve know she had hit a nerve.

"One thing," Jo said.

Maeve put down the muffin tin.

"Did you kill him?" Jo asked. "Because nobody would blame you if you did."

"Jo," Maeve said, "I already told you. Really? You have to ask me again? You know me better than that."

Jo continued to study her. Her voice was barely a whisper when she finally spoke. "Because you're different."

After a few seconds of tense silence, Maeve asked, "Can we go back to work?" She thought after everything she had told Jo that she would feel exhausted, depleted. But she felt lighter than air.

"I don't know if I have the energy," Jo said. "How do you go on each day?"

Maeve didn't know. "With one foot in front of the other?"

"Is it better now?"

"Now that he's dead?" Maeve asked.

Jo gave the slightest of nods.

"A little, I guess."

"It makes me want to kill him all over again," Jo said.

Maeve flashed on Michael Lorenzo's face, a seemingly incongruent thought at an odd time. "Me too." Be back soon, she thought.

Chapter 38

A storm was coming, and it wasn't just the usual fall nor'easter that usually beset the Hudson Valley. Rather, it was being billed as a late hurricane with the possibility of a tornado thrown in for good measure. Jack flipped through the local paper while sitting at Maeve's kitchen table, a glass of Coke in front of him, waiting for his dinner. Even though it was blowing up pretty good down by the river, she had taken Jack on a walk, one that seemed to clear his head and invigorate him even though it left her with a wicked case of windburn.

"Well, if this doesn't make you believe in global warming, nothing will," he said. It cheered Maeve to think that he could still think through the effects of a pockmarked ozone layer. They would have to take walks on windswept paths more often. "Gonna put a damper on the Halloween party at Buena del Sol, though."

Maeve poured some melted butter into the potatoes on the stove and stirred them. "Halloween party? Why so late? Are you dressing up?"

"Yep. Sonny Bono," he said matter-of-factly. "Lila McEntee is going as Cher." He chuckled at the thought of his costume. "And we had a death last week—chair of the refreshments committee—so the party was postponed."

"So you have a date?"

He looked up from the paper. "Yep. A date. Plain and simple." He went back to the blotter. "Your mother's been gone for twenty years, Maeve. I think it's okay if I start dating. Don't you?"

It had been closer to forty, but she didn't correct him. "It's fine, Dad. I'm glad you are seeing someone." She opened the oven and checked the chicken that was roasting inside. "Do you need help with your costume?"

"Still got a fringed vest from when I did undercover in the seventies." He licked his thumb and flipped the page. "What else do I need besides that and a fake mustache?"

"That should do it," she said. "Bell-bottoms, maybe?"

He shrugged. "Maybe. Moriarty may have a pair laying about." He picked up the paper and rattled it, folding it in two. "Blotter is its usual cluster-fuck this week."

"Dad!" Maeve noticed that the older he got—or maybe it was the less aware he became—the more bad language he was starting to use.

He ignored her. "A little mystery at Jo's old place. The house on Cedar Bridge Lane."

"Really?" Maeve asked, getting a wineglass from the cabinet and pouring herself a healthy slug of Merlot.

"Yeah, someone went into the house," he said, scanning the blotter entry, "didn't take anything, but locked the doors on the way out. That's what that skell of an ex of hers told the police, anyway." Jack closed the paper. "There's more to that story than meets the eye," he said, looking at Maeve. "Know anything about it?" He might have been failing mentally, but inside the old guy still beat the heart of an investigator.

"Don't look at me," she said.

"That's right. You never had a vengeful streak. We left that to your mother," he said, laughing.

This was news to Maeve. "Mom was vengeful?"

"You didn't want to cross her," Jack said. "I once left the freezer open and melted your favorite cherry Popsicles, which refroze when I closed it finally. Melted all over the freezer. Stayed that way until two years later when I finally defrosted the refrigerator and cleaned it myself. Woman would have been goddamned if she was going to clean up my mess."

"That's not exactly what I'd call vengeful, Dad," Maeve said.

"I didn't mention the Popsicles she left in my work duffel," he said, smiling at the memory. "You try looking serious with cherry slime on the cuff of your uniform pants."

That wasn't the woman she remembered, but time had definitely burnished her memory of Claire. While in Maeve's mind Sean became more vile and sinister with each passing year, Claire had become sainted, an image at odds with a Popsicle-stowing harpy who just wanted her husband to clean up his own messes.

Cal had asked her each time she had given birth to a girl if she wanted to name her Claire. She opted not to; she wouldn't know until much later if they were perfect enough to be a namesake.

Jack was back to the blotter. "Someone should beat the stuffing out of that guy."

"Which guy?"

"Jo's ex. Leaving that poor girl while she was going through treatment. There must be a special place in hell for people like that."

"She's good now, Dad," Maeve said. "She's got the new boyfriend. The one I told you about?"

"The guy with the khakis?"

"One and the same."

"He love her?"

Maeve opened the oven and pulled out the chicken. "I think he does."

"Tell her that if he does anything to hurt her, I will kill him," Jack said, his eyes on the paper and the other blotter entries. "I will. Wouldn't take much. I've still got it, you know." He dropped his voice to a whisper, seemingly talking just to himself.

Maeve pulled the plastic thermometer out of the thick skin of the chicken, crispy and golden, and turned to her father. "Dad, in light of everything, I think we should lay off the murder threats."

"Then you can kill him," he said, arching an eyebrow in her direction. He folded up the paper and pushed it to the side. "We going to eat anytime in this decade?"

Maeve grabbed a plate and filled it with her father's favorite foods, giving him an extra dollop of mashed potatoes and skimping on the brussels sprouts, a vegetable he hated and which he swore Maeve made just to torture him intestinally. She covered the whole plate with gravy and handed it to him.

"What are you doing tonight?" he asked. "Hot date?"

She took her place across from him and moved the salt where he couldn't reach it. "Yes, Dad. George Clooney is flying me to his romantic hideaway in Lake Como for three nights. The girls are going to stay with Cal while I'm away."

"Don't like that Clooney guy. Too much of a leftie-Commie-liberal. Pick someone else. How about Rush Limbaugh? Or that Hannity fellow?" He dug into his plate of food, finding the brussels sprouts under a puddle of gravy and pushing them aside. "Hey," he said as if he had just remembered something vitally important. "Have you seen that little girl?"

"Little girl?" she asked.

"The one from the park. The one who looked just like you," he said.

"They come into the store sometimes. She's a sweetheart."

"A real cutie," he said. "I saw them at the grocery store on our Wednesday trip and she looked so sad." He drained his glass of Coke. "The mother, too. What goes on in that house?"

He couldn't remember what year it was or how long he had been widowed, but even he was perceptive enough to see that there was a dysfunction in the Lorenzo house that went beyond normal family dynamics. Why did it take years and the onset of dementia to show him something in someone else that he hadn't seen in her? Did old age and the freedom it gave one give him the perceptiveness that he hadn't had when he was younger, working, and raising a daughter on his own? She stared at him, not sure whether to be happy that he was seeing things as they were or angry that he hadn't when he should have. When it had mattered to her.

"I could swear that kid had the tail end of a black eye," he said. "I asked the mom. Said she fell off a swing." He shook his head. "Kid didn't say a word, but after I walked away, I turned around and she was looking at me. Smiling. If she isn't the spitting image of you, Mavy, I don't know who is."

"Funny how that works, Dad." Maeve pushed her plate away, her food half-eaten, her appetite gone.

"He's another one I should kill," he said.

She listened for the joke in his voice, but it wasn't there. "Who, Dad?" she asked, a little shiver of anxiety pulsing through her nerve endings.

"The kid's father." Jack held out his glass for more soda. "For doing that to her."

"Seriously, Dad. Don't say things like that," she said, handing him another napkin after refilling his glass. Food speckled the front of his shirt; he tucked the napkin in under his chin, hoping to stave off more damage.

He dropped his fork on his plate and looked at her, his blue eyes shining. "Just let me do this one thing for you, Mavy."

The conversation was taking a decidedly dangerous turn.

"And what's that, Dad?"

He closed his eyes and exhaled. "Just let me take the fall. I deserve it."

"What does that mean?" she asked, not sure she wanted to know.

He looked at her blankly.

"And do you remember beating up Sean, Dad?" It was a shot in the dark.

He didn't. That was clear from his shocked expression. "Now why would I do that?" he asked. "He was my nephew."

The back door opened, the screen door slamming shut so hard that it almost fell off its hinges. "Grandpa!" Heather yelled, launching herself at her grandfather and giving him a tight hug. She ignored Maeve completely. "I forgot my geometry book," she said, heading up the stairs.

"Hey!" Jack called.

She stopped at the bottom of the banister and peered around the corner into the kitchen.

"Got something to say to your mother?" he asked.

She chewed on that for a moment. "Oh. Hi, Mom." As she went up the stairs, she called down, "And I need a check for the yearbook."

"Rotten little wench, that one," Jack said. "Cute as a button, but rotten to the core."

Maeve was still unnerved from their conversation, her hands shaking. She placed them under her thighs and leaned forward. "How's your dinner, Dad?"

"Excellent," he said, any thought of what they had discussed gone with Heather's appearance. He cleaned his plate, leaving the brussels sprouts hidden under a piece of chicken skin. "I think I'm good. What's for dessert?"

She had made his favorite, tiny pecan pies with homemade ice cream. She put the pies in the microwave for a few seconds to warm them, then scooped rich, buttery vanilla ice cream over the top. "The girls are sorry we couldn't have dinner together. This is their night at their father's." As she said it, she heard Heather thunder down the stairs and run out the front door without a good-bye; she was sure Cal was waiting by the curb, the car idling.

She handed Jack the plate of dessert and watched him scarf it up, the fact that she could still make him happy with her food one thing that gave her a little pleasure. She felt a little sick herself, though. Her dad's comments had put her in mind of Tiffany Lorenzo, sustaining blow after blow with each passing day with no one to protect her, something that reminded her of life before all that ended for her. She rested her head on her hand and studied her father's face, still handsome but carrying the worry lines for the concerns he used to have, the ones that he had long forgotten. Had he worried about her the way he seemed to be worried about this little girl? Had he ever confronted Sean? His parents? Did he even know, or did he believe what he used to say about his "clumsy little Mavy"? She had no recollection of any bad blood passing between any members of the extended Conlon-Donovan family. Their family dinners had been punctuated by drunken laughter, some mild disagreements, and a few lengthy silences over hurt feelings, but nothing dramatic, nothing all that emotional. She often said that the family dynamic swung between two emotions—anger and happiness—with an occasional stop at sad-ness in between. But grow-ing up the way she had, she knew that nobody scratched the surface of a true emotional thought, a psychological breakthrough. Life was lived at the surface, with grudges held and carried in hardened hearts and accusations and recrimina-tions spoken about after the fact and behind everyone's backs.

"You look sad," Jack said, folding his napkin and placing it beside his empty dessert plate.

She smiled, trying to cover up what she was feeling. Not sad, Dad, she wanted to say.

Just angry.

Chapter 39

Maeve dropped Jack back at Buena del Sol after dinner. The rain threatened in the black sky but didn't fall, the wind whipping up and causing a whirlwind of leaves to pool at the front door of the facility. Maeve leaned over and gave him a kiss.

"Night, Dad."

"Night, Mavy," he said, giving her a hug. "Boy, that was a good dinner. If this was my last night on earth, that would be the meal I would want to go out with."

"Dad, don't say that," she said, her voice catching in her throat. At his age, any night could be his last, even if she did everything in her power to make sure he was on the right medicine and taken care of in the best way possible. It had been several days since he had wandered off, and she felt more secure that he would remain at Buena del Sol without incurring the wrath of Charlene Harrison, taking that one worry off her mind.

"I'm just kidding, honey." He opened the car door. "I plan on being here for a long, long time." He turned around, a mischievous grin on his face. "I may not know where I am, but I'll hang out for as long as you'd like."

"Forever?" she asked. She gave him a playful push. "Hit the road," she said. "Go straight to your room. Do not pass 'go.' And no dallying with the ladies."

He saluted her. "I'll be seeing you. Be safe."

She waited until he had walked through the sliding glass doors, had turned around and given her one last wave, and had gone down the long hallway that led to the elevator before she drove off, a feeling that she couldn't shake pressing down on her. The restlessness took her past her own street and out to the edge of town.

She drove down the long drive past the dam, stopping briefly to look at the water surging over the side. The impending storm made it rage more than usual; thousands upon thousands of gallons of clean reservoir water found their way to the Farringville River, a small tributary now swollen to three times its usual size, its banks under a few feet of roiling water. Surely they wouldn't be here tonight—the weather was too dangerous, the conditions not ideal for a romantic rendezvous at a remote location—but there they were, Julie's sports car in its usual spot, Lorenzo's minivan in a secluded corner of the parking lot, its windows steamed up as if two teenagers were necking at a lovers' lane.

Maeve's hand instinctively went to her purse, the tacky pleather number that Jo hated but which had held Jack's old service revolver for longer than she cared to admit, a weapon that had been discharged only once in the fifty years it had been in their possession.

She sat in the car, her head resting on the steering wheel, her heart beating a lonely thump in her chest, her soul asking her what she wanted to do. She had felt this way once before, when she had confronted Sean and not gotten the answers that she wanted, the closure that she had hoped for. It hadn't ended well for either one of them, and for selfish reasons, she was sorry for that. Now would be different; now she would make the difference between one little girl thriving or dying a little bit inside every day.

I'm better than this, she thought. I must be.

Julie drove off after a longer encounter than Maeve expected, longer than any of the other rendezvous on which she had spied. She waited until Julie was out of sight, her sports car making its way past the dam and up to the main road at the end of the drive, and then walked toward the minivan, where she found Michael Lorenzo on his cell phone, yelling at someone on the other end. With one hand, she tapped lightly on the driver's-side mirror; with the other, shoved into the depths of the cheap purse, she touched the handle of the gun, making sure that the fingers grazing it would be able to wrap around it if needed.

Lorenzo turned off the phone and looked at her, the expression on his face a mixture of exasperation and boredom. His hand locked on the gearshift of the minivan, his motivation clear. He was going to drive away. Maeve took the gun from her purse and pressed it to the glass, letting him know that what he wanted to do would have to wait until she'd had a chance to make one final pitch for a little girl's safety.

"Get out," she said.

He stared at the gun and then at her, not sure what it meant that a woman he had known only as a nuisance was now a menace. She stepped back and let him out. He stood next to the back door, his eyes trained on the gun only now, a thin sheen of sweat forming on his forehead despite the cold and the wind.

"Do you know what happens to little kids—little girls—who are abused?" she asked. When he didn't answer, she continued. "They become damaged. They become detached. They become

317

dead inside. Is that what you want?" she asked.

He shook his head. "What are you doing?"

"Teaching you a lesson," she said. She brought the gun closer to his head. "I've asked you nicely. I've asked you firmly. And now I'm asking you one last time to stop hurting that child."

"What makes you think you know what's going on?" he asked. "You have no idea what goes on in my house."

"I think I do. If the dead look in your wife's eyes is any indication, I know exactly what's going on. If the fact that one four-year-old child hurts herself as much as your four-year-old child does is any indication, I know. You're hurting her. You're hurting your wife." She pressed the gun against his head. "You're an animal."

"And what are you?" he asked, his head leaning toward the gun. "You're holding a gun to a stranger's head. What does that make you?"

Beyond the usual descriptors, the things that defined her—wife, mother, baker, friend—she didn't know what she was. An avenger? A vigilante? She tried to think of the word and waited until it came to her, loud and clear. "I'm a survivor," she said. Inside her purse, her phone trilled, ringing six or seven times until it finally went to voice mail. "And I want Tiffany to be one, too. And your wife and the baby. All of them."

"So what are you going to do?" he asked, trying to be tough but weakening with every passing moment that she didn't get in her car and drive away. "Are you going to kill me?" he asked.

"No," she said, throwing her head back in the direction of the dam. "You're going to do it yourself."

Inside her bag, the phone trilled again in agreement. He was going to do it himself. All she was going to do was watch.

Chapter 40

When all was said and done and she watched from atop the dam as his body rolled toward the banks of the Farringville River and eventually into the raging water, she smiled. Maybe once spring came and the thaw along with it, an auspicious diver would find him. But by that time, how much would be left? A femur? Two tibia? It was hard to say. Maybe they'd find him immediately, right after someone alerted the police he was missing. All she knew was that there would be no more Michael Lorenzo inflicting pain on a little girl and a sad woman. What became of his remains was really not her concern.

He had gone willingly to the top of the dam; maybe he had wanted to die. Maybe his pain, the pain that made him the monster that he was, made him want to go into the depths of the river so that it wouldn't be passed on to anyone else.

Or maybe it was just the gun pressed to his temple.

She had given him two choices: a bullet to the brain or a swan dive into the dam. Either way he would die, but the choice was his, giving him a modicum of control over his last moments. He had tried to fight her, but it was no use. She had clubbed him once with the butt end of the gun, effectively making it known that she wasn't to be trifled with, that she would shoot him and dispose of his body, never to be caught, never to be suspected. Who would suspect her? She was a pillar of the community, a woman scraping by, one scone at a time. She donated cakes to the elementary school's bake sale year after year. She let the French exchange students in the high school use the back of her store to make French onion soup for their annual fundraiser. She was Maeve, the cupcake lady.

And no one in town had anything to connect her to Michael Lorenzo besides his daughter's birthday party. Nobody knew that they knew each other, except for Jo, who saw the Lorenzos as customers and nothing more. She would open the bakery in the morning and nobody would be the wiser. Nobody would know that the woman who cheerfully put muffins in a jauntily decorated brown paper bag had blood on her hands.

He begged. He pleaded. He promised, but the promises rang false. She had given him several chances and he hadn't taken any of them. "I warned you," she had said, not feeling an ounce of compassion for someone breathing his last breaths. "I gave you chances." This was the only way out for everyone involved, and she was the only one who knew that, her belief in her righteousness honed over the years of watching Sean Donovan build his financial empire, buy his various homes, and entertain the family as if he ruled it. In her mind were full-color memories of being kicked and hit and tortured, of hanging from a tree until her arm nearly came out of its socket, of being touched in a way that no child should ever be touched. Of crying herself to sleep every night, the sound of Soupy Sales's voice in the background as her mother said over and over in the same reel of her life, "Be back soon."

"If you shoot me," he had said, "they'll find you. There will be a bullet."

"Wrong," she said. "This gun has never been fired. There will be no way to trace it." He had no way of knowing that that was a lie.

In the end, he had chosen to jump, just as she'd suspected he would. At the end, or any time, for that matter, who didn't want to control his own destiny? He went over backward, his eyes boring into hers as he made what seemed like an inordinately slow descent toward the banks of the river, a look she would never forget. He thought he'd survive; she was sure of it. She waited a long time to make sure that he didn't move, his body a shadow down below. There was no way he could have survived the fall, she thought as she walked away, hoping that her instinct was correct. It had to be. She had no time to wait. The bruise that would inevitably be on his head, if he was found right away, would be attributed to the fall.

It was a long way back to the car, still in the parking lot in a darkened corner. Yes, Dad, I'm angry, she thought, listening to the trill of her phone ring for the fifth or sixth time in as many minutes in her purse, ignoring it. Whoever it was could wait. She had things to do at home.

She left the park and went out to the main road, deciding as she had the last time she had gone to the dam that she would go home the back way, avoiding the main road and the traffic that traveled its windy path between her town and the larger one to the east. It hadn't started raining, but it was still windy; and when the storm finally hit, it was clear it was going to be one of the worst they had seen in a long time. She wound her way over the small mountain that framed the town, coming to the main intersection at the very top, hanging a left, and meandering down the other side toward the center of town.

Her thoughts were focused in a way that surprised her. Not "What did I do?" but "Why didn't I do it sooner?" floated through her brain, the thought of a little girl, now fatherless but safe, tucked into her bed, pink wallpaper adorning the room, stuffed animals plush and numerous and arranged around her sleeping frame. And then, out of nowhere, a thought about a special cupcake she would make with bright Tiffany-blue-colored frosting, a little gold leaf to decorate the center. It would be her cupcake, the one Maeve would give her every time she came into the shop and the one that would remind her that once there was someone who cared enough to save her from her own life.

She came around the corner toward the house where Jo used to live. Eric's house was on the sharp bend that always indicated to Maeve to slow down so she could pull into the driveway without overshooting it. There was many a time when she visited Jo that she had missed the driveway and had had to turn around on a street about a quarter mile away. The house was hidden behind a tall stockade fence and a couple of tall trees, making it invisible to the street that it sat right on, dangerously close to traffic. As she got closer, Maeve made out a shape standing by the fence and slowed even more, the outline of the shape becoming clearer and, eventually, in focus.

Jo.

Maeve was going too fast to stop, and given where she had been and what she had done, she didn't want to. In her friend's hand was the can of spray paint that Maeve had spied in the bag by Jo's things on the shelf in the kitchen, and she was writing, fast and furious, the wind proving to be a worthy adversary for her penmanship, a word on the fence that described Eric in a way that was not flattering but completely accurate.

Douche bag.

Maeve was pretty sure it was one word, but now was not the time for a spelling lesson. Anyway, Jo knew better than that; she had gone to Vassar, one of Rebecca's top school picks. She hit the gas and sped past Jo, their eyes locking for a fleeting couple of seconds as she continued down the hill. In her bag, the phone rang again, but she kept driving, slowing her pace and her heart as she got closer to home. She pulled onto her street, most of the houses gone dark, her Prius making its way to the Colonial that she called home, the rain just beginning.

The flashing red lights turned slowly and methodically, cutting through the dark. Several sets, they illuminated her house and the onlookers who had gathered on the street.

It's over, she thought. That didn't take long. She pulled into the driveway and got out of the car, noting that none of the cops rushed her or drew their guns. Rather, they kept a respectful distance as she traversed the front lawn, eyeing her not warily but sympathetically. They were saddened by something, and it wasn't Michael Lorenzo's passing.

"My father?" she asked. And when no one said anything to the contrary, she knew that it was.

Chapter 41

Moriarty was taking it harder than anyone else, and after several hours of hearing him bemoan the fact that he could have prevented Jack's latest walkabout, Maeve gently asked if he wouldn't like to go back to Buena del Sol and get a good night's sleep. It had been a long day and an even longer night, and nobody knew how long it would take for Jack either to wake up or to die. It was one or the other, and either scenario came with a lengthy wait, according to the doctor who was attending the day after Jack had been admitted.

Moriarty finally left the hospital, leaving Maeve alone with her father. He was hers alone to care for, and she didn't call Cal or Jo or anyone in the extended family. He lay in the bed, unmoving, his chest going up and down in a slow but rhythmic motion. He was in good shape, she told herself, but even she knew that the most hale and most hearty person alive would have a hard time withstanding getting hit by an SUV, even if it was going as slowly as the driver claimed it was.

They had been trying to reach her all night, but she hadn't answered her phone, first Charlene Harrison to tell her that he was gone and then the police to tell her that he had been found. While she was dealing with the problem that was Michael Lorenzo, Jack was on his way down the main drag—tons of energy surging through his veins, thanks to a dinner of roast chicken and pecan pie for dessert—to the river, making a wrong turn and ending up on the main route through town, in the dark, the wind whipping around and probably making him more disconcerted and disoriented than he normally was.

She leaned over and touched the leathery skin of his hand, careful not to disturb the tubes and needles that had been placed in and around his body. "Oh, Dad," she said, resting her head on his arm, still warm, a pulse still beating through the skin and muscle. "What did you do?"

She knew that if he were conscious, he would have an excuse, one that would alternately exasperate and amuse her. She took solace in listening to him breathe, wondering if he could keep going after what would have been a mortal trauma for most. But he was Jack. He was, as he proclaimed to her many times over the years, the strongest man in the world. Nothing could keep him down at sixty, or seventy, or even eighty. Although he had let her down, she had to trust that he knew what he was made of.

And if he died? Well, she would have to deal with that. She wasn't ready—she never would be—but if he did go, he would have gone on his own terms, wandering about, free as a bird, his own man. A grown man, as he liked to say, out for a nocturnal jaunt down by the river, not a care in the world because he couldn't remember what his cares were or had been.

A nurse came in and checked his vitals; Maeve didn't lift her head. She wasn't interested in hearing whether or not anyone thought he would live or wonder what he was doing walking around at night or why she hadn't made sure that he was safe at all times. All she cared about was him and what his life would be like if he awoke.

He didn't wake up the next day or the day after that. The Comfort Zone opened up under the guidance of Jo, with the help of Cal and the girls—and presumably baby Devon—and Maeve went home to shower only once, changing out of the clothes that she had worn when she had watched Michael Lorenzo jump to his death. She bagged them up and threw them in a Dumpster outside the hospital's cafeteria before going back up to sit with her father, who didn't seem to be dying but who certainly wasn't fully living, either. When the girls weren't working or going to school, Cal brought them to the hospital to visit, but it was clear that the sight of their once hale grandfather was causing them great pain, a normal reaction to seeing him so broken. The second night that Jack was in the hospital, the girls came, and while they had been stoic the first night, maybe they were expecting some kind of progress that wasn't evident in his status. The two of them went to pieces when they saw their grandfather still in the same position as the night before but now looking weaker and closer to death than he had right after the accident.

Maeve gathered the two of them in her arms and held back her own tears. She knew they were aware enough to know that Jack wouldn't be with them forever, but this kind of situation— where a slow, painful death might be the end for him—was too much for them to bear. While Rebecca composed herself quickly, Heather continued crying, kneeling by her grandfather's bed, imploring him to wake up.

"He's going to wake up, right?" she asked Maeve, the black eyeliner that she had applied that morning now running in streaks down her face.

Maeve got a tissue from the nightstand and wiped her daughter's face. "I don't know," she said. She had to be honest. The situation was precarious, to say the least. "All I know is that your grandfather is in very good physical shape and he is a fighter. I don't think he's ready to leave us yet." Maybe if she said it enough, she would believe it herself. But she couldn't make any promises, and that brought on a new round of crying from Heather.

"They need to lock him up in that place," she said. "So he can't get out."

Sometimes I feel the same way about you, Maeve thought. "They've tried, Heather. They've really tried. Your grandfather is . . ." She paused, searching for the right word.

"Intrepid," came the answer from the corner of the room. Rebecca smiled at her mother. "He's intrepid."

Maeve sank into a chair beside the bed. "Intrepid. That's the perfect word for what your grandfather is."

When Cal came back to get them, Maeve suggested they take the next day off from the hospital. Clearly, it was overwhelming for them to see their grandfather slip away, despite his advanced age. She would leave it up to them if they wanted to come back.

At the end of the third day, Jo called and asked if she could come to the hospital, and Maeve relented, realizing she needed her friend. When she arrived, a panini from Maeve's favorite salumeria was in one hand and four-pack of little wine bottles in the other. She hoisted the wine bottles in the air and proffered the sandwich.

"You don't know what I had to go through to find your favorite cheap Chardonnay in a four-pack," she said, taking a foam cup from the table beside Jack's bed and pouring Maeve a glass of wine.

"I don't really feel like drinking," Maeve said, but at Jo's insistence, she took a sip and found that maybe she did. "Join me?"

Jo poured two of the bottles into her cup and drank half of it down, making an exaggerated sound of pleasure when she finished. "Hospital rooms and good vino. Ain't nothing better."

Maeve smiled for the first time in what seemed like forever. She peered into the bag and smelled roasted peppers, mozzarella, and some kind of cured meat, realizing that she hadn't eaten in a very long time. She unwrapped the sandwich and took a bite. "Thanks."

Jo squeezed her thin frame onto the window-sill, wrapping her arms around her legs and looking out the window, the Hudson in the distance, the best view any of them would ever have. "Not my best hour," she said.

Maeve put the sandwich down and took another sip of the wine.

"The spray paint. The fence," Jo said, explaining further.

"Oh. That."

"The wedding is this weekend," Jo said. "The tent is up."

"And the fence is vandalized."

"And the fence is vandalized," Jo repeated. "I'm sorry. I have a vengeful streak."

You're not the only one, Maeve thought. "I'm getting that impression," she said.

"And you?" Jo asked. "Where were you coming from that night?"

It was a question she should have been expecting, but she didn't have a ready answer. "Target," she finally said. "They're open late and the girls needed some things." It was as reasonable an explanation as she could come up with on short notice and one that seemed to satisfy Jo. "Is the paint still there?"

Jo gave a satisfied smile. "It is. Indeed. You can't get rid of that many 'douche bags' in a few days." She clapped her hands together, a sound incongruous in the silence of the hospital room. "Mazel tov to the happy couple."

"By the way, it's one word, I think," Maeve said. "Douche bag, that is."

Jo shook her head. "I checked *American Heritage*. Either way is acceptable."

"Good," Maeve said. "As long as you spelled it correctly, that's all I really care about."

Jo nodded in Jack's direction; she had yet to look at him directly. "So how's the old goat? He going to make it?" she asked, the words not conveying what her tone did: she loved Maeve's father and would be almost as devastated as her friend if he passed.

Maeve shrugged. "It's anybody's guess. I think he'll pull through. I hope . . . ," she started, her voice thick with the tears she had been holding back. She cleared her throat. "I hope so, anyway."

"The girls been here?"

She shook her head. "Yes. I don't want them to see him like this, but he's their grandfather. I told them to stay home today." His nose, broken, had turned his eyes black. Other bruises bloomed across his once ruddy complexion, some already turning a green not unlike the shade of his favorite St. Patrick's Day socks. One leg was in traction, and the opposite arm was set rigid on a board. When he woke up, as she knew he would, he would be in a world of pain with many months of physical therapy ahead of him. She wondered if she should pray for his death so that she didn't have to witness that.

"How's the store?" she asked.

"Best few days you've had in a long time," Jo said. "I think maybe you should leave it to us from now on."

"Fat chance," Maeve said. "You'll eat all of the profits and then where will I be?"

Jo slapped her head, remembering something. "Oh! I forgot to tell you. You remember that family who had the birthday party? The Lorenzos?" she said.

"How could I forget them?"

"Get this," Jo said. "He killed himself."

Maeve rearranged her features so that she looked suitably shocked. "He did? What happened?"

"They found his van at the dam and him at the bottom. He jumped off the fence, apparently. His wife had reported him missing, but it didn't take long to find him once a park ranger spotted the van."

He *was* dead. There was one less thing she needed to worry about.

"The whole town's talking about it. Can you imagine?" Jo asked. "Jumping from the top of the dam? He obviously meant business."

"I'll say," Maeve said. "That's got to be what? Ten stories?"

"At least," Jo said, warming to the conversation. "And it won't even be in the blotter because it's so big. It will get the front page of the *Day Timer*, don't you think?"

"Absolutely. They can only fill so much space talking about zoning and empty storefronts."

"I don't know. I didn't get a warm and fuzzy vibe from that guy," Jo continued. "I've got a good nose for these things." She looked over at Maeve. "Boyfriends who aren't accountants notwithstanding."

Maeve polished off the last bite of one half of the sandwich. "How's that going, by the way?"

Jo pressed her nose to the window and studied the river. "Good, I guess." She turned and looked at Maeve. "I really like him. Cop or not."

"And he really likes you, I'm guessing."

"I guess." She tried to sound noncommittal, but Maeve could tell it was important to her.

"Does he still ask about me? The case?"

"Hasn't come up," Jo said.

Interesting. "So the case is over?"

"How would I know?" Jo asked. "Now that I know what happened, I don't care if the person who killed Sean is ever found." She let out a string of expletives, ending with "rat bastard."

"You haven't told him, have you?"

Jo shook her head. "I promised you."

That was good enough for Maeve. She would trust Jo with her business, her girls, and her life, and now she trusted her with her biggest secret.

Jo stayed with her until the late afternoon sun slid behind the Palisades across the river and finally, after much prodding from Maeve, relented and agreed to leave. "I've got to get up early," she said. "You know, 'time to make the dough-nuts' and all."

Maeve laughed. She was sorry that this was what it had taken to get Jo to the store on time, but she hoped that this conscientiousness would continue after Jack woke up and got better and Maeve came back.

Jo walked over to the bed and put her hand on Jack's arm. "Wake up, you old coot." She kissed him lightly on the forehead and reached out to Maeve. "Can I give you a hug?"

Maeve stood and stepped into Jo's outstretched arms.

"He's going to be okay," Jo whispered. "He's going to wake up."

"I hope you're right," Maeve said.

She was right. Only moments after Jo left, Jack's eyes fluttered open, staring out into the hospital room, his mind working overtime to get his bearings. Maeve leaned over the bed and put her face in front of his. She talked to him for a few minutes. She told him where he was and what had happened to him. She told him to be strong and to hang on and to make sure that he got better because she needed him more now than ever before. She wanted to ask him where he had been that night, the night that Sean had been murdered, but it didn't matter anymore.

His mouth was dry and she gave him a little sip of water, not knowing if that was what she should do. She knew that she should let the nurses or a doctor know that he was awake, but she wanted a few minutes to herself with him before the onslaught of medical professionals poking and prodding and talking to him in the raised voices of hospital staff. It was as if they thought every patient was deaf.

"Dad?" Maeve said.

He turned his head slightly, as much as he could given the pain, and looked at her.

It was then that she was sure he didn't know who she was.

Chapter 42

The day before Thanksgiving, one of the busiest the farmers' market had in their yearly schedule, was always a good one for Maeve, and she looked forward to it every year. Because she was a two-person operation, she did the market only on this day and was grateful that Margo, the market's coordinator, allowed her to participate one day a year, when customers turned out in droves. The people who approached her little table, under a white "The Comfort Zone" tent, read like a *Who's Who* of the village's most annoying denizens—Marcy Gerson, Julie Morelli, Jody what's-her-name—but Maeve greeted each with a friendly smile that didn't reach her eyes, offering a kind word or two about the upcoming holiday. She noticed that that trio in particular never reciprocated with the questions. Why? Because they really didn't care.

The outdoor market was located next to a DPW base, the one that held the salt trucks and assorted other pieces of snow-clearing machinery; but as night fell, earlier and earlier as the fall days progressed, all Maeve could see were the other white tents that sheltered the vendors from the early sun and then the light drizzle that began to fall.

Jo was back at the store and back to her old ways now that Jack was in a rehab facility and Maeve was running the business again. The farmers' market, according to Jo, made her anxious. The outdoor setting combined with encroaching darkness and the cold temperatures did not suit her skill set. So while she helped Maeve get set up, baking twice as many items for the pre-holiday rush, she opted to stay in the comfort of the store—in her personal comfort zone, as it were—waiting on the slew of customers who wandered in looking for a pie or a cake to bring to their holiday gathering.

It was not the first time Maeve wondered which of them was boss as she shivered in the pair of insulated Carhartt overalls that Cal had insisted she buy for standing long hours in the cold, a fleece jacket under a down coat, and fingerless gloves that made it easier for her to deal with transactions.

Marcy had given her the once-over while paying for her apple pie. "That's a good look for you," she said, attempting to come off light and humorous but instead making Maeve feel like a dumpy farmhand.

"It gets cold here in the evening," she said. "I know forty doesn't feel cold by most standards, but if you stand out here long enough . . . ," she started.

But Marcy had moved on, buying locally

sourced parsnips from the vendor a few tents down. Maeve put the twenty in her fanny pack and thrust her hands deep into her overalls pockets. It was dusk. She would have two hours in the dark, and cold, to fulfill before she could take down the tent, pack everything up, and go home to the bottle of Cabernet on her kitchen counter-top, waiting to be drunk. Tomorrow would bring its own host of challenges, what with the girls going off with Cal and Jack in the rehab facility. Jo was going to her sister's in Scarsdale and was taking Doug of the Dockers. It was just Maeve, whatever was left of the Cab, and a quiche that she had made before leaving the store.

Pathetic, she thought.

She focused on the business of the market to keep her mind off the prospect of spending Thanksgiving alone, but she wasn't successful. Thinking about her father, broken and battered and in rehab, coupled with the absence of the girls, was a little too much to process during the empty spaces that existed between sales of pies and bread.

She took a seat in her camp chair to the side of the table where her goods were arranged with precision, all of the preorders marked with the name of the customer as well as the item inside her signature brown boxes tied with raffia. She surveyed the crowd, seeing a bunch of moms she knew from the one day a year she volunteered

338

at the school bake sale and other people from town who looked familiar but whose names she couldn't conjure up, her sadness filling in the spaces in her brain where information like that used to be. In the distance she saw Cal, his ubiquitous offspring strapped to his chest, emotional napalm to her at that very moment. She sank lower into the chair and watched her ex-husband—now father and mate of the year, it would seem—wander the various stalls, purchasing produce and fresh bread, a growler of microbrewed beer, and an organic chicken that cost more than three regular supermarket chickens put together. Gabriela was the quintessential well-off Westchester woman and had the exacting culinary standards to prove it. Maeve watched as Cal scanned the crowd, looking through the various tents to find her. He finally approached, his arms laden with bags, the baby looking sullen and depressed in his Hanna Andersson one-piece snowsuit and equally dorky hat. When Cal arrived at her tent, the baby let out a long, wet Bronx cheer to illustrate his displeasure at being dressed like a Scandinavian infant in a land where the sun hardly shone.

I feel your pain, kid, Maeve thought.

She rose when Cal approached. "Did you place an order?" she said, jerking his chain. "Everything here is spoken for. You'll have to go to the A&P if you want a pie."

The look on his face was a mix of horror, sadness, and panic.

"I'm just kidding," she said, pulling out a pyramid of boxes, all tied together and bearing his name. She placed them on the table. "A pecan pie, some cupcakes, cookies, and lemon bars. That should be enough, right?" she asked.

Cal went for his wallet. "Yes. Thanks."

"No charge," she said, waving his hand away. "Thanks for helping out with Jack." Cal had come through, finding a space in the closest rehab facility in the county, riding along in the ambulance as Jack was transferred from the community hospital to what would be his home for the next several months. After a marriage filled with disappointment and sorrow, he had come through, his lumbago taking a backseat to her pain and distress.

"But there must be fifty dollars' worth of stuff there," he said, picking up the box pyramid, rocking slightly back and forth to keep the baby quiet.

More like eighty, but she didn't correct him. "It's on me. Enjoy the holiday."

"How's Jack?"

"Coming along," she said, and left it at that. She wondered every minute of every day what the impact of the accident would have on his fading mental agility and waited for the day when he no longer looked at her and saw only an attractive middle-aged mom who could make a mean cupcake and not his dear, devoted Mavy. She prefaced every visit with a loud "It's me, Dad. Your daughter, Maeve," so that he had some frame of reference. She couldn't bear to think that he had forgotten her, his Mavy, the most perfect little girl in the world. She swallowed hard, hot tears pressing at the backs of her eyes, sobs climbing up her throat.

Cal, not one to plumb the depths of despair, or any emotion, for that matter, changed the subject to one that he didn't know was equally fraught. "What are you doing tomorrow?" he asked. He put his wallet back in his pocket.

She was quick to lie, not wanting to see the pity on his face, now ruddy from the cold air. "Going to the parade," she said brightly. "I haven't been since I was little and I wanted to go. I'm meeting some friends in the city," she said.

He looked relieved. "That's great. Who are you meeting?"

"Old CIA friends. Then," she said, elaborating further and creating a nice scenario in her head, "we're going downtown for dinner. Great day."

"Sounds wonderful," he said a little wistfully. She imagined that his day would be taken up with child care and household chores, followed by hours of cooking with only minimal help in the preparation and cleanup. Oh, how the mighty had fallen. Back in the day, Maeve was responsible for all of that and then some, but it seemed that Gabriela had come from other stock, the kind where you married and then lapsed into some kind of domestic semicoma that required some-one else to do the heavy lifting. "Would it help if I picked the girls up after I leave here? That way, you don't have to worry about getting them out the door in the morning."

"That would be great," she said.

"Good," he said, looking down at Devon's Martian-themed hat, the antennae moving with every shake of his little head. "So, have fun at the parade."

"Thanks," she said. Something was off. He was trying to be his usual jocular self, but there was something under the surface, an emotion she couldn't put her finger on. She waited, and in those seconds, a thousand thoughts went through her head. He's sick. He's going back to work. He didn't save enough money for Rebecca's college tuition. He still loved her and had made a huge mistake.

That he was leaving Gabriela wasn't one of them.

Cal looked around. "This isn't going to work," he said suddenly.

"Thanksgiving?" Maeve asked, her hopes up that she'd misread him completely and that she would have the girls for the day. She started compiling a shopping list in her head of everything she would need to prepare the best Thanksgiving meal the girls had ever had, even though in her heart she knew that he was talking about something else entirely.

"No," he said, and she noticed that he was trying not to cry. She had seen him cry only once before, and that was when he told her that he was leaving her for her former friend. He waved a hand around; it landed on the baby's head after a few gestures. "This. Gabriela. My life. It's not going to work."

Behind him, a small line was starting to form and Maeve recognized a few regular customers, some of whom had orders that were ready and needed to be picked up. She shifted uncomfortably, suddenly warm in her workman's thermal overalls. "Cal, let's get together later," she said, dropping her voice to a whisper. "I can't really talk about this right now."

He shook his head, pushing his shoulder-length hair—the longest she had ever seen it—off his face. He rubbed the baby's head as if it were a Buddha belly and straightened up. "Right. I know. I'll go get the girls now."

And then he was gone, no sight of him in the throngs of holiday shoppers milling around the parking lot of a DPW-site-cum-farmers'-market, their arms filled with packages of overpriced foodstuffs that made them feel better about their contribution to saving the environment and local business. Maeve handed out all of the orders that had been placed and surveyed the table, noting that all she had left were three peasant breads, an apple pie, a challah, and a few loaf breads, which would mean that her take for the day would be more than fifteen hundred dollars, something that cheered her in spite of the fact that she was still in a funk over the prospect of a solitary Thanksgiving and now had an ex-husband who would soon be into two women for child support and in Gabriela's case, most likely, alimony, even though she was the primary breadwinner. She wouldn't put anything past her husband's second wife; if anyone could con a judge into that scenario, it was Gabriela.

Maeve's head was down, her pencil tallying the number of items she had sold, when she felt a small, gloved hand touch hers. She looked up and saw blond curls sticking out from under a pink hood and a gap-toothed smile on the face of the girl in question, indicating that Tiffany Lorenzo was happier than she had ever seen her, despite the fact that she was now fatherless. Maeve gave her a big smile in return, looking at Tina Lorenzo at the same time, the baby in her arms. "Well, look who it is," Maeve said, pulling out a cupcake, one with Tiffany-blue frosting, from under the glass-domed tray and raising an eyebrow at Tina, asking for permission to give the little girl her favorite kind of treat.

Tina nodded slightly. Her face wore the expression of someone unused to her surroundings. Maybe now that she didn't live in fear, she felt somewhat unmoored. Maeve knew the feeling well. It was one that she had felt every day for a year after Sean left for college, waiting for the other shoe to drop but not knowing when that might be, when he might return to the area and commence his constant abuse of her. In Tina's case, that wasn't a factor. Her husband was gone for good, and as long as she worked out whatever problems had brought her to a certain kind of man in the first place, she would be fine. The other shoe would never drop.

Maeve handed Tiffany the cupcake and watched her eyes light up.

"This one is my favorite," the little girl said, taking off a glove and placing it on the table so she could unwrap the cupcake. "My daddy is gone," she said suddenly.

Maeve was glad it was dark, because she hadn't expected this statement, nor had she expected her face to flush dark red at the mention of him, the heat creeping up from under the collar of her mock turtleneck fleece and up to her hairline. "I'm sorry," was all she could manage to get out, her voice trapped in her throat with the sobs she had refused to let out earlier.

"Thank you," Tina said, smiling slightly. Tiffany, biting into her cupcake, had already moved on once she had given Maeve that information. It seemed Tina wanted to look a little more jubilant but held that emotion inside. Instead, she went with a hopeful expression, one that manifested itself with a little light that had entered her once dim eyes.

Tiffany waved her arm in front of Maeve's face. "And look! I don't have my cast anymore."

Maeve instinctively went to the place where her arm had been broken, rubbing it unconsciously. "Look at that," she said. She handed Tiffany her glove. "Now you can be a big helper and make sure your mommy doesn't have to do all of the cooking tomorrow."

The little girl giggled. "I don't know how to cook," she said.

Tina pulled the baby's hat down over her ears. "I heard about what happened to your father. I'm so sorry. He is a very nice man," she said. After Maeve thanked her for her concern, she added, "We've both been through a lot."

Maeve struggled for composure, but she was exhausted and it was cold and the things that she had been holding inside threatened to spill out. In spite of using every ounce of self-control that she had, a single tear slipped out of her right eye and traveled down her face before she could reach up and swipe at it. She looked to see if Tiffany was watching, but her attention was on the cupcake and the care it took not to get any of the swirly blue frosting onto her jacket. She offered her baby sister a pinkie covered with icing, which the younger child gobbled up.

"I'll keep your father in my prayers," Tina said.

All Maeve could do was nod. She looked around and noted that the crowd was thinning, the cold and dark getting to the customers as well as the vendors. Only a few cars remained in the parking lot, and it didn't look as though any more would be coming in. She waited until the people at the next tent were out of earshot to ask Tina the question that had haunted her since the day they had met at the grocery store. "When you said it was 'complicated,' what did you mean by that?" she asked.

Tina looked at her sadly and searched for an answer. "I guess it meant that I knew it was bad, but that I knew I would never leave," she said, pulling the baby close. "That I had two babies. I guess that's what it meant." She studied Maeve's face. "How did you know?"

Maeve wondered how Tina knew that she knew, but there it was; they were sisters united by a bond they didn't want to share. "You always know," she said. "You'll know when you see it, too."

Tina stood for a few seconds, and in that silence the bond between them grew deeper, even though Maeve knew that she would have to keep her distance. She had gotten lucky with

Lorenzo—he had never followed up on his threat to file harassment charges against her—but forging a relationship with Tina and her daughter, the one who reminded Jack so much of a young Maeve, would be reckless. As much as she wanted to follow this woman's progress and get in her way if she ever again went down a road that proved dangerous for her and her children, she had to stay away, keeping their relationship professional, friendly, and, most of all, casual and impersonal. Same as it ever was, as the song went.

Tiffany finished her cupcake and asked her mother if they could buy pickles. Tina leaned in before they moved on and gave Maeve a quick hug. "Happy Thanksgiving," she said. "Thanks for the cupcake." She put her hand on her daughter's head. "What do you say, Tiffany?"

"Thanks for the cupcake," the girl responded dutifully in that singsong monotone that children often employed when they were reciting something they were told to say. They walked off together, Tiffany giving Maeve a backward glance and a smile that nearly broke her heart.

Maeve let out a sigh that she hoped no one could hear. "She'll be fine," she whispered to herself. "Remember that. That's all that matters. She'll be fine."

Chapter 43

When the market closed at seven, Maeve was the last holdout, the only vendor who had stayed until the end, braving the cold and the dark in hopes of clearing her table of bread, pies, and cakes so that she wouldn't have to transport the unsold items back to the shop. She was close to achieving that goal. By the time the last person had left the parking lot, she had one challah bread and one apple pie with walnuts and raisins in her possession, a little less than thirty dollars' worth of goods. It had been a fantastic day overall, and she patted the wad of cash in her pocket to make sure it was still there. She'd be able to pay her rent early and put another chunk of change in the bank.

She couldn't figure out why she wasn't happier. Her business was doing better than ever. Sean was gone, and another abuser, one who was sure to inflict more and worse torture on his wife and two daughters, was no longer of this world, thanks to her sharp mind and determination. Jack, hopefully, would return to his former self, a little addled, a lot forgetful, but no less loving. Her best friend was falling in love with a guy who seemed solid as a rock and would likely never leave her, if the adoration he displayed for her continued to grow, as Maeve hoped it would. With the business almost booming, money was less of an object. Tomorrow, she would have the day all to herself. It all pointed to a happiness that should have been radiating throughout her being, but all she felt was empty and alone.

It was a feeling she could never shake, even in the midst of her girls, her friends, the people in the village. It was a feeling that came out of Sean's abuse and the emptiness inside that she always assumed would feel better than what she should be feeling. She was hollow, she decided. She was alone.

She opened the trunk of the Prius and carefully placed the pie and the bread inside, making sure that the pie, in particular, was laid flat. She closed the trunk, surprised to see Rodney Poole standing near the front end of the car, his look inscrutable, his coat looking as if it had been made for someone much larger and who stood much straighter. She put her hands in her overalls pockets to keep her fingers warm.

"Fancy meeting you here," she said. "I hope you don't need cupcakes for tomorrow. I sold out."

"Good for you," he said.

"I've got a challah and a pie, though," she said.

"I'll take them," he said, and pulled out his wallet.

She opened the trunk and used the time inside of the back of the car to collect her thoughts, to slow her breathing. When she emerged with the two baked goods, he was right beside her, a ten and a twenty in his hand. They exchanged what each was holding.

"I owe you change," she said.

"You don't owe me anything," he said. In the dark, his eyes looked even sadder, his face more drawn. "I know this is a little out of the ordinary, but is there anywhere we could go to talk?"

It was out of the ordinary. It was also concerning.

Seeing the look on her face, he held up his hands, surrendering. "Off the record," he said.

She thought for a moment. "My house?"

He considered that for a moment before nodding. "Okay. Your house."

She knew that he knew where it was. He was attentive to detail that way.

She made it there before he did, turning on every light in the downstairs of the Colonial before he arrived. She opened the bottle of Cabernet and set out two glasses. She didn't care if he didn't want a drink or if it broke some kind of police procedure; she would offer him one nonetheless. He rang the front doorbell a few minutes later, and she stripped out of her Carhartt overalls and down to her leggings before letting him in and taking his coat, which she hung in the hall closet.

He followed her into the kitchen. "Glass of wine?" she asked. "This was given to me after I catered an event at the Longwood Country Club, so I know it's better than anything I would normally buy."

He smiled. "I don't drink."

"Because you're still on the clock?"

"Because I'm an alcoholic," he said, pulling out a chair from underneath the white pine kitchen table. "But you go ahead. There's nothing I enjoy more than watching someone enjoy a fine Cab. And that's a fine Cab," he said, taking the bottle from her and looking at the label. A glimmer of the old Rodney, the one she had met at the speed-dating event, the one who told her—who lied to her—that they would soon share a bottle of Côtes du Rhône, peeked out for a second.

She took the bottle back from him and poured herself a healthy glass, leaning against the counter. "I've got seltzer, diet soda, and juice. Pick your poison."

"I'm good," he said. Even though it was her house and she should have been inviting him to sit, he was already seated and beckoning her to join him. She pulled up a chair. The only sound as they sat there was the lonely call of a train whistle down by the river and the distant sound of cars traversing the main thoroughfare that headed north.

"Cheese?" she asked. "Crackers?" The silence between them was discomfiting, and it occurred to her that all she really knew how to do was feed people.

And kill them.

"No," he said. "Thanks."

She took another sip of her wine and rolled her head around to loosen the tight muscles that came with standing all day in the cold. She put a hand to the back of her neck and rubbed it, feeling the knot that was always there and that would never loosen, no matter what she tried. "You're welcome to stay as long as you like, Detective," she said, "but I'm guessing you probably want to get home to start celebrating the holiday with your family."

"Call me Rodney."

"Okay. Rodney." She took in the bags under his eyes and the sad-sack expression that seemed to have gotten progressively sadder the longer she knew him. "I'm alone tomorrow," she confessed. "Just me and the rest of this wine. I told my ex I was going to the parade so he wouldn't feel sorry for me, but the truth is I'm staying home. All day. By myself."

He listened as she continued, telling him about her plans for the quiche and how his buying the bread meant she would have to start a new batch from scratch so that she had something to go with the egg dish. After listening for a few minutes, he stopped her. "I was ten the first time."

She stopped talking, midsentence, and let him continue.

"First, it was roughhousing. Then, it became

something else. He was my stepfather. Meaner than a junkyard dog, just like the song said." He looked down at his hands. "Did you think it was your fault?"

She couldn't answer. She had turned to stone.

"I thought so. Takes a long time to shake that feeling, if at all," he said.

She pushed the wine aside, the sight of it making her nauseated.

"So I drank. A little at first. Then, a lot." He leaned in conspiratorially. "There were some drugs, too. Don't tell the PD. Or Colletti." He smiled. "She seems tough and loose, but she's a Catholic schoolgirl all the way. Very ingrained sense of right and wrong."

"I don't know—"

"Yes," he said. "You do. You know all about it. Remember? You told me."

She tried not to let anything show on her face, but she knew it was impossible. This man, someone she had met under strange circumstances that had just become even stranger, could see into her soul. Even if she hadn't told him, he would have known what had happened because it had happened to him, too. Just the way she knew what had happened to Tina Lorenzo and what was going to happen to Tiffany at some point until Maeve did something to stop it.

"I thought if we went after your father, you would crack. But you're good at acting and even better at lying, and I could never get to you." He leaned back in the chair again. "I think I'll take some of that cheese you were offering."

She stood on shaky legs and walked to the refrigerator, the act of making a simple plate of cheese and crackers with some pear slices in the middle steadying her. Her mind went on auto-pilot. *I'm doing what I know how to do. I'm making food. I'm going to serve a plate of cheese and crackers to this very nice man, the one who understands me better than anyone ever has. The one who knows me better than anyone ever has even though he only met me a little while ago. He's going to eat the cheese and tell me what he knows and then he's going to leave. He's going to let me live my life.*

She was sure of that.

She put the plate on the table. "The whitish yellow one is Jarlsberg and the soft one is a St. André brie. Very rich. I hope your gallbladder is working properly," she said, letting out a little laugh.

He spread some of the brie on a cracker and took a bite. "Rich," he agreed, before changing gears so rapidly that Maeve wasn't sure what they were talking about anymore. "It was torture. Every day. Am I right?"

She figured the less she said, the better off she was.

"I couldn't believe that even after we threatened

to throw Jack in jail, you wouldn't budge. I felt like I was playing the most competitive game of chicken ever," he said, the admiration for her steely nature evident. "Or the most intense game of chess."

"My father had nothing to do with this," she said when she found her voice. It wasn't the first time Poole had heard her say it, but it was going to be the last.

"You win."

"I win?"

"Yep," he said. "You win. I got nothing. I don't have a gun, I don't have a witness, and although you have the worst alibi in the world, I still can't pin it on you even with the long blond hair we found in the car. You're the only blonde in the family, Maeve. I noticed that at the wake."

"You were there?" she asked, remembering a couple of cops but not him.

"In the parking lot. Not inside." He smiled. "Don't worry. No hair root."

She didn't know what that meant, but it was clearly significant. "And speed dating? Why were you there?"

He looked at her, nothing to say.

"Me," she said.

"We were following you," Poole said matter-of-factly and without emotion. "Just a hunch on my part." He chuckled. "I was working with Doug that day. You should have seen his face when you got to the hotel. Speed dating," he said, laughing again. "Took some fast talking to get us into the queue of daters but we're creative like that."

Unlike Poole, she didn't find any of it funny at all. Rather, she felt weak at the thought that she had been followed and never knew. She wondered about other times—when they were, where she had been—but she didn't ask.

"It was always a crime of passion to me," he said, changing the subject. "This wasn't a random killing. Too much violence behind the murder. If you know what I mean."

She did, but she wasn't going to let on.

He closed his eyes and took a few deep breaths. "I still can't pin it on you, though," he said again. "Not that I'd want to even if I could." He chuckled. "Watching Food Network," he said, shaking his head at her flimsy alibi.

He was right. She had motive. She had opportunity. But there was nothing he could do to prove that she had done it. And now that he had revealed their bond, the one she had with a countless number of nameless, faceless strangers walking the earth alongside her, he was loath to make her pay.

"Your going to the ash scattering was inspired," Poole said, obviously an unidentified voyeur at the event she had attended begrudgingly. "Not too many people have the stones to do something like that."

She didn't know why she needed to tell him, but she did. It came out in a sob-filled croak that surprised both of them. "He killed my mother. Sean. He hit her with his car and left her to die on the street."

Poole took a break from eating the food that Maeve had put in front of him to look at her, confused by what she said. "No, he didn't."

"Yes, he did." She was crying openly; the memory of being told that her mother, the one who left her to watch Soupy Sales while she went to get milk and cigarettes, was dead, that a red car had hit her and taken her life, was too much. She didn't care what she revealed to Rodney Poole, only that he know that whatever Sean Donovan had done to her, what he had done to her mother had been much worse.

"A man named Marty Haggerty killed your mother."

Marty Haggerty was Dolores Donovan's and Margie Haggerty's father. He was a bartender at the Dew Drop Inn in Yonkers and a drunk. He was that horrible type of addict that was always mean, sober or soused, and the kids in the neighborhood stayed away from him, giving him a wide berth on the street when he parked his bright red Rambler after a night at the bar and sauntered on home to scream at his wife and two daughters in their Bronx row house. Maeve had always cut Dolores the slimmest of slack because of her life with Marty Haggerty and his drunken, booming voice calling her a fat cow in the middle of the day at the height of summer when all of the windows were open and everyone could hear. Maeve didn't like Dolores but she did feel sorry for her.

Maeve realized her mouth was open and that she was trying to speak but no words were coming out. She closed her mouth slowly and let the impact of Poole's words sink in like a heavy shroud that was cutting off the light and eventually the air. She rested her chin on her hand, letting her fingers cover her mouth. In her mind, her voice screamed that even in death, Sean was still controlling her, still controlling the lies. He had let her believe, year after year, that if she told, the only other person she loved as much as her mother—Jack—would be dead, too, and that he would get away with it again. Her stunted mind, the one that held on to this and believed him, had become more twisted with each passing year, and the fire, the one that she thought she had lost, burned anew, her grief stoking it until it could no longer be ignored.

Poole was looking at her, his eyes a mix of sorrow and understanding. He ate some more cheese as if it were the most normal thing in the world to be doing and chewed thoughtfully. "I'm guessing they kept that from you."

She nodded slowly.

"It was all in the file when I got it. A detective named . . ."

"Pepe Pollizzi."

He tried not to look surprised but couldn't help himself. "Right. Pepe Pollizzi."

"He told me a few weeks ago that they never figured it out."

"They didn't want you to know." He gave a little shrug. "Deathbed confession. Told your dad, of all people. Always suspected, never proven until the day he died. Guy got away with murder."

More lies. Lies on top of lies. She wondered where the truth began and ended and when the lies would stop. If they would ever stop. It would be no use asking Jack; he didn't even remember where he was right now, never mind when he was finally back at Buena del Sol, if he ever got there. This last transgression, the one that landed him in the hospital, may have effectively ended his days at the assisted-living facility. She stared at Poole, the realization of what this new development meant sinking in. She let the thoughts run through her head and ended up at the same conclusion: Whether he had killed her mother or not, Sean Donovan had deserved to die.

"Funny," he said. "It was right after Haggerty died your father beat the stuffing out of Sean Donovan. I wonder what else the old guy told your dad?" Rodney looked at her as if she would know. She didn't.

But she could manage a guess. The timing of the beating, which she finally put together with a black eye she had observed years ago at a family christening, had coincided with a protectiveness that Jack had started to exhibit even though she was no longer a child by that time. Like a good Irishman, he had never brought it up, preferring instead to do what he thought he knew how to do best: take care of her. Beating Sean for whatever he thought had happened was the first thing he saw to. The next came in increasingly incessant phone calls and "check-ins," as he liked to call them, the drop-by when he still drove. She caught him looking at her occasionally with a sadness that she could never figure out, and she wondered if she had started to remind him of her mother. Now, with all of the pieces in place, she knew why his gazes had turned apologetic and morose; he knew what had happened, or had an idea, and he would never feel the same again.

Forgetting the past, even if the memories came back every now and again, was a gift that had been given to Jack, in her opinion. He just didn't know it.

Maeve could only wonder. Did Marty Haggerty know something about Sean that no one else did? Maeve turned that over in her mind. If he had, why did he let Dolores go with Sean, a cruel and depraved individual? Was it like Margie said? Was it just all about the money and nothing else?

Finally, Rodney spoke, and his voice, which had been true and sincere just moments before, took on a tone that Maeve didn't recognize at first but which told her everything she needed to know. He stood. "So, I'll be going, Maeve, my warrior queen." He went to the closet and got his coat, pulling it closed, buttoning a few buttons, and putting up his collar against the night chill. "You were right: your cousin was a horrible person. I think I'll focus my energies on more worthy homicide victims. You know, the drug dealers and the jilted husbands. Solve a few of those cases. Put in my last five and then get out. Head down to the Keys, where I can forget about everything I've seen and all of the money Colletti owes me. The change-of-life baby will be going to college soon after that, so I can move on."

She couldn't get up. She was glued to her chair. "Good night, Detective."

"Please. Call me Rodney."

"Rodney."

He leaned over and gave her a peck on the cheek, whispering two words into her ear, the force of his breath ruffling her hair.

"Good work."

Chapter 44

Maeve waited until the next morning, Thanksgiving Day, to peel back the carpeting in her closet, the carpet that she had laid painstakingly at the end of September and that, if she did say so herself, looked as good as if a professional had done it. It was a nubby Berber and really classed up the look of the closet. She was sad about ruining such a wonderful job, but there was something beneath the carpeting and the floorboards beneath it, and she needed it now.

She wasn't sure why she'd kept it. Maybe to remind her that it had really happened, that he was really dead? Well, that as well as the insurance policy it provided. If she ever needed to skip town, the money would help. But she had no intention of skipping town, and she didn't need the insurance policy now. What she needed was a dress that was fit for her best friend's wedding, and this time, H&M wasn't going to suffice, nor was Target. She was going downtown to a boutique and buying something befitting a warrior queen.

She was on the down side of forty. How many offers to be a maid of honor would she get after this one? This was probably her last, and she needed to make sure that she was dressed to kill.

Jo had called the night before to say that Doug of the Dockers had proposed. It had taken her aback, she'd said, but she couldn't find a reason not to say yes. Maeve didn't think that was the best reason to get married, but Jo had been madly in love with Eric and she knew how that had turned out. He had turned out to be a scoundrel of the highest order and a heartbreaker, leaving Jo's in little pieces after he left. Maeve had a good sense of people, a honed set of antennae, and Doug of the Dockers seemed like a gentleman. Even though Jo had hung her hopes on marrying a boring C.P.A., finding out that she was really dating a cop had made Doug even more attractive to her and had "sealed the deal," in her words. Make no mistake—he was still boring and she still felt betrayed that he had lied to her; but that was something she would use to her best advantage over the next few years. He'd be making it up to her forever. He would never set the world on fire, but he didn't need to. He only needed to make Jo happy and keep the fire of contentment burning inside of her.

The floorboard came up easier this time because she hadn't glued it back in place. She reached down under the floor and pulled out a worn but expensive wallet. It was Burberry, a wallet that a captain of industry, a man of distinction, would carry. In it was two thousand dollars and a condom.

"Fancy meeting you here," she had said to him that night, right before she had put a bullet in his temple and then smashed the gun down between his legs, the extra violence that Poole had referred to the night before.

She pulled the money out of the wallet. She didn't know why she had kept it. Now, though, it had to go, along with the gun—Jack's service revolver—the one that she planned to throw into the river when she was way up north buying apples for the store. She hoped it wasn't discovered by an auspicious diver. Boy, she had loved that gun. She would miss it, even. But it was evidence, and it had to go. Although she had told Michael Lorenzo that it had never been fired, making it clean, it had. If she had been forced to shoot him, there was the chance that some eagle-eyed ballistics expert would make the connection between the man who had been murdered in the park and the one who had been found floating in the Farringville River.

She wouldn't have to go far to get rid of the wallet. She would have a fire roaring in minutes, a Bloody Mary chilled and ready to go, and she would watch as the last material connection she had to Sean Donovan went up in flames.

Maybe that would make her feel better. Maybe that would help her let go.

Or maybe not. Maybe the warrior queen would continue to avenge, the thoughts of what she had been told and what had been done to her a fire that she wouldn't ever be able to extinguish but which she could continually stoke and use to her—and others'—advantage with some careful planning and detailed execution.

She went downstairs in her pajamas and mixed the Bloody Mary just as she liked it, extra horseradish, no celery. There was a cord of wood right outside the back door, and she chose a couple of dry, seasoned logs from the top of the stack, waving to her neighbor through the trees.

"Happy Thanksgiving!" she called, not waiting to hear her neighbor ask if she had an extra pie that she could buy; she had been too busy to go out the day before, apparently. Maeve set about making the fire, and satisfied when it was lit and crackling to a full roar, she got her drink.

Her iPod was plugged in in its dock on the dining room sideboard and she turned it on, wondering which song would shuffle to the top. She would take it as a sign, whatever it was. A loud drumbeat came out of the speakers, announcing a song that she had listened to over and over again because it was one of the girls' favorites. Something about a fire deep inside. Deep inside the singer's heart, her broken heart. It was a song the girls played repeatedly and sang along to, the crescendo building to a point where their voices cracked and the notes proved too long to hold.

Maeve threw the wallet in the fire. The song played on.

She made Sean wish he had never met her. Michael Lorenzo, too.

In that knowledge lay power.

Sean hadn't killed her, emotionally or physically.

He had made her stronger.

Center Point Large Print
600 Brooks Road / PO Box 1
Thorndike ME 04986-0001 USA

(207) 568-3717

US & Canada:
1 800 929-9108
www.centerpointlargeprint.com